SMALL TOWN D.A.

SMALL TOWN D.A.

BY
JOHN VOELKER
(ROBERT TRAVER)

A&M
Altwerger and Mandel Publishing Company
West Bloomfield, Michigan

Published by
A&M
Altwerger & Mandel Publishing Company Inc.
6346 Orchard Lake Rd. #201
West Bloomfield, MI 48322

ISBN 1-878005-48-0

Cover design by
Judith White and Vivian Bradbury

TO GRACE

AND

THE LITTLE WOMEN

CONTENTS

8 **CONTENTS**

PREFACE

THIS BOOK is the story of my fourteen years as D.A. District Attorneys extract so many confessions from others that it should be refreshing to at last behold one himself in the role of confessor. Since people who run afoul of the criminal law frequently fall short of exemplifying the loftiest aspirations of mankind, any candid account of the D.A. and his work is bound to be rough and earthy. And this account is candid if nothing else.

The setting is the rugged iron-mining, logging and dairy-farming county of Iron Cliffs lying in the equally rugged and sprawling Lake Superior district of the Upper Peninsula of Michigan. The people are mostly Finns, Scandinavians, Italians, French-Canadians, Irish and Cornishmen—and some interesting scramblings thereof. Throughout the Upper Peninsula (simply U.P. to its inhabitants) these nationalities predominate roughly in the order named.

"Young man," Judge Belden sagely warned me when I first launched my criminal career, "now you will have to learn to prosecute your cases in seven dialects." He was right. Evidently by way of compensation for good deportment I also learned to swear a little in Chippewa Indian, but Scotch (the brogue, not the beverage), totally eluded me. All Scots accordingly went free.

In Michigan the D.A. is officially known as the Prosecuting Attorney, a rather pompous and ominous title that never charmed me. Other states bestow even fancier names, such as State's Attorney, Commonwealth Attorney, County Solicitor and similar daisies. But whatever his name his job is the same, and I somehow prefer the classic simplicity of D.A. For one thing, thanks to the magazines which immortalize authentic crime and to TV, radio and the movies, nearly everybody nowadays knows who the D.A. is. The rest learn about him by colliding with him. I am wryly aware that this latter group has even choicer names for him because, at one time or another, quite a few of them were pelted at me.

Fourteen years is a long time to survive as D.A., an occupation with a high electoral mortality rate. Since nearly every young lawyer in America who ever recited *A Message to Garcia* in high school aspires to be D.A., naturally at every election there is a mad scramble for the job. All during my time in office a small regiment of these aspiring youngsters pursued me, baying and snapping at my heels. At last political arthritis set in and one of them finally brought me down.

D.A.'s generally either get licked after a term or two or else, using the job as a ladder, ascend to the loftier political plateaus inhabited by judges, attorneys general and governors and the like. Some, like Tom Dewey, even aspire to be president. No class is politically more on the make than ex-D.A.'s. Washington is far and away their favorite Valhalla, where the halls of Congress bulge with their number and resound with their din. Judging from some of the current emanations from Washington I sometimes disloyally think that quite a few of my fellow ex-D.A.'s should have remained home as notaries.

This ex-D.A. is not typical in one respect: I happened never to be bitten by the political bug. Like the new girl at Hurley Gertie's, asked how she got that way, I can only reply: "Jeez, mister, I was just lucky, I guess." I liked being D.A. and I loved—and still love —living full-time in my native Upper Peninsula. A clue to my eccentricity perhaps lies in the fact that the U.P.—besides being a wildly beautiful place—possesses three of Nature's noblest creations: the white-tailed deer, the ruffed grouse and the brook trout. I photograph the deer, mildly hunt the partridge, and endlessly pursue the elusive trout. Thoughts of Washington have left me rather cold ever since I learned that fishing in the Potomac is more apt to produce a despondent and mildewed congressman than a trout.

The D.A. is inevitably in daily collision with life at its most elemental level. His job is somewhat akin to that of a young intern on Saturday night ambulance call: he is constantly witnessing the naked emotions of his people—raw, unbuttoned and bleeding. His is a tremendous experience with life itself, and he must leave his job either a better man or a lethargic bum. There is no middle way.

Finally to all district attorneys comes the awesome realization that there are times in the affairs of men, of your neighbors and mine—of you and me, if you will—when no law and no threat of punishment, however severe, will for a single moment deter or prevent the most frightful explosions of primitive passion and violence. At such times the D.A. merely attends at the official cleaning up of the human debris lying all about him. For he has finally learned a sobering and chastening thing about people and about his work: that this thing we call civilization all too frequently lies but skin deep.

By virtue of his job the D.A. is the keeper of the public conscience, a sort of father confessor to his people. Before him in an unending line tramp the foolish and the wise, the fox and the lamb, the wrongdoer and the wronged, the arrogant and the bewildered, the informer and the reformer. By popular desire he is the community symbol of the three wise monkeys.

In this book I propose to get one of these monkeys drunk and tell you some of my experiences and observations, in court and out, during my fourteen tumultuous years as D.A. If I have drawn any large conclusions from these exciting years of watching my fellow men in trouble and in suffering, then certainly the outstanding one is an abiding belief in the essential goodness and toughness of human nature. If I have not been compelled to learn that—humbly and irrevocably—then indeed I have wasted my time in an elegant course in despair.

ROBERT TRAVER

SMALL TOWN D.A.

Chapter 1

THE LITTLE MATCH BOY

THE FIRST TIME I ran for District Attorney I had so much company that it looked like the start of one of those traditional Parisian bicycle races: the kind entered by every other adult male in the community. *Bang!* went the starter's gun. We were away. . . .

All of us rival candidates were political virgins, and during the race we kept tripping over each other in our puppy-like zeal, picking ourselves up, dusting ourselves off, bowing and apologizing—all the while wishing that the other had snapped his whizzle string. But I was fortunate: I was young, eager, and singularly unencumbered by the weight of such extra baggage, say, as campaign funds. My only problem was to conduct a hotly contested political campaign without money; pay the rent on my empty law office; and in the meantime prevent Grace, my despondent—and pregnant—young wife, from filing for a divorce.

During the nightmarish months of that first campaign I haunted every mine, farm, lumber camp, ore dock and railroad shop in Iron Cliffs County in my dogged quest for votes. I simply had to win. Since my county is one of the largest east of the Mississippi—twice as large as the whole state of Rhode Island and nearly as large as Delaware—before the thing was over I developed the leg sinews of a floorwalker in Macy's basement. Tramp, tramp, tramp . . . I must have trudged the entire circuit five times—and, so it seems in retrospect, at least twice on my hands. I wouldn't even take yes for an answer.

In my boyish enthusiasm I once spent a day and riotous night in the logging village of Ralph, spreading campaign goodies—and

15

free drinks—in my wake. Ah, such friendly, thirsty people. About midnight, finally focusing on a sportsmen's map in a tavern, I was horrified to learn that I had been campaigning twelve miles across the border in a neighboring county. The streak I made getting back to my own bailiwick may best be described as luminous. After that I always carried a compass and a map.

My campaign strategy was simple: seek out and accost an un-suspecting citizen and thrust a campaign card or folder of matches under his nose before he could escape. "Elect Robert John Traver your new D.A." the legend ran. This solemn injunction was ac-companied by an equally solemn portrait of the candidate almost as large as the union label. For some odd reason, everybody called the youngest candidate "Johnny." Wherever a knot of innocent people gathered there was the ubiquitous Johnny Traver gravely passing out his campaign gimcracks like a gaunt and feverish gnome. I had no money for the usual election publicity splash, so I had to reach each voter the hard way. It was probably also the best way.

I covered so many high-school football games the autumn of that first campaign, sniffing and rooting for stray adults, that towards the end the kids used to cheer me whenever I entered the playing field, as though I were a wounded star. "All right! Nine rahs for Traver!" So stoic and humorless was my quest for fans over twenty-one that I failed ungratefully even to pause and ac-knowledge their cheers. Getting votes for Traver was my business and I tended to it. "What's the score?" I'd occasionally ask as I prowled my lonely rounds. Sometimes I got too close to the gladi-ators and longed for a pair of shoulder pads.

As the campaign got hotter I even took to lying in wait at beauty parlors, loitering outside movie houses, and lurking around depots and bus stations. "Have one of my campaign cards, Madam?" I'd leer, suddenly popping out from behind a pillar. Sometimes madam would squeal in terror and I recall at least one lady that sighed, spun, and fainted dead away in my arms. Since this sagging voter was a large one and I found myself growing weak over the suddenness of her surrender, I involuntarily lowered her to the curb, propped her against a hydrant, snatched up my fallen campaign card—and fled like a rapist. Or again I would confront some benumbed citizen emerging from a double feature. "Have some of my matches, Mister?" I'd quaver, for all the world like the Little Match Girl's little brother. These forays were always accompanied by one of my most forlorn smiles. One confused drunk was so moved by my appeal that he tossed me a quarter and then noisily demanded a pair of shoelaces. I knelt and gave him mine. All in all it's a wonder I wasn't challenged to a duel or popped in the eye or picked up and booked on suspicion of accosting and soliciting or something.

One of my more disgruntled opponents started a low and baseless rumor that I was bothering the patrons in—of all places—pay toilets. The whole thing was of course a thin tissue of lies: I merely lay in wait outside an occupied cubicle in respectful silence until the occupant's lease had expired. Then, as he emerged flushed and happy, I thrust a book of matches at him, nimbly seized the door—"ran out of change, Mister"—and cloistered myself within until I had impaled my campaign cards with thumbtacks to the inside of the door. The thing had to be timed just right, of course, but soon I grew quite expert at it. This strategy not only saved me a nickel on each toilet but thoughtfully provided future tenants with something more stimulating to contemplate than the usual venereal literature and greetings from Kilroy. (Sly fellow that I was, I had read somewhere that American males did their most effective reading in the can.) Since each of my cards bore my picture, by-and-by in some irreverant quarters my campaign slogan became known as "The Face on the Toilet Door," a diverting variation from the more venerable "The Face on the Barroom Floor." All was grist to my mill. It was only months after I got elected that I first learned that this latrine maneuver of mine made the candidate for D.A. guilty of breaking not one but *two* misdemeanor statutes. In my enthusiasm I had not realized that the entrepreneurs of pay toilets had a lobby in Lansing.

Then there was the hilarious time the phony official of a nonexistent railroad brotherhood called at my office and sold me forty dollars' worth (my last dime) of election advertising in a mythical brotherhood house organ after pledging me the entire thousand-odd votes of his brotherhood and inviting me to give a speech at the big brotherhood picnic to be held three weeks hence. (That was before I gratifyingly learned that no man, whether he be head of the Union League Club or the Amalgamated Makers of Dropseat Union Suits, could ever deliver any group's vote for anything or anybody.)

I toiled on my speech to the picnicking brotherhood for days. It was a honey. When I arrived at the picnic grounds on the appointed day—with the new Gettysburg Address of all the unsung railroad workers folded carefully in my pocket—my sole audience was a knot of all the other candidates for District Attorney, each carrying the typescript of *his* speech, along with a sheepish smile. Then and there we made a solemn pact not to expose each other. "All candidates for D.A. rooked by smalltime con man" was one headline none of us cared to read just about then.

But perhaps my most glittering election memory of all from that first campaign was my part in the Fall Festival and Baby Parade held at Hematite, the neighboring town just east of here. I never did learn precisely what the Fall Festival was all about, but I doubt that I shall ever forget the Baby Parade.

The three-day festival was to be concluded by a free-for-all parade of prize-seeking offspring entered from all over the county. The master minds of the festival knew that no baby parade could possibly ever miss, based as it was upon the sound psychology that even the most leaky and evil-looking brat is regarded as a picture of matchless beauty and charm by its parents. For days I pondered a way to get in on the act. Then the day before the parade while campaigning in a Hematite tavern—by then I stopped nowhere—I ran across Big Buller Beaudin, a 300-pound local slave to Old Cordwood, the Peninsula's favorite blended whiskey.

"Look, Johnny," rotund Buller said as I dubiously handed him my cards and matches, "I'm shick today. Terrible hang-over. Gimme a quarter an' I'll vote for you twiced."

In his travail Buller drew his lips up into a moist rosebud pout and blew out his enormously fat pink cheeks. He looked like an unfortunate cherub whose thyroid had run amuck. Then the inspiration came to me and I suddenly pictured him in a nightgown and a fringed baby's cap. . . .

"Look, Buller," I said, my voice grown hoarse with animal cunning, "how'd you like to make yourself ten bucks instead?"

"What doin', Johnny?" Buller said, rallying swiftly.

"Just sitting on your fat prat and riding in the big parade tomorrow."

"You don't mean the *baby* parade?"

"Sure, sure, Buller," I mollified him, dangling more bait. "All you got to do is sit there and fork down a fifth of Old Cordwood. Nobody'll recognize you."

"Hm," Buller mused, pondering my offer as my mind raced. Let's see: I'd rent an old carriage—the kind with wavy fringe on top—and one of those ancient donkeys (the symbol of my party) from McVannel's Livery Stable; hitch the donkey to the carriage; install Big Baby Buller and his bottle of Old Cordwood in the carriage; drape "Traver for D.A." signs from the carriage and over the donkey's back—and let the people laugh me into the District Attorneyship. "Hm . . ." went Buller, rocking thoughtfully.

"Of course, Buller," I said, "if you don't *want* the ten bucks and the free fifth . . ." I turned to go.

"Look, Johnny!" Buller shrilled in terror. "Don't be hasty. I'll do it! I—I was jest gettin' up my courage to hit you fer five bucks on account."

"Nothing at all, Buller," I said, airily whipping five dollars off the roll of six I happened to be carrying. "I'll meet you right here at ten tomorrow morning. The parade starts at eleven. I'll have everything ready—even to the diaper!"

"O.K., Johnny," Buller said, reaching out for the five dollars with eager trembling hands. "Ten o'clock here tomorrow—sharp on the dot."

"O.K., Buller," I said, and away I darted, filled with dazzling plans for rented donkeys, carriages, baby clothes, bottles of Old Cordwood—and irresistible political signs.

Sharp at ten the next morning one of McVannel's drivers and

I carefully threaded our way across Iron Street, guiding the tired donkey through a maze of baby buggies and weeping passengers to the rear of Torreano's Tavern, there to pick up Buller Beaudin and dress him for the baby parade. "Whoa!" said the driver to the disconsolate donkey.

"Wait out here, Fred," I told the driver, leaping gaily from the carriage with my satchel of props and darting into the tavern's family entrance. "Hello, Joe," I hailed the proprietor. "Where's Buller Beaudin?"

"Hm," Joe said, shaking his head and leading me to the back card room and switching on the 25-watt overhead bulb. "There's your Buller—if you can find enough help to move him."

There was an inert Buller, half sitting and half sprawled across the billiard-green card table—out like a light. "Buller!" I shouted, as I shook him wildly. "Wake up, Buller! The *parade* starts in forty minutes!" Vast Buller just rolled from side to side as I shook him and then came back to rest, like a huge, soft, gyroscopic toy. "Blub wah," he muttered, in a kind of a rumbling five-dollar burp.

There I was out all my money—the rental of the donkey and the driver and livery equipment and all my props—and I had no baby. "Joe," I murmured, turning white-faced to the proprietor. "Before I try moving this wheezing alcoholic slob—or delivering a baby of my own—would you mind bringing me a double-shot of Old Cordwood? I—I think I need a drink awful bad!"

"Blub wah," Buller went again, doubtless trying to rally at the magic name of his favorite drink. The effort caused a relapse for he shortly began to snore. I shut my eyes and wagged my head and sank to a chair beside him.

The parade went off on schedule. Sharp at eleven the Mayor's attendants finally hoisted him up on his horse and balanced him there, the Hematite American Legion band burst into a jazzed-up and slumber-chasing version of Brahms' *Lullaby*—and away rolled several hundred moist, squalling and unhappy offspring, pushed by an equal number of anxious and perspiring mothers. At the very end of the parade, drawn by a donkey, rode the biggest, fattest and wettest baby of all—laughing, bawling, cooing, gurgling, hiccuping, burping, patting his damp bangs—all the while beatifically sluicing down a bottle of Old Cordwood through a red rubber nipple.

The huge baby occasionally paused and, like a princeling bestowing largess, carelessly flung a handful of campaign matches to a scrambling and grateful populace. In all the excitement and jollity nobody noticed that the baby's nightshirt was stuffed with wine straw and old newspapers and that his cheeks were distended with huge wads of tin foil. In fact to this day nobody but good old Joe Torreano and McVannel's driver knew that this baby—who incidentally won a special prize—was none other than the dignified candidate for D.A. himself.

The election came and went. With considerable humility I report that I was elected—yes, by a larger majority than any candidate running on either ticket. The nightmare was over. Grace wept.

Chapter 2

WILLIE THE WEEPER

WHEN I FIRST BECAME D.A. there was a fabulous old criminal lawyer still practicing in these parts called Old Crocker. In his day he had been the Clarence Darrow of the Peninsula, the victorious hero of hundreds of criminal defenses. He had also been a constant thorn in the side of my predecessors in office. By the time I arrived upon the D.A. scene (via the Baby Parade) he was a very old man; crotchety, deaf and alcoholic; his fires banked, his day nearly done. He sat at home with his Shakespeare, his whisky and his memories, roaring at his equally deaf old housekeeper. But occasionally the old war horse could be lured out of retirement (like wee chuckling Harry Lauder cannily making his fiftieth farewell tour) if the fee was large enough and the case happened to interest him.

Old Crocker was more familiarly known among the legal profession simply as The Voice or else Willie the Weeper. Besides his booming bass voice, tears were the secret of his success; he wept his way through every trial; and for years sniffling, lachrymose jurors had been rewarding him and his amazing tear ducts with verdicts of acquittal. He was said to set his fee by the amount of tears he shed, and the one and only time I met him in court his rate was reputed to be $500 a pint.

About all I can remember of the trial facts was that the case was a rape case in the classic tradition: the defendant was a wandering married man who wouldn't take no for an answer, and the girl wouldn't say yes, so perforce he raped her. All during the trial I felt the same thrill to be pitted against this grand old campaigner

23

that a young actor might feel given his first walk-on part with one
of the Barrymores.

Despite his age and deafness (he disdained wearing a bean in
his ear) Old Crocker was still good on examination, especially
cross-examination. But as the trial wore on it was plain to see that
he wasn't too much interested in the facts of his case; facts were
for fools and young D.A.s; *he* was waiting for the third and final
act—the jury argument—when the great Crocker himself, ignoring
mundane facts, could strut and fret and fume and shout and weep
down all opposition. When he finally had his man on the stand he
paused and cleared his throat and suddenly asked his client: "Are
you married?"

"Yes."

"Is your woman stickin' with you in your trouble?" In court
Old Crocker, really a well-educated man, frequently affected the
one-gallus, cracker-barrel talk of a small-town feed merchant.

"Yes."

"Is your woman here in court?"

"Yes."

"Will you point her out?"

"Sure." Pointing.

"Will you ask her to stand up?"

"Stand up, Amanda," the witness ordered.

Amanda obediently stood up, a plump, matronly, pleasant-
looking woman in her late thirties. In her arms she held the sweet-
est golden-haired baby I'd ever seen outside of my own kids or a
movie. "Goo," gurgled the baby. The women on the jury cooed
with adoration. The D.A. wanted to boo.

"So that's your woman standin' there holdin' the infant?"

"Yes."

"Tell her to sit down!" Old Crocker barked.

"Sit down, Amanda!"

Amanda sat down.

All this gluey and obvious play for sympathy had nothing whatever to do with the case, of course, and I doubtless could have successfully objected to it. But I knew that the jury was consumed
with curiosity and would have resented my blocking its gratifica-

tion, so I remained silent. It was one of Crocker's oldest tricks: if I objected I made the jury mad at me; if I remained silent he accomplished his purpose. Either way he won. Yet I couldn't help but admire the crafty old fox. It was all corn, but damned effective corn.

When it came my turn to cross-examine the defendant, deaf Old Crocker didn't even deign to come over and stand near his client so that he could hear my questions and hear his client's answers. This rankled me. So that's what he thought of the young D.A.'s capabilities! Instead he sat at his table putting on a diverting side show: taking elaborate notes (on what I know not, since he couldn't hear); clearing his throat, trumpeting into a large silk handkerchief; and tossing off a series of white pills with bumpers of tepid water. (Courtroom water is always tepid.) Half the time the absorbed jury sat looking at him rather than listening to the fumbling and exasperated young D.A.

As I monotonously examined the defendant, who blandly denied everything, something in the back of my mind kept bothering me, striking a faint warning bell, a tinkling little bell which seemed to chime: "Johnny, aren't you overlooking something? Think, Johnny, think!" Suddenly it came to me: of course, the *baby,* the little golden-haired baby! Old Crocker had barely *mentioned* the baby. I and everyone had naturally assumed that it was the defendant's child. But was it? And why had crafty Old Crocker neglected to cover such an important sentimental point in his corny bid for sympathy? Was it deliberate?

I glanced at Old Crocker, who was busy rearranging his silk handkerchief in his lapel pocket, just so. Then I drew near the defendant and lowered my voice. Just as Old Crocker didn't want to listen to me, so now I wanted to make sure he couldn't hear me. I spoke in such a low voice that even the jury had to pay close attention to follow me.

Speaking out of the side of my mouth like a movie mobster: "That baby your wife is holding—is it your child?" I asked the witness, almost stealthily.

The witness glanced anxiously at oblivious Old Crocker, who

was now elaborately swallowing a new crop of white pills. "No. No it isn't," he answered.

"I see. Perhaps the child is adopted?"

"No."

"Is it a boy or a girl?"

"I haven't the faintest notion."

"What's it's name?"

"I dunno."

"Is it any relation to you or your wife?"

"Not that I know of."

"Hm. . . . Do you and she *have* any children?"

"No."

"Does your wife work?"

"Yes."

"Is she self-supporting?"

"Yes."

"Are you and she living together?"

"No, we're separated. Over five years."

All this was equally objectionable, but oblivious Old Crocker had partially opened the taboo subject and I felt I had an equal right to exhaust and close it.

"Why is the child here?"

Shrugging: "You got me. I don't know." Innocently: "My lawyer asked my wife to bring a small baby to court. They made their own arrangements. She and I ain't talking. That's all I know."

So the baby was just a Crocker stage prop. The diabolical old goat!

I turned to the jury to make sure they had heard all this. From their quick glances at each other and their broad smiles I knew they had been listening. I then retreated quickly to my counsel table and stood facing the judge and said in a loud voice: "That's all. No further questions of this witness."

Old Crocker forsook his pills and got up, gracefully flowed his silk handkerchief through his forefinger and thumb, and then trumpeted: "May it please the Court, the defense rests!" The old boy could lend drama to a burp.

"Very well, gentlemen, you may proceed with your arguments," Judge Belden said, smiling gravely.

My opening argument was brief and routine. Old Crocker came over and stood listening to it, cupping his ear. I felt flattered. I was also pleased that he had had no time to exchange vital statistics with his client. Acting on a hunch I could not then have explained, I was careful to at no point refer to the defendant's wife or the baby she held. I simply reviewed the bare facts in the case and abruptly sat down. It was now Old Crocker's turn.

Old Crocker arose and bowed low to the judge—"May it please the Court"—and strode before the jury like an arthritic old Roman senator. "Esteemed members of the jury," he began in that melodious soothing voice, like a pipe organ warming up. Then he was away. . . . The oratory flowed from him like sap from a girdled maple in May. He discussed everything under the sun but the facts in his case: quotations from Shakespeare, the roll of drums at Valley Forge, the spat of muskets, Betsy Ross and the furling flag, the deathless Constitution, the dampness of those gray prison walls, the defendant's lonely wife, the ashes in the cold hearth, the empty home with the lamp gleaming in the window. . . . Sometimes the voluptuous rhetoric itself grew inaudible and there was just the deep growl and boom of the Voice, vibrant and muttering, like a cathedral organ during a transitionary passage—and then away soared the words in another verbal flight. I found myself nodding. It was a form of hypnosis.

"Ah, yes, the hearth, the home!" he repeated dramatically, slowly savoring these folk-laden words. At this point he sniffed and shook his head and produced his silk handkerchief and buried his face in it—and promptly emerged miraculously convulsed with tears. He turned and pointed tearfully at the defendant's wife. "Who's going to take care of this little mother and her suckling babe?" he quavered tremulously down the scale. It was superb: by comparison Pagliacci himself would have been ejected for unseemly laughter. At this point—and equally miraculously—the suckling babe let out a sudden stricken wail, for all the world as though some one had deliberately stuck a pin in it.

"Hear, hear!" Old Crocker thundered, his face contorted with grief, the tears coursing down his cheeks, "already this innocent child senses the danger lurking over its poor father!" Between the duet of wailing of the old lawyer and the baby, the din was terrific. Judge Belden frowned and surreptitiously turned down his hearing aid. Pointing Old Crocker was too absorbed with the lines and diction of his big scene to observe that a hardhearted jury was convulsed with mirth. On and on boomed Old Crocker, picturing the sad fate of the little mother and her suckling babe. "Think of this poor child growing up to sweet girlhood the daughter of a convicted felon!" he rolled on. All the while he dripped so many tears that I feared he would skid on the wet tile and fall in a heap.

Old Crocker paused electrically, shed another $500 worth of tears, and then, gathering himself, swung into his resounding conclusion. "Breathes there a man or woman on this jury with soul so dead," he wept, his voice cracked with grief, "who can bear on his conscience the knowledge that by his guilty verdict he will have torn this innocent man from the loving grasp of this little mother and the tiny plucking fingers of this bereft infant?" He paused and straightened. "Ladies and gentlemen, I thank you and may God bless you."

Old Crocker turned and strode tearless back to his tepid water and white pills. By this time some of the jurors in their unholy mirth were stuffing handkerchiefs in their mouths and hiding their faces behind their hands. It was my closing turn to talk. But what was there to say? I slowly arose to my feet.

"The People waive any closing argument," I announced, and slumped down. Enough was enough. Far from feeling any sense of triumph, my main feeling was one of embarrassment and guilt: embarrassment that a venerable old lawyer—whose reputation I had esteemed for years—could make such a gorgeous ass out of himself and his profession; and guilt that I had to be a party to the old Roman's decline and fall.

Verdict: alas, the plucking fingers of the suckling babe were torn from its borrowed foster-father. Old Crocker retired permanently to his Shakespeare and his whisky and his little white pills.

Chapter 3

THE EDUCATION OF A D.A.

JUDGE BELDEN summoned me to his book-lined chambers just before my first circuit court term as D.A. "Shut the door and sit down," he said, slowly filling his pipe with a shaggy supply of that working man's marijuana known as Peerless. I sat watching the man.

Despite his advancing years he was as erect and slender as a young man. His powerful neck and shoulders were a heritage from his early days of strenuous physical labor. (He had put himself through law school and had worked hard at all manner of jobs after he got out.) He had the head of a Roman emperor, with deep-set piercing blue-gray eyes, a strong, curving, flaring nose, a firm chin, and a full, mobile mouth. His thinning hair was white, as was his mustache and small, well-trimmed beard. The strength of his features was tempered by an expression that may best be termed kindly; the man radiated awareness and good will; he had that Albert Schweitzer look.

As he sat there he looked more like a judge than any man I ever knew. In the long professional years that lay ahead together I was to find that he *was* more like a judge than any judge I ever knew. I was to find that he was wise, patient and humorous; simple, tolerant and kindly—a fine lawyer and a gentle man. I was to find that he abhorred pomposity, bombast and fake like some congressmen embrace those qualities. I was also to find that he was my friend; that Judge Belden was every inch a man. . . .

"Young man," he said, his pipe finally stoked and billowing smoke, "you are embarking on a tough job, a poorly paid job, and one in which you will receive far more criticism than praise. Criticism is the lot of all men in public life, but particularly that of a public prosecutor." He paused and added dryly, "I know that is so because I was prosecutor of this county before you were born. On the other hand few people will know whether you are doing a *good* job and fewer yet will care." The Judge puffed reflectively on his pipe. "I will know and I will care." He held out his hand and smiled. "Good luck, Johnny."

"T-thank you, Judge Belden," I said, peering at him through the haze of Peerless smoke and swallowing hard from mingled emotion and nausea. I was thrilled that this grand old man of the law should care what happened to this latest upstart young D.A. He had seen so very many. The knowledge was a tremendous lift —as well as a challenge—and one that stayed with me during all my time in office.

"Another thing," Judge Belden continued, "you will lose cases that you will think you should have won. At first it will be hard and you will frequently smart with self-reproach. But you will have to learn to take these lickings with a smile or else quit." The Judge smiled—I thought a little wistfully—perhaps recollecting his own early days as prosecutor. "You will have to learn to do this because you will be dealing with that strange and wonderful— and unpredictable—beast, the *jury*." I sat there trying to visualize a writhing creature with twelve leering heads, all mechanically repeating, "Not guilty" like a telephone exchange announcing a strike. "And remember this," he continued, "jurors in criminal cases always ask themselves not one but two questions: 'Is the defendant guilty? If so, do we want to see him punished?' Remember this and your way may be easier. The road will be rocky at best. Now let's get to work, Johnny."

One of the first things I found I had to work on, fast and hard, was the problem of lying witnesses. There is a constant flood of perjury in all of our courts all of the time; a flood that reaches its crest in our criminal courts where the stakes are high, being usually for freedom instead of money. One of the big trial jobs of every D.A. is to spot and expose perjury wherever he encounters it.

And he encounters it often. It was only after years of rough and tumble criminal trial work against some of the best trial lawyers in the Peninsula that I became a little perjury spotter and exposer from hell. I had to in order to survive.

One of my first lessons in the ungentle art of trapping liars came when I prosecuted Gordon Bliss for manslaughter with a car. The People claimed Bliss had hugged the wrong side of an inside curve and collided head on with an approaching car, instantly killing the other driver. Since it was vitally important for the People to establish that the defendant did indeed drive on the wrong side of the road, I called as witnesses the two survivors in the other car and the three investigating state police, all of whom testified that just after the accident the broken glass from both cars was almost all confined to the "wrong" side of the highway. This naturally showed that the accident had occurred there.

In defense the defendant Bliss called the keeper of a tavern in the vicinity of the accident, who, being sworn to "tell the truth, the whole truth, and nothing but the truth," blithely proceeded to testify that he had heard the crash; had hurried from his tavern; that the accident appeared to him to have occurred on the defendant's side of the road; and that most of the broken glass was on his or the "right" side of the road.

"Did you see anyone move any of that glass following the accident?" the defendant's lawyer asked this surprise star defense witness. It was an objectionable leading question but I wanted to know the answer so I remained silent.

"Yes," the witness answered.

"Who?"

"I saw the state police kicking and scraping the broken glass over onto the wrong side of the road," the witness calmly answered. The defense lawyer turned to me with an ill-disguised smile of triumph. "The People may examine the witness," he said.

This bombshell witness was a serious blow to my case and I knew it. In court as elsewhere, truth is not measured by the quantity of those who profess to tell it, but by their quality, and if the jury believed this man's story or if his story raised even a reasonable doubt in their minds, my case was out the window. And technically he was the only strictly disinterested witness in the case. While I never subscribed to the consoling notion that the People's witnesses were the sole repositories of truth, or that the defense witnesses were all liars, it struck me as rather odd that this man should tell the exact reverse of the story already told by five apparently credible witnesses.

His story seemed too damned neat. I had already observed that the state police had quite enough grief on their hands without rigging their cases; in other words, these fine officers ordinarily left their broken glass where they found it. At any rate, it was my turn to either question the witness or let him go. I had to believe someone so I chose to believe the trusted officers with whom I worked. I plunged ahead on the theory that this witness was lying by the clock.

"Did you ever tell me or any law enforcement officers your version of the accident before you testified here today?" I asked, floundering for an opening.

"No."

"Why?"

Bridling: "I didn't think I had to. I'm no cop. Anyway, it was none of my business and nobody asked me."

"*Nobody* asked you?" I prodded this winning fellow, taking a shot in the dark.

"That's right."

My opening had already appeared and I seized it. "Not even the defendant?" I asked.

Perjuring witnesses frequently guiltily think it is somehow wrong for them to admit the natural fact that they of course had words with the side they maintain. There is nothing wrong about it; it would be wrong if they hadn't. But this witness fell for the rusty old trap. "No," he answered after a pause, reddening. "We never discussed it."

I knew then that I was on the right track. "Nor with his lawyer?" I bored in.

"No," he answered, committed now.

"Nor with any of his relatives?"

"No."

"Nor with any person whatever?"

Grown complacent with falsehood. "No, that's right."

I now had him pinned down. I would drive a final spike through his lying heart. "So, Mr. Comber, the fact is that you have never discussed what you saw at the accident that night with any living person—before you testified from this witness stand here today, a few minutes ago?"

Glancing quickly for succor at the defendant's table. Then back. "That's correct." His face was lobster red now.

I paused to let this sink in. Positive now that I was dealing with a liar, and a clumsy one, I moved quickly away from my table and got over to the side of the jury box so that my liar would have to look directly at the jury as he spun his fantasies. That way the jury would not only get an unobstructed head-on view of him as he testified, but they would also get the full psychological effect of the wide swing of his head that the witness would have to make as he cast his beseeching, guilty glances over at the defendant's table. It was a trick I had learned early to use to deal with perjurers. The stage set, I pressed on.

"Now, Mr. Comber, who asked you to come here to court and testify?" I asked him quietly.

This was a loaded question: If he said the other side had summoned him he would have shown that he must most likely have first communicated the nature of his testimony to them, which he had just denied; and if he said no, he further exposed the extravagance of his falsehoods.

The witness made another barn door swing of his head at the defense table and then back at me: "W-what did you say?"

"I said, Mr. Comber, 'Who asked you to come here and testify today?' "

"Oh! Oh, that. Why—er—nobody, nobody at all. I just read in the paper that the trial was on, so I decided it was my duty to come and tell what I knew."

"I see," I said, touched by such unselfish devotion to the ideal of good citizenship. "You have no interest in the case, or in its result, you've never discussed the facts of the case with anyone—

your sole interest is that truth and justice shall prevail—is that right?"

Nodding, considerably relieved: "Why, yes. That's exactly it."

"You realize of course that by your testimony here you are not only imputing perjury to the two survivors in the other car, but to the three state police as well; and that you are also making the serious accusation that the police have framed this case against the defendant?"

Airily: "Yep." This native Socrates carried his responsibilities lightly.

"Did it never occur to you, in your laudable zeal to uphold justice and truth, to remonstrate with the state police when, as you claim, you saw them moving the glass?"

"What's remonstrate mean?"

"Kick, my friend, kick."

"I didn't want to get them down on me. You see, I run a tavern. They could give me a bad time."

"You thought maybe if you waited to pop this serious charge at them before everyone here in open court everything would be dandy and they would somehow learn to love you?"

Uneasily: "I dunno . . . I thought it was time for me to come in here and tell what I knew."

This answer opened up glittering new vistas and I went baying along the scent. "Hm. . . . You wanted to tell what you knew, did you? Now I don't think I called you to the stand as a witness, did I?"

"No, of course not." He looked at me regretfully. How stupid could a D.A. get?

"The fact is the defendant Bliss' lawyer called you, isn't that right?" I pressed on.

Again the forlorn glance at the defense table. But since everybody in the courtroom had plainly heard the defendant's lawyer call Comber to the stand, there was only one possible answer. "Yes," he mumbled.

"I see. Now will you please explain to the jury and me how come the defendant's lawyer happened to call you to the stand if you never spoke to him or the defendant or anyone about your professed knowledge of the case? How would he ever know about you?"

The witness was growing very unhappy. He mopped his brow and again glanced guiltily at the defendant's table. I glanced too. Bliss' lawyer sat looking at the floor with his eyes winced shut, his hand to his troubled brow. Such grotesque falsehoods had floored even him.

"Did you hear me, Mr. Comber?" I prodded gently.

"Yass, I heard you. Ah. . . . Well, it was this way," he floundered. "I met the defendant in the hall during recess and told him I knew something about the case and would testify to it if he wanted to call me to the stand."

"I see. But you naturally didn't tell him what it was or what you were going to say?"

Seizing at a straw now. "Yep, that's correct—nary a word."

I paused and the ancient words of Quintelian came to me. "It is fitting," he had wisely said, "that a liar should admit as much truth as he can." I returned to the perspiring witness. "So you want us to believe, Mr. Comber, that an experienced and able defense counsel like the defendant's lawyer called you to the witness stand this afternoon without having the faintest notion of what you might say?"

Defiantly now. "That's right!"

"Or whether your testimony might help his client or harm him?"

"That's right."

I again glanced at the defendant's lawyer. He had revived a little and rolled his eyes up in his head at me in mute resignation. I then walked over and consulted the court stenographer. He searched his notes and at my request read back one of the early questions asked the witness by the defense lawyer. " 'Did you see anyone move any of that glass following the accident?' " the stenographer intoned in the monotonous dead-pan voice court reporters seem occupationally compelled to cultivate. I moved back before the witness.

"Do you remember the defendant's lawyer asking you this question [repeating it] and your answering that you saw the state police kicking and scraping the glass over to the wrong side of the road?"

"Yes," the witness replied, because he had to.

"Will you please explain to the jury and me, Mr. Comber, how the defendant's lawyer could *possibly* have asked you that question if you had not first discussed the details of your testimony with him or with someone?"

Again glancing unhappily at the defendant's table. He moistened his lips. "Ah," he said. Another quick glance at counsel, then at the clock, and then back to me. "I dunno. He musta took a shot in the dark, I guess."

Judge Belden spoke up at this point. "I see that it is nearing five o'clock. Perhaps we had better adjourn until 9 A.M. tomorrow. The prosecuting attorney can resume his cross-examination then. Mr. Sheriff." The sheriff banged his gavel, everyone arose, "Hear ye, hear ye, hear ye . . ." sang the sheriff, and court adjourned until the following day.

But there is no rest for the D.A. during a term of court. I still had to finish my preparation for the trial of a murder case that followed this one. I phoned Grace that I was trapped down at court and hoped to be home "before the spring breakup." I lit an Italian cigar (an antidote to Judge Belden's eternal smogs of Peerless) and, supperless, buried myself in the law library.

About 9 P.M. I had my chores done and stopped and grabbed a hamburger and a beer and got in my car and hightailed for Chippewa—and bed. My route took me past the scene of the accident in the case we were trying, and as I boiled around the curve where the accident happened my swinging headlights momentarily swept the front of the tavern. By the merest chance I happened to glance over that way and was enchanted to see, of all things, the defendant Bliss getting out of a car and heading for the tavern door. It was 10:17.

"My, my," I murmured. "Skull practice for Humpty Dumpty."

The next morning court convened, Witness Comber climbed warily back on the stand, and I resumed my heckling post by the side of the jury. I wasted no time.

"Mr. Comber," I began, "is it still true that you have never discussed the facts in this case with the defendant or his lawyer or with anyone on his behalf?"

"Yes," he snapped defiantly. "I told you all that yesterday."

"Pardon me. And that holds true right down to this very moment?"

"That's right."

"You have never any time up to this moment conferred with the defendant or his lawyer about the details of this case?"

"Right!"

"And all that is just as true as your testimony here yesterday about the position of the cars and the broken glass?"

"You bet."

I decided it was time to lower the boom on this clown. I shot my cuff and glanced elaborately at my wrist watch as I spoke. "Tell us, then," I began, still absorbed by my watch, "just what you and the defendant Gordon Bliss *did* talk about when he called on you at your tavern at 10:17 last night?"

This was the closest I ever came to seeing a jaw drop. The witness shifted and glanced and reddened and puffed and blinked and glanced again. How much did I know? he was obviously asking himself. It was plain even to him that I certainly knew that the defendant Bliss had been there. But did I have someone spotted in the tavern? One could almost hear the rusty clank of his cranial gears.

"Ha . . ." he finally answered, perspiring freely. "Oh, Bliss—he just dropped in for a beer or two. Didn't stay too long."

"Suppose you tell me your version of how long he stayed?" I said, playing on his doubt of how much I knew.

"Maybe an hour or two," he ventured vaguely.

"IIm . . . I see. Just popped in and just popped out. And of course you and he didn't refer to the pending case, then?" I had already committed him on that one.

"Oh, no."

"If I am not prying, what did you talk about?"

Airily, relieved to think he was over another bad spot: "Oh, the weather, high prices, deer hunting. Stuff like that."

"Didn't the defendant even thank you for volunteering to testify for him yesterday?"

"No," he snapped.

In mock wonderment. "Didn't he even congratulate you on the splendid way you handled yourself on the witness stand?"

"No, no, no, I said!" I was fast getting to him.

"Oh, you mean there was no reference whatever to the case by either of you?"

Grimly. "That's what I've said a dozen times."

"Not even *one* little word about the case?" I persisted, goading him.

Exploding angrily: "No. Why should we talk about the case! The guy means nothin' to me. I tole my story and I'm done." Suddenly shouting: "It's the truth, I say! Every damned word is the truth, I tell you!" Bristling angrily: "What you tryin' to do, fella, call me a liar?"

"I scarcely think that is necessary, Mr. Comber," I said, surveying this maddened dolt. "But do you think it unnatural that I should suspect that a man who is on trial for a grave felony might want to discuss his case with the only witness that may stand between him and a verdict of guilty?"

Glaring: "I dunno nothin' about that." Sullenly: "I'm tellin' the truth, I tell you."

"That's all," I said, figuring that by now there was surely another school of thought on that subject.

2.

There was, and Bliss was promptly convicted. The testimony of his star witness had been so far blasted that the jury would have had in effect to convict itself of gross stupidity to have freed the defendant. This is always nice work if the D.A. can maneuver it. The jury has a certain low pride. . . . The interesting thing is that all this was accomplished solely by cross-examination, showing its tremendous value in smoking out courtroom liars. The case shows something else: the witness Comber's testimony had been pretty well blasted by cross-examination before I had ever seen the defendant Bliss enter his tavern. The rest was merely a fortuitous assist to the final coup de grâce, but it shows that the D.A. during the trial must be as alert to see and cash in on the breaks as is the quarterback of a bowl-bent football team.

All this sounds about as modest as a gravel-voiced congressman astride a sound truck shyly persuading his constituents why he should be paroled back to Washington; as though I should have pontifically entitled this meditation *What Every Young D.A. Should Know.* I do not mean it that way. Manifestly I can best tell about those cases that happened to me, that were burned into my memory, and the Lord knows I doubtless missed many beautiful chances to trip up other lying witnesses. But somehow I'd rather tell you about my little triumphs. Spotting and exposing liars has always been one of my greatest courtroom delights.

Another strategy I developed, as do all D.A.'s whose heads are not loaded with Crisco, was the fine Latin strategy of the—ahem—*reductio ad absurdum,* that is, of making the lying witness's story look silly, of giving a lying witness enough rope to hang himself, of finally making the witness himself look like a liar or fool or both. I had partly used this with Comber. This strategy is especially valuable where one feels certain that the witness is lying but cannot quite catch him at it, as I had luckily been able to do with Comber of the broken glass. But he was really no match. Not all courtroom liars are so witless. Let me tell you about a smarter operator, one who drove me to the limit before I finally nailed him.

One night twenty-three-year-old Carl Manfred of Hematite got a romantic seizure and drifted over to Chippewa in his Chev to do something about it. He finally lured a seventeen-year-old seamstress into his car on the pretext of driving her home, instead whirled her out to the brambles, stopped the car and turned out the lights, turned abruptly to the girl and said seductively, "How about it, Toots?" Perhaps he had wasted too much time in wooing her; at any rate she said no and started to get out of the car.

Manfred grabbed her and whirled her around and struck her on the jaw, breaking it. "How about it, Toots?" he repeated. "Yes," the girl mumbled, wisely succumbing to his blandishments—whereupon Manfred promptly tried to do his stuff. Due however to the fact that the girl happened to be a virgin the engagement did not come off very well. After repeated attempts sturdy young Manfred gave up and drove the girl near her home and dumped her off and sped away—but not before she had spotted his license number. The hysterical girl staggered into her home. When her jaw was set and she was able to mumble her story through gritted teeth, the police went out and joyfully gathered in Manfred. The girl identified him as her assaulter, he was charged with assault with intent to rape, pleaded not guilty, and the D.A. had another nasty case to try.

Manfred's defense was consent, that is, that the girl herself had wanted to get laid. How did she get her jaw broken? Easy—she'd evidently been drinking before he picked her up and had fallen on her face when she got out of the car once to relieve herself. But first I had showed that the girl was a virgin; that she did not drink; that the physician who set her jaw later that night detected no signs of drink; and that she was badly bruised and torn in the genital area. When the People's case was in Manfred took the stand and told the above "consent" story. When it came my turn to get my verbal claws on him I soon found I could not shake him from his story. He was an intelligent, clean-cut-looking, well-educated little punk who came from a good family. I soon felt that he was scoring heavily with the jury. After all, why else would a girl get into a car late at night with a strange man? he cleverly inferred. I swiftly decided to change my tactics. Why keep butting my head against the stonewall of his clever denials?

"You were out looking for some scratching that night, weren't you?" I asked him.

"If you mean sexual intercourse, no," he answered swiftly. "Just excitement. I admit I like girls"—here he paused and smiled in sheepish modesty—"and-er-I guess they like me."

So far no good. Some of the jurors tittered a little at this, a bad omen for the D.A.'s case. Here was a smart little bastard and I had to find and expose his weak spot and do it fast. He sat looking confidently at me. I studied him through squinted eyes and decided his greatest weakness was egotism. If I could only get him talking and overconfident. . . . The defendant sat there watchfully awaiting my next question, like a clever and wary young boxer waiting for the bell.

"You mean that you were just a normal young man that wasn't particularly looking for anything, but wasn't throwing anything over your shoulder, either?" I asked.

He smiled. "Yes," he answered. "I think you have precisely stated my feelings in the current idiom."

Current idiom, indeed! The insolent little whelp! I decided to pitch him some fast idiomatic curves.

"Did you know this girl before?"

"No."

"Did she know you?"

"No."

"Perfect strangers?"

"Yes."

Suddenly: "Did you use any male contraceptive device during your sexual engagement?"

"Please repeat that?"

"Did you use what we old idiom-slaves call a French safe?"

The defendant shot a quick look at his lawyer—his first bobble—and back at me. "Yes," he said, smiling shyly. "At first I did—later I didn't."

"Hm . . . And are these rubber devices standard equipment with you when you go out in your Chev looking for—er—normal young American excitement?"

This was a loaded question and he immediately sensed it. He quickly chose the lesser evil. Easily: "As a matter of fact, no—it happened that night was the first occasion I ever carried them."

"But of course you still had nothing in mind but good clean American fun?"

"That's correct. Also, with so many fast young girls running around these days I thought I had better carry some protection." He had a clever faculty of enlarging his answers to his own advantage. But at least I had him talking now and gaining confidence.

"Protection perhaps from fast young girls like this one?" I quickly shot at him.

"Well, yes," he admitted.

"And protection for yourself, you mean—not for the girls? Is that right?"

"Well, no—protection all around," he swiftly countered. "You see, I—I'm not very experienced at this sort of thing." Again the whimsical, boyish smile which was part of his American boy act.

"I see. Why did you stop the car and turn out the lights? Or did this fast girl in her eagerness grab the brake and turn out the lights for you?" But I was forcing him too fast.

Smiling: "No. . . . You see, she was pretty—is pretty—and I thought we could sit and smooch a little before I drove her home."

"And of course this fast girl started the smooching?"

"As a matter of fact she did."

"And smooching is *your* idiom for what an old ex-smoocher like me might call petting or necking?"

Smiling: "Yes."

I felt I had him coming nicely now, so I speeded my questions. "Was she good at it?"

Shyly: "Quite."

"And this fast girl, good at smooching, finally managed to get you interested in something more than your normally innocent parking activities?"

"Well, yes," he admitted, shyly embarrassed at such a crass question.

"Who made the first business pass?"

"What do you mean?"

"Who first indicated that he or she wanted to get laid?"

Thoughtfully, with a nice air of wanting to be fair: "I believe it was the girl. Hm. . . . Yes, it was. She got awfully close to me—lay tight against me. Perhaps her drinking made her bold. She was quite intoxicated."

"Anyway, she was a hot little number?"

"I believe that is the term *you* might employ," he shot back.

The little bastard, I thought. "What did she say?"

"She kept repeating, 'Darling, darling, darling . . .' "

"And you?"

"I don't recall that I said anything."

"Like one of the Rover Boys, you remained cool, calm and collected under fire?"

"Well, not precisely."

"My, my. You finally got up a head of steam?"

"What do you mean?"

"Pardon my archaic idiom. You finally wanted to lay her?"

"Well, yes."

"At what point did you introduce your new rubber purchases?"

"She kept asking me if I had anything. I finally understood that she meant a rubber."

"Come now, you never thought that meant anything else, did you?"

"Well, no."

"So you finally consented to lay her?"

"Yes."

"But with considerable reluctance?" I said, cautiously feeding out more rope.

"Well, yes. She seemed so—so sort of bold and forward, I was a little afraid."

"Afraid of what?"

"Afraid of contracting a venereal disease."

"But she finally overcame your boyish reluctance and fear?"

"Yes."

At this point I took up my favorite spot at the side of the jury. It was now or never. "The fact is, Mr. Manfred, this fast girl was the aggressor in this whole thing, was she not?" I held my breath, for on his answer depended whether the defendant, in his lardy ego, was coming all the way or not.

The answer finally came. "Yes," he said quietly.

"As a matter of fact it was the *girl* who started things; the *girl* who pushed things beyond the smooching stage; the *girl* who virtually forced you to lay her? Right?"

"That's right," he said, finally grabbing all the rope I was giving him.

I paused to deliver my fastest ball of the trial. Slowly: "So that it would be fair to say, Mr. Manfred, would it not, that *it is the girl who should be standing trial here today for the crime of assault with intent to rape rather than you?"*

By now his answer was inevitable. "Yes," he finally answered, after some rapid SOS glances at his attorney. I could almost feel the revolted jury stiffen and grow tense at this brazen answer. At last the egotistic little bastard sat exposed for all to see. I paused to let the moment sink in and then veered away before he could try to patch things—veered, that is, to my clincher.

"You heard the doctor testify here earlier that the girl was what we idiomatic laymen call a virgin?" I asked.

Warily now, a little gun-shy: "Yes I did."

"Do you question the correctness of that opinion?"

"No," he answered, because he had to.

"You also heard the doctor testify as to the tears and bruises the girl had in the genital region?"

"Yes."

"Do you question the correctness of those findings?"

"No—but I must admit she tried awfully hard."

Now was the time to strike. "Mr. Manfred," I slowly asked, "will you please give the jury and me your explanation of why this seventeen-year-old virgin should choose *you*—a perfect stranger—as the altar at which she should sacrifice her virginity?"

Suddenly: *"How in hell do you expect me to read her mind!"* he shouted. At last I had stung him to the quick and he sat there with clenched fists, white and shivering with anger. He looked as though he might even want to break the D.A.'s jaw. The jury's eyes were glued on him.

Pressing: "But that's what she tried to do, didn't she? She threw herself at you? She wouldn't take no for an answer?"

"Yes," he said softly, trying desperately to cover his revealing flash of temper.

I could speak softly, too. "Perhaps it was your irresistible male glamor about which you have already modestly spoken?"

In a low controlled voice: "Perhaps."

"Perhaps she just couldn't resist your clean all-American sex appeal?"

Darting me a look of sheer hatred. "Perhaps."

Still softly: "Perhaps, too, she was just a little slut at heart, anyway?"

"Perhaps."

Very softly: "You really *believe* she is a little slut, don't you, Manfred?"

Quietly: "I do."

I glanced quickly at the members of the jury, all of whom now sat glaring balefully at the defendant. "That's all," I said, figuring his goose was now cooked to a turn.

My jury argument was brief and without histrionics. Naturally I stressed the absurdity and the enormous egoism of the defendant's claim that this young girl would fling her virginity at the first stranger who came along. Since it was a danger factor to be reckoned with, I also freely admitted that this poor working girl was foolish to have gotten into the car with this young stranger (I had long since learned to take human nature in court and out as I found it), but I asked the jury whether they felt that the proper penalty for such lack of wisdom was to subject foolish virgins to unpunished rape attacks.

"Are not these poor girls who frequently and perhaps foolishly snatch at a fleeting chance for romance to relieve the drabness and tedium of their lives—are they not precisely the sort of young women who most need the protection of the law," I asked, momentarily mounting my soapbox, "rather than the happy and carefully sheltered daughters of the well-born and wealthy?"

Then there was the defendant's American boy act, the danger that some lingering sympathy for his youthful good looks and faked shyness might still confuse some of the jurors. It only takes one holdout juror to throw a case. The defendant's lawyer had wisely stressed this sympathy business in his argument. Ah yes, his client: so young, so clean, so shy. . . . Sympathy was about all he had left to talk about. But that is frequently plenty. More criminal prosecutions founder on the rocks of sympathy than on anything else. I had learned to always face the issue squarely.

"Compassion is one of the grandest impulses of mankind," I told the jury, and I meant it. "Not for one moment would I suggest that you ever forsake it, here or elsewhere. But," I told them, "I wonder what there is in this case that should arouse your sympathy for this defendant, unless it be the natural pity and sorrow and dismay all of us feel in the face of gratuitous evil exhibited by one's fellow men?

"Has this defendant shown the slightest contrition or remorse to warrant his claim of sympathy at your hands?" I asked. "Let us examine this sympathy business," I said, spreading my verbal wings a little for a brief flight through purple clouds. Jurors expect it so away I roared. "He not only broke this girl's jaw, then tried to rape her, and then forced her through the final degradation of this public trial, but—as though he had not already harmed her enough—in his effort to save his precious hide he is willing and even eager to further lacerate this girl, to publicly picture this seventeen-year-old admitted virgin as a drunken slut, a female so depraved that *she,* not *he,* should be standing trial here today for this offense. What monstrous, massive egotism! Ask yourselves: Has he himself felt the slightest shred of sympathy for this poor girl? Yet he prates of sympathy. Sympathy, indeed!"

Unlike most D.A.s, it was never my habit to ask for a conviction. I had given the subject a lot of thought. First I never felt it was properly a prosecutor's place to ask for a conviction, and second I felt that it was not wise strategy to join issue with the defense and voluntarily reduce the People's case to the competitive level of wrangling civil litigants. I felt that only thus would the jury become properly aware of its responsibilities to the People as well as to the defendant himself. Anyway, whether a matter of principle or of strategy, the approach seemed to work. "Ladies and gentlemen," I concluded, "the case is now yours. I ask only that you judge it well—with your hearts as well as your minds." I sat down. The verdict was "guilty."

Chapter 4

THE DRUNK DRIVER

ALL ACROSS this vast country, day and night, blear-eyed citizens attended by tired cops are filling up little bottles with an appalling quantity of urine, blowing thousands of cubic feet of their hot boozy breath into assorted paper bags and toy balloons, and shedding torrents of blood into test tubes—all of which is whirled away to the nearest police laboratory to determine whether or not Joe Blow is guilty of drunk driving.

Drinking drivers not only constitute the biggest traffic hazard in America—they are also the biggest headache a D.A. has. When is a man intoxicated? Ah, there's the rub. All of us recognize a drunk when we see one, but how are the police later going to project this befuddled picture before a jury in the cold daylight of a courtroom? Many tests have been devised, scientific or otherwise, but all of them suffer from the fact that at the trial there is really no way to *show* the jury that this contrite defendant, now so well-scrubbed and full of shame, was the same lurching, shambling imbecile those awful cops are now trying to picture to the jury.

All good citizens are violently against drunk driving in theory. But once they are chosen to sit on a jury to determine whether or not this particular defendant—their neighbor or fellow-townsman—was besotted when he wrapped his Chev around that hydrant last Saturday night—that becomes a different story. While I have no figures on the subject except my own sad experiences as D.A., I would venture the guess that the percentage of jury acquittals in drunk driving cases in America exceeds that of any other crime on the books.

47

Why is this so?

There are, of course, a number of reasons. For example, many jurors believe that the penalty is too severe. (In most states revocation of a driver's license is mandatory upon conviction, and since most people must drive a car these days to make a living the juries are quite humanly hesitant to convict.) Another reason is a wry feeling of sympathy for the defendant which may perhaps best be summed up by the saying, "There but for the grace of God . . ." Is it the shock of recognition? Then there is the difficulty, as I have suggested, of projecting the picture of a drunk before a jury. (Perhaps the harried cops should develop Technicolor movies with a sense of smell.) If a man slugs his neighbor or robs a filling station it becomes largely a question of proving his identity or simply describing what he did, whereas so many subjective factors enter into the composite picture of an intoxicated man.

Added to all this is the fact that drunk driving, bad as it is, is not inherently bad, like rape or armed robbery, but is bad because of the potentially evil results that may flow from it. (Lawyers, like druggists, like to couch their trade secrets in Latin: here they call it the difference between offenses termed *malum in se,* and offenses *malum prohibitum.* Freely translated, this means the difference between those offenses which men commonly recognize as bad in themselves and those deemed socially bad because, damn it, the legislature bloody well says they are.)

Also there is the jury's knowledge, common to all of us, that there are many degrees of drunkenness, varying from mellow to swacked; that different men react differently to the treacherous therapy of seven Martinis; and also the fact that saloonkeepers and their employees, when called in as witnesses for the defense, are understandably reluctant to admit that they sold drinks to a drunken man—which in most states is a rather serious crime in itself. Perish the thought. "Yass, my customer was as sober as the Judge sittin' here" is a favorite tavern testimonial in my bailiwick.

Things are vastly different, however, if the same drunk driver, with the same symptoms, should hurt or kill someone as a result of his drinking. American jurors, swiftly reversing their field, are then almost ferociously callous in their zeal to convict. But then the charge against the defendant is manslaughter or negligent homicide or some similar offense at or near the felony class, whereas in this essay I treat only of the common or beer-garden-variety of drunk driver.

I must have tried hundreds of these drunk driving cases in my day—and I have yet to hear more than a handful of defendants ever admit to having had more than two nickel beers. Presumably the grand defense strategy here is to account neatly for the odor of alcohol without making too damaging an admission of guilt. "Yup, I just had two nickel beers. Small ones, too. Mostly foam."

This two-nickel-beers business is an unvarying formula, an involuntary response, like a man muttering "yes sir" when he encounters a stranger at the door of a public toilet. It matters not that nickel beers disappeared permanently from my ken with Pearl Harbor—it's still *two nickel beers*. (Where, oh where can one get such a beautiful glow for a dime—that's what I yearn to learn.) It finally got so bad that for a time I thought seriously of posting a public reward of acquittal to the first brave drunk driving defendant who would rear up and defiantly admit, just for once, to inhaling *three* nickel beers. None ever did.

The bearded men who study this sort of thing and construct elaborate charts and graphs and diagrams about it say that the plastered drunk driver is not nearly as grave a highway menace as the one who is merely on the road to achieving plasterhood. The plastered driver, they reason, is usually caught before he fairly gets away from the post. Or he shortly succumbs to slumber and parks his car for a snooze or else promptly runs it off the road and sits there in a shower of broken glass, stolidly blowing little plastic bubbles of alcohol until the wrecker arrives. In any event, they say, he rarely can drive at excessive speeds and his eccentric progress down the road, like unto a wounded potato beetle, is a plain warning to all beholders.

No, they say, it is the "in between" drunk driver that is the menace. The alcohol in his radiator has not yet become a depressant; he is stimulated and exhilarated and filled with a false and overweening sense of confidence. It is not the weaving drunk driver that is the greatest menace; it is the chap who feels like Nero when he puts his hands behind the wheel, the fearless fellow who claps the accelerator to the floor and runs stop signs and passes cars on hills and curves until he finally winds up by depositing his dripping radiator, if not perchance himself, onto your very lap. It is not so much his actual manner of driving on any given section of the road, they say, but the beclouded judgment, the constant taking of chances, that constitutes the greatest menace from the middling drunk driver.

In other words, the experts imply, at a certain curious stage the "sober" drunk driver is more dangerous on the highway than the "drunk" drunk driver. Yet, when he is caught, his comparative lack of extravagant symptoms of drunkenness makes him all the harder to convict. The drunker he gets the "safer" he becomes— and the easier to convict. If all this is true, it certainly is a hell of a situation in any drinking man's language. And I dolefully think the bearded boys may have something there.

Some years ago I thought I had heard every possible defense story any drunk driving defendant could ever tell. I was wrong. For as a class these stout people show a fertility at improvisation and a soaring quality of imagination that would be the envy of any Hollywood script writer and one that has constantly amazed me. There *is* something new under the sun. Here are some of the engaging courtroom yarns I have heard from the troubled tribe of drinking drivers:

One drunk-driving defendant, a tearful lady, testified that her alleged inebriation came from taking medicine prescribed for her "female trouble," a broad subject upon which I gallantly refused to dilate or further explore. A seagoin' cab driver who had impulsively headed for Lake Superior and who had subsequently, in his extremity, regurgitated all over the flower of the rescuing Iron Bay night patrol—and then had played a very childish trick on himself in his cell—ascribed his series of misadventures to his allergy to, of all things, pickled pigs' feet. Yes, I said pickled pigs' feet. . . . Another Happy New Year's casualty swore he had mistaken a bowl of Tom and Jerrys nestling in his girl friend's icebox for that of curdled Bulgarian goats' milk, a concoction to which he was an apparent slave; another claimed he was in a state of shock over the death of his wife's mother; another ditto over a contemplated visit by his wife's mother; another that he had unwittingly tossed off a bumper of gin, thinking it was soda pop. All freely admitted drinking. All were promptly set free.

Because of the expense and cumbersomeness and complexity of the various scientific tests (and also the poor trial results), many police are shying away from them and getting back to blunt, idiomatic descriptions of the simple and classic symptoms of drunkenness. "The guy was plastered." Jurors, they say, understand this sort of language and feel a certain hostility to those smooth-talking expert witnesses who use all those confusing sixty-four-dollar scientific words. And some courts are reluctant to admit these scientific tests on the general ground that such tests (as one state supreme court so masterfully put it in such limpid English prose): ". . . have not yet attained such standing and general scientific recognition as to justify the admission into evidence of expert testimony subsequently deducted from experimental tests performed under such an underlying scientific theory." Whew, I'm weak. . . . Thus the Michigan Supreme Court in volume 325 of the Michigan reports at page 270 heaved Harger's "Drunkometer" high out of the courtroom—and the happy alleged drunk along with it.

Accordingly, many of the weary and discouraged cops are getting back to describing just plain good old American burps and hiccups and belches; the various Saturday night heavings and weavings and staggerings; the delightfully simple symptoms of fetid breath and mumbling talk; and the sheer naked beauty of the alcoholic drooler with his matted hair and bloodshot eyes. Again they are trotting out the old blindfold test, the walking-the-straight-line test, the stooping-and-picking-up-a-coin test, and all the old reliables. They're even getting back to having the suspect recite old-fashioned alliterative tongue twisters. Did I say tongue twisters? Let me *tell* you all about tongue twisters.

I was trying a routine drunk driving case in the municipal court at Iron Bay. The defendant's name was Georgie Porgie, let us say. Georgie was driving home from a country dance when, for some droll reason, he suddenly left the highway and calmly drove over the hills and into the trees. There he was found and chopped away by the state police, who discovered him trying unsuccessfully to sing both parts of *The Tennessee Waltz*. At the trial the police rolled in quite a sordid story. He had had all the symptoms, all right. They even found the tag end of a fifth of whisky on the seat beside him. Things looked *bad* for Georgie.

"When you got him back to town, what happened?" the suave old D.A. purred on. "Did you conduct any tests?" (As though I didn't know.)

"Well, he was in such obviously bad shape we only asked him to repeat one of those simple tongue twisters," the desk sergeant replied.

"Ah, a tongue twister," I said. "Which one was it?"

" 'Charlie Kaplan shaved a cedar shingle thin,' " the sergeant promptly replied.

"And how did he do?"

"Got it all balled up. Couldn't get past the third word. We helped him away and locked him up. The man was plastered, that's all."

I glanced at poor red-faced Georgie, who sat, very unhappy, staring down at his hands. "That's all," I said. "The People rest."

Georgie took the stand and his attorney grimly took him over the jumps. He had a tough one and he knew it. Georgie, true to tradition, admitted having the two nickel beers; blamed his singing on a bump on the head; blamed the empty fifth on the mischievous fairies of the night; and ascribed his failure with the tongue twister to the excitement of his arrest. "Dey got me all rattled," he said. Then he again sat staring down at his hands, which seemed to fascinate him.

His discouraged attorney shrugged and turned to me. "You may take the witness," he said.

I arose and moved before Georgie, contemplating him more in sorrow than in anger. It wasn't a fair match, but a job was a job—

and the sterling voters had elected me to do it. It shouldn't take long.

"Mr. Porgie," I began, "do you recall the police sergeant asking you to repeat a simple little tongue twister after they brought you in to the jail?"

Glumly: "Yes, sir."

"And could you say it?" I pressed on.

"No, sir. I guess I was too rattled."

"And yet you deny that you were drunk that night?"

"Yes, sir."

Suavely: "You are sober now, aren't you?"

"Why, yes sir, I'm sure I am, sir."

"Do you think you could repeat that little tongue twister for us now, Mr. Porgie?"

"I could try, sir."

"Then go ahead," I said, stepping back and folding my hands complacently. In one brilliant swoop I would show what a drunken and inert bum Georgie must have been on the night of his arrest.

Georgie was troubled. "I—I'm not sure I remember all of it—" he began.

"Do you want me to prompt you?" I volunteered generously. I did not want him to slip out of my clever noose.

"Please, sir."

"All right, Mr. Porgie," I said, closing in for the kill. "Just take it slow and easy, now, and repeat after me. . . . Are you ready?"

"Ready."

"Not a bit rattled?"

"N-n-no."

"Okay. Here goes," I said. " 'Charlie Chaplin chaved a cheedar chingle chin.' "

After a stunned pause a faint titter ran through the courtroom. The judge glared and pounded his gavel. Georgie looked greatly distressed for me.

"Er—ahem," I began, and plunged again. " 'Sarlie Saplin saved a cedar single sin.' "

The titter became a roar. The judge ducked his head into volume two of Gillespie's *Michigan Criminal Law and Procedure,* revised edition, where it remained. It was a cowardly abdication of judicial responsibility. The defendant, Georgie, sat looking at me mournfully, more in sorrow than in anger. His lips were moving. Perhaps he is praying for me, I thought wildly.

" 'Charlie Kaplan shaved a cedar shingle thin,' " he suddenly blurted, like a delayed action fuse.

"That's all!" I hissed, turning and groping blindly for my papers.

Upon retiring the jury didn't even pause to have the usual smoke. "We the members of the jury find the defendant *not* guilty!" the foreman announced, looking severely at me as he carefully enunciated every syllable of every word.

I hung my head and studied my toe. I saw that Charlie Kaplan's executioner needed a shine. I also saw that I needed two nickel beers—fast.

Chapter 5

WHAT'S HAPPENED TO ADULTERY?

OLD JUDGE BELDEN once sagely remarked: "I sometimes think that most men go through three stages in life: puberty, adolescence and adultery." Yet, while practically every state in the Union still makes it a criminal offense to violate the Seventh Commandment, reports of criminal prosecutions for adultery have virtually disappeared from our newspapers. This is not to suggest that our newspapers have suddenly got religion, the Lord knows, or that roving spouses have suddenly got fidelity. The fact is, according to my runners and my interpretation of the reports of Dr. Kinsey, that the actual incidence of adultery has sharply increased. This is so, I suspect, not because our national morals have sagged, but because, in this age of the combustion engine, coeducational bars, and the overnight cabin, the facilities have vastly improved.

The sad truth is that most newspapers continue to print all the marital dirt they can dredge. If this is so, and if it is also true that wandering spouses are today wandering ever farther afield, then why aren't we reading more news of adultery prosecutions, at least in our sensational press? The answer to that one is simple: There just aren't any adultery prosecutions to report. This poses another question: If adultery is increasingly on the march and is still made a crime in most states, then why aren't such cases criminally prosecuted?

The answer to that one is hard and cuts deeply across the changing mores and folkways of American life. If some wealthy and discerning foundation (Ford, Guggenheim and Rockefeller please note) will please kindly grubstake me for five years I might come up with some fine sonorous sociological answers. This I do know: I have been D.A. for fourteen years in a boisterous community harboring its fair share of extramarital rompers of both sexes, and I have had less than a half-dozen really serious adultery complaints made to me during all that time.

Prosecutors as a class form a pretty sensitive litmus paper of public opinion. They seem to have sensed here that an entire population has tacitly agreed, by some sort of curious extrasensory process (this amazing phenomenon is witnessed mostly in our presidential elections), to tacitly repeal one of the country's most basic and ancient criminal laws. Due to this silent conspiracy prosecutions for the crime of adultery have virtually disappeared from our criminal courts.

Impulsive amateur researchers might leap to the conclusion that the reason there are so few adultery prosecutions these days is that the irritated spouses generally pump the guilty pair full of lead—and there simply isn't anyone left around to prosecute. They would be wrong. While fumbling adulterers are indeed occasionally tagged by a stray bullet fired in anger, this sort of bedroom heroics has grown distinctly ham, all fireworks are strictly in bad taste. Cuckolded spouses no longer fire pearl-handled pistols at their mates; they race to their lawyers and fire a divorce summons instead.

Other television-side researchers may take issue with one of my premises, namely, that news of criminal adultery cases no longer blaze across the front pages of our newspapers. They may distinctly remember licking their chops several times during the past year over the erotic newspaper details of this love triangle or the lurid exposure of that love nest, complete with photographs. They would still be wrong. What they were reading was incidental news of adultery that grew out of some five-alarm café society divorce, or out of some drag-out court battle over the custody of a little child (usually accompanied by a photo of poor little Pamela forlornly clutching her stuffed doggie), or out of some plea, usually defensive, in some *other* type of criminal case (the most common being the murder defendant who claims he shot Joe Blow because

—to use a favorite newspaper cliché—Joe was "molesting" his wife).

Our divorce courts today furnish by far the greater part of the titillating adultery news you read, and the vast increase in the grounds for and rate of divorce is, I suspect, one of the main reasons why there are so few criminal prosecutions for adultery. In the old days—and not too long ago, at that—when divorce was frowned upon in many states on any grounds, including adultery, about the only recourse the offended spouse had was to flourish the pearl-handled pistol or trot to the D.A. for an adultery warrant. Adultery is now almost universally recognized as a ground for absolute divorce, except, Suh, in the die-hard state of South Carolina, a resourceful commonwealth which appears to have exterminated sin by ignoring it. In New York adultery is the only ground for divorce, and a whole modern industry composed of detectives, photographers and horizontal actresses has sprung up there, devoted to staging intimate little boudoir tableaux of adultery to appease its reluctant divorce courts. At any rate, aggrieved spouses (except in South Carolina) now have another place to go, or, if they are hesitant, the D.A. has another place to shove them.

This brings me to another reason why there are fewer adultery prosecutions. Due to the enlarged facilities for adultery that I have mentioned, fewer of the transgressors are caught—er—red-handed, so to speak. In other words, the proof is lacking. I may boldly dance and get potted night after night in the Rumpus Room of the Tarleton Arms Hotel with a dubious blond of equally dubious virtue, but unless there is proof that I later squire her upstairs for a demonstration of her new foam rubber mattress, and tarry there for an indecent interval, I can not be prosecuted for criminal adultery. Dancing and drinking with strange blonds is doubtless "adulterous conduct" which would give my poor wife grounds for divorce in most states, at least on the ground of cruelty. But it is still far from sufficient proof of criminal adultery. Suspicion and conjecture are not enough.

Acts of adultery, from their very nature, normally occur only in secret. (Nobody seems to give a rip about those transgressors who don't trouble to hide.) While the law does not precisely require that the guilty pair be discovered *flagrante delicto,* there must be some rather cogent proof of actual skulduggery. Propinquity alone is not enough. Propinquity plus opportunity is the magic formula. There is a fine line that must be crossed before there is enough proof of criminal adultery. In the pragmatic legal profession this fine line is commonly known as the threshold of a bedroom. Once across that line—boom!—you are guilty of adultery on circumstantial evidence—although in fact both of you sat there in your overcoats and galoshes, bored to distraction, playing canasta all through the night. The law charitably presumes that no man and woman could possibly ever find themselves alone together without at once joining hands and leaping gaily into the sack. There are doubtless those faltering knights of the strange bed who wish wistfully that the law occasionally presumed correctly. . . .

Leave us face it. Prosecutors do not like adultery cases. They shun them as they would avoid having Charles Addams sit on their murder juries. Perhaps they reflect that when a true married pair get so snarled up in adultery that one of them has to run to the D.A. for a criminal warrant they are attending upon the liquidation of a marriage that is already on the rocks. What good can now be done by a public prosecution? Even where the marriage isn't already finally wrecked, D.A.'s know that popping an adultery warrant—with its attendant unleashing and baying of the hounds of the press—will often destroy the last possible chance for reconciliation. Prosecutors rapidly get a pretty steady, if somewhat squalid, view of life as it is lived, and they come quickly to realize that one cannot prosecute a wandering spouse into moral rectitude. They also realize that innocent persons, such as relatives and children of the parties, can be permanently scarred by the accompanying publicity and commotion.

Of the few serious adultery complaints that do come before prosecutors, most of them are from spouses sent by sly divorce lawyers who would like the poor D.A. to build up for them an airtight divorce case, with its attendant claims for custody, alimony, *attorney* fees and property settlement. For American divorce has now entered the realm of big business. . . . Others are moved to complain largely from motives of revenge—especially in the case of the woman scorned. However, even in her case it is remarkable how rapidly her rancor cools in the soothing spray of a subsequent alimony and property settlement.

In short, prosecutors realize that most adultery prosecutions accomplish little good and often cause much harm. Surely no one is punished in the ordinary sense. In all my time as D.A. I cannot remember seeing, reading or hearing of a single adultery defendant, anywhere, that ever spent an hour in jail. (I am not talking here about those curious folk we read about, and worse yet, occasionally stumble over, who are jailed for relieving their romantic seizures on bridle paths, park benches, public beaches or in unfortunately parked taxicabs. These impatient people are not run in for adultery: they are carted away for their bad taste in selecting a site.)

Final reasons why there are so few adultery prosecutions are largely procedural. Today in many states such prosecutions may be instituted only by one of the offended spouses (who is frequently the last person to know the true state of affairs). So even the legislatures are making it tougher to prosecute adultery cases. Then again, in many states the criminal prosecution must be brought against both parties to the adultery. Even when armed with all kinds of evidence, offended spouses frequently hesitate to drag their guilty mates through the criminal courts along with the other bedwarmer. Then, too, as is often the case with an erring married man, the partner in his night errancy is quite often relatively innocent—mind you, I said relatively—and prosecutors, gallant to the end, generate little enthusiasm for taking her over the bumpy criminal jumps along with the suave married male.

But none of these "reasons," or all of them put together, really explains the national reluctance of both our prosecutors and the public to bring prosecutions for criminal adultery. I suspect that the real reason is at once deeper and simpler. At any rate, for better or worse our public attitude toward adultery has changed sharply in the last twenty-five years. Perhaps, in this case at least, it is evidence that we are slowly reaching a state of sexual maturity and realism. Heaven knows we still have a long way to go.

2.

Once when I was young, misty-eyed D.A., still laboring under the delusion that an expression of the basic appetites of people could long be curbed by law, I got smoked into an adultery prosecution. I have regretted it ever since. Let me tell you about it.

Mrs. Maida Logan swept into my office, sank into the chair opposite me, lowered an avalanche of furs to expose a heaving bosom, and spoke in a dramatically vibrant contralto voice: "I want my husband Marvin and his paramour arrested for adultery."

"Here we go again," I ruefully told myself, wincing inwardly, studying this dazzling creature, this stunning, flashing, fireball of a brunette. I managed to bestow one of my more secretly understanding boudoir leers. "Suppose you tell me all about it," I finally panted, weak with admiration and most un-D.A.-like thoughts.

"Suppose you ask me the questions," she parried throatily, regarding me with all the uncurious warmth she might bestow on a gnat.

Questioning this beauty developed that she and her husband Marvin had been separated for many months; that they had two young sons; that he was a middle-aged salesman and that his girl friend was a young unmarried woman who did clerical work for an industrial concern. Further questioning developed that Mrs. Logan, doubling as a lady detective, had, at various times shortly before visiting me, seen her husband and the girl friend dancing together, dining together, drinking together and driving together. Altogether it was all very sad. I clucked my tongue.

She paused and carefully dabbed her eyes. Could she please sign an adultery complaint right away? Her large doe eyes glistened with tears. She sat there looking so appealing and innocent and helpless that I got a lump in my throat. Sighing with relief I carefully explained to her that as distressing as she might find her husband's conduct, it did not amount to proof of criminal adultery. Not by a long shot. I then gratuitously suggested that she might find better success in the divorce courts, and that, even if she had proof of criminal adultery, there were the children to be thought of.

She sat up and her eyes flashed sudden forks of fire. "I did not come here to seek and I do not need your advice on how to conduct my personal affairs. Please tell me what proof I need," she demanded. Her voice was edged with ice. The defenseless damsel had suddenly taken a powder.

I retreated behind a rolling dark cloud of smoke from my black Italian cigar. "Mrs. Logan . . ." I began when the cloud had lifted. I went on to explain to her the business about propinquity and opportunity, the fine line that must be crossed, and all the other resounding legal platitudes surrounding criminal adultery. I repeated that I could not accept her complaint until she or someone produced adequate proof.

"Very well," she said, arising and grimly jutting out her handsome profile like a female General MacArthur. "I shall be back." She swept out of my office leaving behind a disturbing trail of perfume and confusion. I puffed furiously on my Italian reefer.

In two weeks Mrs. Logan was back at my office, handsomer and grimmer than ever. She marched in like an avenging goddess and sat down and again threw back the furs, again exposing the throbbing expanse of bosom that had me longing to turn sculptor—or something. (I also longed to see what manner of superwoman Marvin Logan had traded her in for.)

"Here's your proof, Mr. Traver," she began, whereupon she opened her purse and took out a roll of typescript as thick as an Easter sermon. She then proceeded to read me the movements— and I use the word advisedly—of her husband and his girl friend for the past two weeks. She had them dead to rights. She had them in bed and out; rumple-haired and curried; robed and disrobed; vertical and unvortical; zipped and unzipped. Here is one of the milder entries she read me from her lengthy catalogue of sins:

Wednesday, 11:25 P.M.

My three witnesses and I trailed Marv and X to X's apartment. After an interval we tiptoed up the back stairs of her apartment. The kitchen was dark and there was a single light burning in a hallway leading off the kitchen.

At 12:03 A.M. Marv came out of a doorway entering upon this hallway, presumably leading to the bathroom. His hair was mussed, he was carrying his glasses, and all he wore was the bottoms of his shorts. My witnesses whispered to me that they recognized him. [I sniggered a little over this last, and again hid behind a cloud of smoke.]

At 12:07 A.M. Marv recrossed the hall. This time his hair was combed and he wore his glasses. Almost immediately X crossed the hall from where Marv had disappeared, clad only in panties and a brassière. My witnesses also recognized her.

At 12:21 she recrossed the hall, extinguishing the hall light. She was wearing a black and red kimono. It was a duplicate of a kimono Marv had given me on our last wedding anniversary. [Here she paused and glanced at me, her beautiful dark eyes flashing daggers of fire. Her voice shook ever so little as she resumed reading.] We waited another hour and then went and waited in the car. It had grown chilly. At 4:37 A.M. Marv left X's apartment alone and drove to his hotel.

Mrs. Logan read me this and all the other counts of her lengthy indictment in a low monotone. She had everything down to the split second and must have used a stop watch. On and on she calmly read and I debated getting her a pitcher of water. But her rising color and flashing eyes somehow belied her apparent calm. My private guess was that she was inwardly consumed with jealously and hate. As she read on in her flat monotone I mentally rechristened the amazing man she had married as "Marvelous Marv." Mrs. Logan finally got the pair through seven nights of staggering boudoir gymnastics. "Well," she paused triumphantly, turning the full blaze of her burning dark eyes upon me, "do you think I *now* have enough proof to get my warrant for adultery?"

I sat there blinking. "I—I rather think perhaps you have," I answered weakly, reaching nervously for another cigar to bolster me. The woman in fact had enough proof to give each of them six months in the electric chair—in the latest double or love-seat variety. Still I groped to find some way to slow down this handsome human dynamo. I liked her and admired her spirit and I wanted to try to save her from doing something I was sure she would regret. "But first I'll have to go over the situation with your witnesses and take their statements," I sparred. "That is, whenever it is convenient for you to—"

"All my witnesses are sitting outside in your waiting room now," she blandly interrupted. "We'll give you all the statements you want right now. I'd like to get my adultery warrant today." She arose and stood smiling insistently down at me. "Please," she purred silkily. I blinked some more, completely melted. I was her slave.

Since she had me trapped I saw her witnesses then and there; heard their supporting version of the saga of Marvelous Marv; took their signed and sworn statements; reluctantly drew the court papers—and in two hours the sheriff was on his way to arrest her husband and his paramour for adultery. "Thank you, Mr. Traver," Maida Logan again purred, once more a defenseless female kitten. "Aw gee, shucks, M'am, it ain't nothin'," I almost answered her.

I asked Judge Williams to phone me when the pair was brought in for arraignment. In due course he phoned me and I drove over and there was the great Marvin himself flanked by X—a mousy, wan, flat-chested, nondescript little blonde. I stared at her. So this was the woman for whom Marvin Logan had forsaken his dashing beauty. Baffling are the forces of mutual attraction. . . . It seemed my day to blink so I blinked some more.

The pair waved a preliminary examination and were bound over to circuit court. Judge Williams set their bond, which they promptly posted, and in another hour Marv and his blonde were free as the wind and hurried on their way—presumably to resume their interrupted relay race across the hallway of her apartment.

When the case first came up in circuit court Mrs. Logan wrote me pleading illness and asking that the case be continued. I gladly shoved the case over the term. In the meantime she had retained a smart divorce lawyer and had filed for divorce. Through the legal grapevine I next learned that she was bearing down hard on Marvelous Marv—apparently she would only agree to leave him with his indoor track suit, that is, his glasses and the bottoms of his shorts. I winced, blinked and shook my head. I knew then that my office was being used as a pawn in the little divorce game of bigger alimony. I didn't like it.

The next term of court the other side moved for a continuance and, turn about being fair play, Judge Belden granted it. Each time the courtroom was loaded with expectant women—expecting a Roman holiday of sex, that is. Each time the case was continued the expectant women grumbled and went back home to their soap operas and tales of authentic Romance. In the meantime Mrs. Logan evidently relaxed in her divorce demands to the extent of agreeing to throw in the tops of Marv's shorts. The parties and their divorce lawyers still strained at their grim tug of war. Another term of court grew nigh. I could visualize the horde of expectant women getting their make-up back on. Developing a slow burn I sought out Judge Belden and told him I thought Mrs. Logan was using her adultery charge as a wedge to pry more alimony out of her husband.

"Write her lawyer that you insist upon trying the adultery case the next term of court," Judge Belden suggested. "Then add that you are going to move to nolle (dismiss) the case if she is not ready to go ahead." Judge Belden paused and smilingly added: "My guess is that you will get a request to drop the criminal case in the return mail."

"Thanks, Judge," I said, and sped to my dictation.

Judge Belden was wrong. Mrs. Logan's request to drop the adultery case didn't arrive by return mail. It came a day later.

I, Maida Logan, wife of Marvin Logan, complaining witness who signed the adultery complaint against my husband and the other defendant, wish to advise the Prosecuting Attorney and this Honorable Court that I was angry when I signed the complaint; that I would not have signed the complaint unless I had been urged to do so; that I made the complaint against my own feelings and wishes; that I have two children and that for the sake of my children and my own happiness and peace of mind I ask that the defendants be discharged and the case against them dismissed.

(Signed)   Maida Logan.

There it was. I wondered vaguely who the scoundrel was that had "urged" poor Mrs. Logan to prosecute. Doubtless that old devil prosecutor himself! At any rate, I did the only thing I could do: I moved to dismiss the case and Judge Belden granted my motion. In due course Mrs. Logan got her divorce and her alimony —"acrimony," I call it—and everybody lived unhappily ever after.

What had my adultery prosecution accomplished? Nothing that I could see, outside of possibly winning Mrs. Logan some additional alimony. With her time-clock proofs she could have got that anyway. As for Marvin Logan and his little blonde, the heat proved too much. She left town and I heard later that Logan's company fired him and he followed shortly. The adultery prosecution had done only this: caused a lot of unhealthy tongue-wagging and gabble in the community; disappointed a lot of frustrated women; brought considerable distress and humiliation to all of the parties involved; and finally chased two of them out of town. I was not proud of my part in the unhappy farce.

Chapter 6

DETECTIVE STORY

THE CORONER met Detective-Sergeant Greerson of the state police and me at the kitchen door of Frank Gutchek's shack. We "hi-ed" each other around appropriately and quickly huddled over the crackling fire in the kitchen stove. It was midwinter and zero outside, but inside the damp shack it felt at least twenty degrees colder. Perhaps it was the knowledge of what lay in the other room. . . . The coroner, an old hand at scenes of violent death, briskly got us up to date. He was positively joyous. As he spoke his breath made little bluish jets of vapor as though he were exhaling the thin smoke of a Turkish cigarette.

"Body's in there," he said, jerking his thumb at a curtained doorway at the bottom of a narrow stairway. "Froze stiffer'n a board," he added, coining a phrase. "Looks like a clear case of suicide. . . . Shotgun. . . . Thought I'd better notify you before I moved 'im. . . . Looks routine, but you guys are always givin' me hell when I don't call you. . . . Sorry to bother you."

The detective and I had been conferring on an approaching murder trial when the coroner had phoned him. I had tagged along mainly so that we might continue our discussion. "Who notified you?" Detective Greerson asked the coroner.

"Neighbors," said the coroner, who was evidently a man of few words and used them sparingly. It seemed that the neighbors, as neighbors have a way of doing, had noticed that no smoke had emerged from the chimney of Frank Gutchek's shack for three days—from the Sunday morning before. Since old Frank was crippled and ill and during all that time the thermometer had registered zero or below, on the morning of the third day one of the more imaginative neighbors suspected that something might be amiss. So that same Tuesday morning he had pounded and "hallooed" outside Frank's door and finally entered and found old Frank lying in bed, still clutching the shotgun—"deader'n a mackerel," the coroner concluded, coining another colorful phrase. The neighbor had promptly fled and phoned the coroner. The coroner had phoned us.

"Hm . . ." Detective Greerson said. "Did you touch anything?" He glared balefully at the poor coroner. I was touched to witness this flowering of their beautiful friendship.

"No, of course not," the coroner snapped, wounded to the quick. "You boys an' Traver there are forever dingin' at me to call you first in these here violence cases. So I called you, damn it."

"Good. Supposing we go look, then," the detective said. The coroner scrambled to lead the way. It was one of the less gruesome prerogatives of his office.

"Wait!" I shrilled, pointing horrified at the kitchen ceiling. An irregular patch of red stain covered an area a foot wide. As I looked a droplet fell to join a similar bloody patch on the kitchen floor. "Good God, man, is there another body upstairs?"

"Naw," said the coroner, pausing, delighted to see his D.A. grown so jumpy. "Just some jars of preserved raspberries what froze up an' busted. The fire's thawin' 'em again."

"Let's go look at our man," Detective Greerson said dryly, himself leading the way.

Old Frank lay there in his tousled bed, half sitting up, indeed stiffer than a board and deader than a mackerel. His wildly staring eyes had taken on the opaque gun-metal blue of a dead buck's. I looked away. His left hand clutched the barrel of the shotgun, pointed at him. The butt lay towards the foot of the bed. A cord was tied to the trigger of the gun, thence running around the bedpost at the foot of the bed, thence running into Frank's right hand. Anyone could observe plainly just how the poor sick old man had ended his life. . . .

"See," said the coroner, bustling professionally, advancing toward the bed, "he took an' held the gun this way an'—"

"Don't touch that gun!" Detective Greerson barked at the coroner. I thought for a moment he was going to slug the bustling little man. "Please," he continued more moderately and with weary patience, "please just try to stay to hell away from the bed until I have made my investigation. Suppose you go out to the store and call the state police post to send out the photographer and a spare man." It was not precisely a request.

"Okay, okay," the coroner pouted, like a little boy dismissed from the sand-lot gang. He withdrew in a sulk to the kitchen, rattled and banged the stove lids, and thence stamped out the back door, slamming it. "Thank the Lord," the detective said, closing his eyes and shaking his head like a sorely tried man. Despite the intense cold and the rigid and staring dead body lying there on the bed, I lingered so that I could watch a trained police investigator do his stuff. I was then a comparatively young D.A. What I saw was a revelation and showed me why so many trained police officers resent the blundering inefficiency of the average politically elected coroner, whose only discernible equipment for office is often merely a strong stomach, an invincible ignorance, and a tenacious ability to garner votes.

Detective Greerson first carefully examined the manner in which the dead man's left hand grasped the barrel of the shotgun and the right hand grasped the cord. Both the gun barrel and the cord lay loosely and rather more on the rigid fingers than in them. "Hm . . ." said the detective, nodding. The dead body was clad in a thick woolen cardigan sweater under which there was a thick woolen shirt, both buttoned to the neck. The detective carefully unbuttoned both garments and exposed the wound. The chest for an area of about six inches across the region of the heart was peppered with fine shot from the shotgun blast. There was very little blood and no gaping wound.

"My, my," Detective Greerson murmured to himself, quickly rebuttoning the garments. Using his handkerchief he next broke the gun and looked in the breech and carefully removed the empty shell. Holding the shell in his handkerchief he carefully examined it and returned it and then closed the gun. He glanced at me. "Number six bird shot," he said. "Luckily it was printed on the shell. Many shells don't have it." I nodded wisely, wondering what in hell this was all about. He then paced off the distance from the head of the bed to the curtained bedroom doorway. "Slightly over fifteen feet," he said, nodding significantly. "Let's go out by the stove and get warm," he added. "We can't do much more now till we get the pics and the measurements. We'll do the fingerprints and the rest at the morgue."

Huddled over the kitchen stove I thought it was about time for mystified Traver to assert himself. "Sergeant," I said, giving him one of my keen D.A. squints, "do you think maybe"—I spoke slowly—"do you think maybe by any chance this *wasn't* suicide?"

Detective-Sergeant Greerson smiled grimly. "Johnny, even at the first glance I was pretty sure it wasn't. That's why I jumped that poor dumb coroner so hard. But now it really looks like murder to me, made all the stronger by the clumsy attempt later—quite a bit later, I think—to make it look like a suicide."

"Look, Sarge," I pleaded, casting professional pride to the winds, "supposin' you give your stupid D.A. a clue so he won't appear quite so damn dumb when the others arrive. Just give me a clue, pal. Frankly it looks like a plain case of suicide from where I sit."

"Okay, Johnny," Detective Greerson relented. Crouched over the dead man's stove he gave me a five-minute cram course on the mysteries of homicide investigation. "The first clue we have is based upon the psychology of suicide itself—a clue which I admit, taken alone, wouldn't be of much use to us in court," he explained. "That clue is that suicides using firearms generally fire at the head, and when they don't they invariably expose their bare flesh to the discharge. It's a curious thing but a suicide will frequently even open or remove a thin cotton shirt," he explained. "They rarely if ever would shoot through a thick woolen sweater and shirt. I've never seen such a case." Detective Greerson had won his spurs in the teeming Detroit area and I had to concede that he had seen plenty of gore.

"Go on," I said, still unconvinced. I tried to imagine myself cut adrift in court trying to convict someone of murder by trying to explain to the average jury the modern psychology of gunshot suicides. The picture was not good. Detective Greerson went on with his lecture.

"The second clue—and this is physical, not psychological—is that *someone* obviously tried to make this look like suicide. They tried to place the gun and the cord in the dead man's hands *after*— I would guess considerably after—rigor mortis had set in. It was a poor hurried job. In any event it's an impossible thing to do. If the dead man were a true suicide he would either be grasping one or both of these objects in a grip of steel or he wouldn't be holding them at all. That's our second clue."

"Hm," I said, less skeptically, but still far from sold. "And what else, Sherlock? Watson is all ears."

"The strongest physical evidence right now is the character of the wound itself. At the close range that the fatal shot must have been fired, were this really suicide, the load of shot would have been concentrated and there would have been one central gaping bloody hole—perhaps the size of a silver dollar—right through the sweater and shirt and the body tissue itself. Here we can be sure that the shot was fired from a much greater distance because the pattern of individual shot was able to spread; hence there is no single perforating wound in which the tissues have been completely torn away." He gestured at the curtained doorway. "My guess is that our murderer—when we find him—fired the shot from about there."

"Guilty as charged," I said, smiling in submission. As he spoke I remembered the bloody havoc wrought by close-range shotgun blasts at other murder and suicide investigations I had reluctantly attended.

"Johnny," Detective Greerson said, giving me the clincher, "just recall what happened to a partridge or rabbit you may ever have shot at even five times the range that we have here."

"I surrender, officer," I said, remembering some unfortunate snap shots I had made at close range. "It's murder, sir. Now where in hell do we find the guy what done it?"

There was a frosty creaking and tramping on the kitchen door-step and the coroner arrived with the state police photographer and the fingerprint man. "Hi," "Hi," "Hi," went all around the frosty room. That is, from all but the coroner who was still deep in his little pout of professional jealousy. "These damned new-fangled cops," his glum expression seemed to be saying.

Detective Greerson phoned me at my office the next morning. "Just want to make a preliminary report," he said.

"Shoot, Sergeant," I said, "but not at too close range." New murder cases always made me giddy with hilarity. The sergeant proceeded to shoot.

Photographs and measurements were complete on the scene; a complete autopsy had been performed at the morgue; pellets of number 6 bird shot were recovered from the wound; some shotgun shell wadding had been found imbedded in the wound; one piece of intact paper wadding had been found *behind* the muzzle of the gun; a box of identical shotgun shells had been found on the scene; test shots had been fired from the same gun at a dummy target; the closest matching pattern, including distribution of shot and carry of wadding, showed the fatal shot to have been fired at or slightly beyond the curtained doorway. . . . Detective Greerson paused for breath.

"Go on," I said, taking macabre notes like crazy.

"No powder burns or singeing or charring of tissues found at wound or on surrounding flesh or garments, further indicating distance from which shot was fired; lead pellets from shot found to have perforated bedclothes and clothing in spread pattern impossible at indicated range; a few pellet perforations found in bedclothing *behind* muzzle of gun as held by deceased; two spent pellets identical-sized to those taken from wound and from sample shell found in clothing; all tests demonstrate conclusively impossibility of suicide. No discernible fingerprints found on brass jacket or elsewhere of empty shell in gun. Smudged fingerprints of deceased found on gun, some covered by later fingerprints of suspect . . ."

"What suspect?" I interrupted, nearly swallowing my soggy Italian cigar.

"Tony Sleezak," the detective answered. "Woodsman with a four felony record including two felonious assaults. Tip from a neighbor that he was deceased's only friend. We've got the character here now taking his first statement. He's lying beautifully. It's murder, all right, and I think we've got our man." I thought I detected a thin note of triumph in his voice.

"Detective Greerson," I said, "you shall be duly knighted the next night I have off. In the meantime I wish you would please try not to sound so goddam superior and virtuous."

"Aye, aye, sir."

In a half hour Donna announced that Detective-Sergeant Greerson was again on the phone. Wanted to read back the first statement. "Fire and fall back, Sarge," I said, my pencil poised.

Tony Sleezak, age sixty-seven, was the best friend of the deceased, the statement read. He worked in the woods but generally spent the week ends visiting at the shack of his old crippled friend, Frank Gutchek, age sixty-nine. Yes, he had visited him the Saturday before but the deceased had seemed so ill and depressed that Tony had left the shack before midnight and spent the week end on a rather mild binge around the local taverns.

Where had he slept? Oh, he didn't remember that, was a little too drunk, he thought. Perhaps he slept in the depot. Yes, poor Frank had mentioned committing suicide, but he had been threatening that for years. It was an old story. . . . Yes, Frank owned a single-barreled 12 gauge shotgun. He kept it largely as a pest gun to protect his chickens. No, Tony hadn't touched the gun or used it in years. No, he hadn't fired any shotgun or any other firearm in months.

This was the burden of Tony Sleezak's first statement as given to the state police. In taking this statement Detective Greerson had cleverly not shown his hand. He was all bland and inquiring innocence. With a lying suspect this was sound strategy for now he had his man committed to his first important lie, the demonstrable lie that he had not touched the fatal weapon. It also showed his guilty state of mind. There were still plenty of gaps to fill, of course, but the important thing was that we now knew we were tracking the right man. The pattern of *our* shots would not be scattered.

"Thanks, Sarge," I said. "I'll be down this afternoon to sit in on the next session."

The next few days were perhaps among the strangest in my D.A. career. In all investigations of murder and similar cases I had learned early the hard way that it was best to rush in and get a bulldog grip and hang on. It was easier in the long run. . . . The jailers brought Tony Sleezak up to my office in the courthouse. They left him and waited outside the closed door. "This is the D.A.," Detective Greerson said. It was more in the nature of a necessary explanation than an introduction.

"Ya, ya," Tony Sleezak said, staring at me with the unblinking wariness of a trapped animal.

At sixty-seven Tony Sleezak was not a man I would have chosen to smite me in anger. His thick squat neck set on defiantly square shoulders and accentuated by a bristly bald bullethead, gave him the curious look of a sort of human battering ram. He had long curved simian arms that hung away from his body. As he stood there he kept kneading his fingers loosely in the palms of his powerful hands as though he were restlessly seeking something to rend. He radiated brutality and power and with his flushed expression he looked like a permanently angry man, like something escaped out of prehistory itself.

"Won't you sit down?" I said, contemplating this awesome lower primate dressed in man's clothes.

"Ya, ya," he said, thudding abruptly into a chair across the desk from me, banging his two clenched hands together on the desk in front of him. His little angry gray eyes continued to bore me from under bristling gray eyebrows. D.A.s must try to remain objective but here was a man, I felt, who possessed all the emotional control and moral equipment of a starved hyena.

I shall not go into all the weird exchanges and "ya-ya's" of that second session more than to say that he still vehemently denied having used or touched old Frank's shotgun or having himself shot any firearm for many months. We wanted to get him well committed on that one. We were not yet ready to show our hand on his fingerprints being on the shotgun. Cornered with that isolated fact he might have had a sudden saving recollection. It was better to wait until we had considerably more to throw at him. I wanted at first to measure him more for size.

"How ever't'ing out dere?" he suddenly asked, near the end of the session.

"Out where?" I countered.

"Out da shack?"

"Okay, I guess," I said, wondering idly at his macabre interest in the scene of his crime.

"You fellas lock da goddam door, ya?" he asked.

"The door's locked," Detective Greerson answered.

"You water an' feed da chicken, ya?" he pressed.

"The chickens are being cared for," the detective answered.

"Better off kill dose chicken, ya, ya. Goddam neighbors he steal dem."

"We'll see, we'll see. Maybe we'll do that, Tony."

With this his fingers momentarily stopped their endless kneading and a glacial smile of brutal cunning flitted across his granite features. I quickly decided that I much preferred to take him frowning. I wrote down this latest exchange and read back the entire statement and asked him to sign it and initial each page. "Ya, ya," he said, angrily grabbing up the pen. This done the powerful fingers again began kneading away like writhing serpents. I observed that his hands were streaked and filthy, the square horny fingernails clotted with dirt. In a land dedicated to cleanliness, where soap suds daily foam out of our radios, where the very snow flakes are rapidly turning to falling soap chips, there are still occasional fugitives from cleanliness who will apparently wash their hands only when manual dexterity is impeded. Such a rebel was Tony Sleezak. He was as soiled and unkempt as a wild hog. And the scent he gave off was growing overpowering.

"That's all for now," I said, weakly summoning the jailers. "We'll see you later."

"Ya, ya," he said, rising and lunging out the door like a trained ape. I threw open the window—freezing was preferable to asphyxiation—and turned to Detective Greerson.

"Phew!" I said. "No jury could possibly survive long enough

to convict him. I'm afraid we'll have to hog-tie and throw him—
and then bathe him. Either that or set him free."

"I'm with you, Johnny," he said, wrinkling his nose.

"By the way, Detective Greerson," I said, a thin note of triumph
creeping into my voice. "How about first taking a paraffin cast of
his hands and running a dermal nitrate test to see if he's recently
fired a gun? We'd better do that before we dry-clean him." I
paused expectantly. My little triumph was short-lived.

"It was the first thing we did when we got him in yesterday—
in all his unwashed elegance. We're waiting for the laboratory
returns. Here. . . . I'll call the post now." He talked cryptically
into the phone for a few moments and hung up smiling. "Relax,
Johnny. The test was positive. The cast of his right hand showed
nitrate particles which have been identified as granules of powder.
Thank God for a dog-dirty defendant."

"Nice work, Sarge," I said admiringly, for that it surely was.
"There's only one thing," I mused. "Why did he do it? Was it
money? Did they quarrel? We seem to have everything now but a
motive."

"That's right, Johnny, that's our weakest link so far—but at
least now we *know* he did it."

"I wonder," I continued to muse, "why Tony kept asking about
the shack and the chickens. I wonder. . . . I wonder . . ." Suddenly
I sat up. The nasal edge of triumph crept back into my voice.
"Sarge, I wonder just who owns that damn' dump out there?"

"I dunno, the victim I guess," Sarge answered. "The only thing
against that being true is that the coroner told me so. Apparently
the dead guy had no relatives."

My hunch was growing stronger. "We've got to check this title
business right now!" I said, rising. "C'mon downstairs with me
now to the register of deeds' office."

We clanked and echoed around the register's hollow vaults and,
with considerable rummaging and a timely assist from the title
sleuths that inhabit those catacombs, finally tracked down the
precise plot of ground. Entry: The deceased, Frank Gutchek, had
purchased the property some ten years before. Entry: Frank

Gutchek had deeded the property to a local notary public just two months before. Entry: On the same date the notary public had reconveyed the same land to Frank Gutchek *and* Tony Sleezak, as joint tenants with *sole rights to the survivor!* In plain English a deal had been set up that meant that if one died the survivor automatically acquired sole ownership, without any red tape, wills or probate proceedings—or lawyers.

We now had found a motive with a vengeance and next we swooped through the filed copies of bills of sale of personal property and soon dredged up a similar flurry of papers creating the same survival setup as to the personal property, including all furniture and furnishings and down to "all chickens and chicken feeds and one 12 gauge single-barrel shotgun. . . ." By shooting his partner with his own weapon Tony Sleezak had acquired all of his property, including the shotgun, lock, stock and barrel. It was a neat way to inherit. No wonder Tony had been concerned about locking the shack and feeding the chickens. He was merely showing the normal qualms of proprietorship.

"Nice going, Johnny," Sarge said.

"Ya, ya," I said, kneading my fingers and blushing prettily.

That night we endured and survived another aromatic session with Tony Sleezak during which we at last let him know that we knew his fingerprints were on the shotgun. When he got the full import of that he stared down wildly at his two clenched hands as though he were about to devour them. "Goddam son-a-bitch," he muttered savagely.

"What'd you say?" Sarge prodded softly.

Then came the horrible grimacing smile followed by a gibbering torrent of words. "Ya, ya . . ." Tony had been wrong, he said, when he had told us he hadn't returned to Frank's shack that Saturday night. "Ya, ya, ya. . . ." It all came back to him now. He had come in late, quite drunk, and had gone upstairs to sleep in the spare cot among the raspberry preserves. The next morning he had come down and found the fire out (which Frank usually attended) and had glanced in at Frank and saw him lying there with glazed and staring eyes. "Poor fella musta been dat way when I'm goin' on my bed, ya, ya."

"What'd you do then, Tony?" Sarge asked.

"I'm goin' in dere an mak' sure he's dead, poor fella. I'm looking in dat gun an' fin' empty shell, ya. I'm going on town report police but den I remember I'm been prison t'ree-four time an' I'm scare as hell to tell. Maybe police dey t'ink ol' Tony *I'm* shoot ol' Frank, ya. 'Stead I go on town an' get dronk, ya, ya. Poor ol' Frank . . ."

When I had finished writing that up—I always took my statements in long hand (the slow scratch of the pen and the long pauses seemed to stimulate recollection)—I read it back and had him initial each page and sign it. Tony sat staring at me for nearly a minute, gripping the arms of his chair. It was like looking into the fathomless eyes of a Bengal tiger.

"That's all for tonight, Tony," I said, reaching eagerly for the window. "But tomorrow morning you can tell us how come the fresh gunpowder got on your right hand. Think that over during the night."

Again the horrified and maniacal stare down at his telltale hands. Then he crouched in his chair, taking quick furtive catlike looks at Sarge and me as though deciding which way to spring. By then Tony sensed that the baying hounds of the law were inexorably closing in. . . . Sarge casually kept his hand resting on his shoulder holster like a chronic cardiac case taking his heartbeat. The man made me shiver just to watch him. Surely he represented a discouraging form of gratuitous evil in a disorderly world. ! . . I rang for the jailers. "Take him away, boys."

There is an engaging legend abroad in the land that advancing years mellow one and somehow bring out the kindliest impulses of one's nature; that the countryside swarms with repentant native Scrooges. My own observation has been that when a bastard grows old he simply becomes an old bastard. Tony Sleezak was a standing vote for my side. I sighed and reread out loud the afternoon statement. It is frequently a productive exercise. Something made me pause over the part where Tony had asked us about the chickens and suggested that they be killed. "Hm," I mused, pondering, staring sightlessly across the room at the tidy rows of systematically unread law books. Why, why, why?

"Sarge," I said, suddenly sitting up. "I don't want to go psychic on you, but I'll bet you a steak dinner that the deed to the shack is hidden somewhere in that chicken coop."

Sarge debated a moment. "You're on, Johnny—and I've got a feeling I'm going to lose."

"I won't narrow the bet this much—but I think you'll save time if you'll look first in the chicken feed itself. Tony's getting damned afraid that his chickens are going to eat him into trouble before he can get back out there. Remember this? 'Better kill off dose chicken, ya, ya.' "

"Let's drive out there now, Johnny. I'm getting plenty hungry. We'll have our steaks later tonight at Dinty's, win, lose or draw."

"Okay, Sarge," I said, zipping shut my trusty leather case.

Rummaging among the sleepy clucking hens with a flashlight we found a burlap feed bag. In the bottom of the bag we found an envelope marked "Property of Frank Gutchek." In the envelope we found the deed to the property. I felt like setting up in business as an elder swami. . . . The steaks at Dinty's were particularly swell that night. And the French fried onions were delicious.

The next morning Tony appeared before us as scrubbed and shining and fragrant as a choir boy at Christmas. Even his nails were spotless and gleaming. It was good to breathe again without pain. The only trouble was that Tony's conversion to cleanliness had come a little late for all of us.

"Now about the gunpowder found on your right hand, Tony?" I began, abruptly renewing hostilities.

"Oh, dat," Tony began, and away he went. Tony had been doing a lot of remembering last night, he said. Tony was all wrong about old Frank committing suicide, ya ya. The fact was Tony had accidentally shot Frank in defense of his own life. It had all happened this way: Tony had come there that Saturday night and Frank, who had been drinking, had picked a quarrel over some money matters. Frank had grown very threatening and abusive. Tony, ever the gentle peacemaker, had gone upstairs to bed. The next morning when he had come down Frank was sitting up in bed with his shotgun trained on Tony. Frank had said he was going to kill Tony, ya, ya, unless Tony immediately paid him the money that he wrongfully claimed Tony owed him.

"What I'm gonna do?" Tony shrugged, acting beautifully. "I'm say 'Hokay, Frank' an' I'm going in dere my purse in han' pretend like give him money, but quick I jomp on Frank an' razzle for dat gun. I'm on'y try to stop Frank from shoot me, I no try shoot him," Tony said, all the while wrestling and writhing in a death embrace with an imaginary adversary, "an' some way dat gun he get twist 'roun' for Frank but Frank he no stop an' *'Boom!'* dat gun she's go off accidental. Poor ol' Frank give a couple of puff an' he's gone." Tony paused and sought to control his grief. My pen scratched slowly along.

"How far was the gun from poor old Frank when it went off?" Sarge put in.

"Right up against him, poor fella. No chance to miss. You see, we razzle dere on da bed."

Sarge shot me a contented look. I duly entered this damning statement. "So you faked the suicide, Tony?" I asked.

"Well, I got bad prison record—maybe nobody believe on Tony. But now I see I got to tall da trut'. I t'ink maybe it's bes'."

This rapid conversion to the policies of Poor Richard left me cold. "So you faked the suicide, Tony?" I repeated.

"Well if you want to call him dat."

Patiently: "So you faked the suicide, Tony?"

Nodding the bullethead. "Ya, ya."

I read back the statement and Tony ya-yahed it and signed it and initialed the pages.

"Tony," I said, "this afternoon I want you to tell us how Frank came to be shot from a distance of between twelve and fifteen feet away. *And that, Tony, we can prove!*" I buzzed the jailers while Tony again went through his animal crouch and Sarge again stood quietly feeling his heart.

In the afternoon installment Tony soared to new heights. He could have made a fortune writing science fiction—for the inmates of zoos. . . . Frank hadn't threatened to shoot Tony. No, no. Tony was all wrong about that and it was always better to tell the truth, ya ya. What *really* happened was that Tony had been after Frank for several weeks to show him a certain "business paper," but Frank wouldn't show it to him. So Tony thought he would just sort of scare Frank to make him show the paper so he had come down that Sunday morning and picked up Frank's shotgun on a whim (not knowing it was loaded, of course) and had gone and stood in the curtained bedroom doorway and ordered poor old Frank to produce the paper. Just a little joke, ya ya. But Frank hadn't enjoyed the prank and had suddenly reached down and hurled, of all things, a loaded chamber pot at Tony who flinched— ya, ya—as one well might, and *"Boom!"* the gun had gone off and accidentally killed poor old Frank.

Sarge stole a look at me and slowly nodded his head and wrinkled his nose. I nodded. We were tacitly agreed that at last a gleam of truth had crept accidentally into his astounding narrative. We were all in solemn agreement that Tony's last bath but one had been in anything but water.

"Did you ever find the business paper, Tony?" I asked, trying to forget the chamber pot.

"Hm . . . After dat I'm feel too bad to look. I go feed dem chicken an' den go on town an' get dronk."

"And *when,* Tony," Sarge interposed softly, "when did you come back to the shack and rig up poor Frank to look like a suicide?"

"Who, me? Oh dat. . . . Early nex' morning, she's still dark."

"Hm . . . Did you have any trouble?"

"Ya, ya. Frank's han's he's like froze stiff. I'm do bes' I can— I'm strong man—I can't open dom goddam finger."

Sarge was practically purring with contentment. "So you did the best you could—and placed the barrel of the gun in his left hand and the cord in his right?"

"Ya, ya."

"Tony," I took over, hastily veering away from perfection, "what was this business paper you and Frank quarreled over?"

"Oh, jus' some ol' paper—I'm not speak very good Englis'— jus' some ol' paper."

If Tony didn't like to talk about the paper we'd play ball and talk about something else. "So after poor old Frank gave a couple of puffs and was gone, Tony, you went out and fed the chickens and then went to town?"

"Ya, ya."

"Now about those chickens, Tony," I pressed, "if we have them killed, as you suggested yesterday, shall we give the chicken feed away or just throw it out on the dump?"

Almost lunging at me: *"No, no, no!* Don't t'row him away! Tony want dat bag chicken feed! Chicken feed him cost moaney!" He sat there glowering and swaying his torso from side to side like Bushman raging in his cage.

I produced the deed. "Funny thing, Tony, we got curious last night and happened to look in that chicken feed sack and found this deed—a little business paper under which you became sole owner of the shack when poor old Frank puffed and died." Sarge moved in at careful attention. "What do you say to that, Tony?"

Tony sat blinking for a moment and then he let out a wail that must have been heard for seventeen blocks. He gripped his temples and rocked in his chair. "Poor Tony caught, poor Tony caught," he moaned, rocking and rocking. "Ya, ya, ya, poor Tony he caught, he *caught!*"

We finished the statement swiftly, lashing Tony to the mast. He recovered enough to sign it and I called *four* jailers to take him away. He was beginning to look a little too much like Bushman.

The tragic part of the whole thing was that Tony did not need the fatal deed. Like a lot of better educated people than he, he did not realize that the *records* in the register of deeds' office were not only quite sufficient but controlling as to ownership. While his main motive was to get the property by hook or crook, he had apparently killed his best friend to obtain a deed he didn't need.

Tony pleaded guilty to killing Frank Gutchek and now sits brooding in a place where business papers are scarcely necessary.

The case stands out, among its other implications, as one in which a brutal killing was cracked by intelligent and *timely* police work of a high order. Police and prosecutor had really worked as a team. The case also points up the obvious necessity, which should long have been plain to even the most stupid legislator, that the important office of coroner would better be served if the incumbent learned something more about his business than the schedule of his fees. *That* they learn by heart immediately. In the meantime only the Lord Himself knows how many criminal homicide cases have been lost or gone unsolved—indeed unsuspected—because of the officious and innocent blundering of untrained coroners and police.

Chapter 7

GEEVE ME DE MORGAZHE

ONE DAY Donna announced Frank Paquette, an old French-Canadian of my acquaintance. Old Frank was a bachelor in his mid-seventies and still active and spry. In his younger days he had worked at various jobs around the iron mines and lumber camps. Unlike most lumberjacks, he had saved his money and was reported to have lots of it. He lived alone modestly in the village of Spring River, in a neighboring township of the same name. What could he want with the D.A.? I wondered.

"Show him in," I told Donna.

Old Frank came in—" 'Ello, 'ello"—and sat down heavily across the desk from me, his squat, broad frame filling the chair. His shock of white hair and the massive gold watch chain he wore across the vest of his black broadcloth suit made him look like the mayor of a small French village. Old Frank spread his powerful hands on my desk, palms up, and launched his lament without further ado.

"I am in *baad* trouble. You know Reechar' an' Rosie LaBeau?"

I nodded. I had known of this fine pair by reputation for some years. It was not good. Mr. and Mrs. Richard LaBeau skated constantly just within the law. They ran a small hotel at the crossroads in Spring River, catering to hunters, fishermen, tourists and lumberjacks. Rumor had it that they regularly rolled drunken lumberjacks but the police had never been able to catch them dead to rights. "Yes, I know them," I said. "What have they been up to now?"

"Dey come on my place last summaire an' dey want me to

85

borrow dem eight 'ondred dollaire," Frank continued. "Dey have leetle 'otel in Spring Rivaire near my place. Den de 'ighway she's change. Dey got chance to buy lot on new 'ighway, so dey can move dere 'otel dere. Dey want me to borrow dem eight 'ondred dollaire to get new lot."

"What'd you do, Frank? Borrow them the money?" I asked, sinking naturally, like the sly politician I was, into the argot of the proletariat.

"I tole dem I got no money to borrow dem. Dey say, 'Well, Frank, you know she's har' tam to borrow eight 'ondred dollaire on bank. You ain't work now. You borrow us dat money and we geeve you job help move de 'otel.' "

"Yes," I said, relaxing, realizing that all hell wouldn't hurry this old Frenchman, or prevent him from telling his own story in his own way. "What'd you do?"

"Well, I borrow dem dat eight 'ondred dollaire an' I go help dem move dere 'otel by new lot on new 'ighway. Dey put in new cellaire, new furnass, new watching machine, new refrigidaire, new bat'room an' feex a lot o' t'ings. W'en she was all done Reechar' an' Rosie dey owe me t'ree t'ousand one 'ondred eighty-fi'e dollaire an' 'leven cent. Dey geeve me good firs' morgazhe on de 'otel an' I come home."

"Did they ever pay up the mortgage?" I said, hoping to arrive at the point of the narrative by sundown.

"Den wintaire come an' dey pay no princypall, no intras', no nossing," old Frank continued. "I go on bank an' I tell bank if dey don't pay hup da morgazhe I 'close on dem."

"Did you foreclose the mortgage?" I ventured.

"Bank write dem strong lettaire an' Rosie and Reechar' come see me an' dey say, 'Look, Frank, you know she's har' tam start out new 'otel on new 'ighway. We got no money to pay you. You leeve here alone all wintaire. You come leeve wit' us. We geeve you good boar' an' room. Dat will pay de intras'. Bettaire you get somet'ing dan nossing."

"What did you do?" I said.

"Well, I go."

"What happened after you went to live with them?"

"De firs' morning I go Pos' Offis an' get my papiere from Montreal. I go my room an' sit on bad an' read my papiere. Den w'at you t'ink? Pres soon dat Rosie come in an' sit down 'side me, real clos', too clos' for decan' woman. She pretend like read. I say nossing. By an' by she go."

"My, my," I murmured, remembering that Rosie was a comely, flashing-eyed, well-stacked woman of about forty. I was beginning to see daylight. "What happened then?"

"Dat night on suppaire table Reechar' 'e say, 'Rosie, I got good job go on Xavier Beauchamp lombaire camp an' shoe some horse.' Rosie, she say, 'Reechar', w'en you go?' 'E say, 'Tomorrow morning four-fi'e o'clock.' Rosie say, 'How long you stay?' 'E say, 'Maybe t'ree-four day. Beauchamp 'e got some sleigh to make an' odder job to do.' "

"What happened then?" I said.

"Well, nex' morning I go Pos' Offis an' get my papiere from Montreal. W'en I come in Rosie she smile an' say, 'Frank, doan go upstair. Is col' up dere. Sit down here on sofa an' read your papiere w'ere is nice and warm. Dere's no one here 'cep' you an' me. An' Rosie awful lonely wit' 'er 'usband way out Xavier Beauchamp's camp.' "

I saw that the plot was thickening rapidly. "Did you stay and sit on the sofa?" I asked, knowing.

"I sit down on sofa an' try to read my papiere. My han' she shake 'ard t'inking of dat 'andsome Rosie an' me dere all alone. I can't read de word—papiere she's might as well be print in Henglish. Pres soon by an' by Rosie come in from badroom and sit down 'side me on sofa, real clos', too clos' for decan' woman. I feel her breat' on my neck an' my han' she shake some more. I say nossing."

"What'd Rosie do then?" I said.

"Den she go badroom an' queeck she come stan' on door wit' jus' leetle t'in t'ing on, too t'in for decan' woman. Den she smile an' wink an' moshaw me to come on dat badroom. I say no—Reechar' 'e's my fren'. Den she go on badroom an' pres soon she's stan' on door wearing nossing but beeg smile—an' she moshaw me."

"What did you do?" I said.

"Well, I go," old Frank said, panting over the very recollection. "I forget all 'bout my fren' Reechar'."

"What happened then?" I said, breathing a little hard myself.

"We sit dere on bad an' pres soon Rosie she's 'ug me an' kees me on de mout'. Den she lay down an' smile dat sleepy smile— you know—an' moshaw me, an' den I lay down, too. We lay dere fi'e-ten minoot an' den dat badroom door she's fly ope' and dere's my fren' Reechar'. Reechar' 'e look lak wil' man an' 'e 'oller: 'W'at de 'ell go on 'ere? You, Frank Paquette, my ol' fren'!' Den 'e call me all kin' *baad* name—I doan say dem name 'cause I b'long 'Oly Name Society. Den 'e 'oller: 'I shoot you, I shoot you, I shoot you!' W'at can I say? I say 'Go 'ead, Reechar', shoot me.' Den 'e 'oller: 'I sue you, I sue you, I sue you! I sue you twenty t'ousan' dollaire. If you doan pay I tell poleeze for harrest Frank Paquette, 'e break my 'ome!' Den I say, 'I got no monay. All I got is U. S. Bon'.' Den 'e say: 'Bon,' she is no good, jus' scrap of papiere!' Den I say, 'Den you bettaire call poleeze an' harrest me. I got no monay.' Den Reechar' 'e put 'is face close on me an' say: 'GEEVE ME DE MORGAZHE!' "

"What did you do?" I said, leaning forward, completely absorbed.

"W'at can I do?" he shrugged. "I'm force'. I tell him I geeve him de morgazhe. So we go on bank, me an' Reechar', an' I tell bank, 'Geeve him de morgazhe, she's all pay.' De bank 'e look on me kin' o' funnay so I say: 'Geeve him de morgazhe. She's all pay.' So bank 'e's make dischar' papiere an' I sign papiere dat morgazhe is all pay. Bank 'e give dischar' papiere to Reechar' an' Reechar' 'e smile an' say: 'So long, Frank. Come see me an' Rosie again som' tam.' I t'ink dat's kin' o' funnay an' bank 'e say: 'Tell me da trut', Frank. Dey nevaire really pay hup de morgazhe— instead Reechar' catch you on bad wit' Rosie, no?' I 'ang my head an' I tell bank dat's da trut', how you know?—an' bank 'e smile an' say, 'Bettaire you go on District 'Torney an' harrest dem crook.' "

"So that's why you came here?" I said, already running a slight temperature to think of what a crude badger game these two knaves had worked on this likeable old Frenchman.

"Non, non," he said. "I wait whole year. I doan like to go for law an' den 'ave headline on papiere say ol' Frank Paquette go on bad wit' wife of 'is fren' Reechar'. An'way, den I still got U. S. Bon'. But dat fox Reechar' he remembaire dem U. S. bon' and pres soon he come visit on my place every mont' an' make me cash hup de U. S. bon' or he will go on poleeze an' tell dem 'bout me an' Rosie an' send me on prison. Las' mont' all dem U. S. bon' is cash hup an' I look for Ol' Age Pensyown an' 'e take me on bank an' bot' bank an' Ol' Age Pensyown 'e tell me Reechar' an' Rosie blackball me an' bettaire I go on District 'Torney an' harrest dem crook. So I go." Old Frank paused and looked across at me with a kind of a sheepish smile. "Dere should ought to be some law for dat, no?"

There was indeed some "law for dat." Even though old Frank called it "blackball," this appeared to be plain old-fashioned blackmail of the crudest sort. Lawyers, abhorring simplicity, generally label the offense extortion, but by whatever name it is one of the shabbiest and most cowardly criminal offenses on the books.

"Are you willing to sign a criminal complaint and testify in court against Richard and Rosie?" I asked old Frank.

"You mean, instead Reechar' harrest me I harrest Reechar'?" old Frank inquired.

"That's right," I answered.

"I sign da papiere," old Frank said, finally making up his mind.

I made an appointment to see old Frank later, and in the meantime checked the mortgage records and talked with the bank and the old age assistance people, and confirmed that my old Frenchman had told me the solemn truth. Of course I could have instead sent him away to retain his own private civil lawyer to file a bill in equity to cancel the discharge of the "morgazhe," foreclose the mortgage, and for other relief; but thanks to Rosie and Reechar', old Frank was now broke and had no money to hire lawyers or anybody, and anyway I felt that the time was way overdue to really crack down hard on Mr. and Mrs. Reechar' LaBeau. I prepared the papers charging extortion; old Frank signed them;

the criminal warrant was issued; Rosie and Reechar' were arrested. They promptly and loudly pleaded not guilty and hired a good lawyer. The show was on.

When the county clerk called the case of the People versus LaBeau for trial in circuit court it seemed that every adult resident in Spring River Township was on hand for the trial. They had arranged themselves into informal cheering sections—the Frank Paquette rooters on one side and the LaBeau rooters on the other. The LaBeaus' lawyer and I tugged and hauled and pettifogged most of the morning and finally selected the jury. I then made my opening statement and called old Frank to the stand. He arose and marched resolutely to the witness stand like a white-maned old lion, was sworn, sat down and, under my usual brilliant questioning, slowly told his story to the jury just as he had told it to me in my office.

"That's all," I said, whereupon Merciful Mike Moriarity, the lawyer for the LaBeaus, arose to take over the cross-examination of old Frank. This crafty old campaigner was the hero of many a criminal trial. It soon became evident from his questioning of old Frank that he was trying to show that Rosie was a woman of spotless virtue; that she had stoutly resisted old Frank's advances for some time; and that a lecherous and calculating old Frank had waited until Reechar' was absent and had finally crumbled her defenses by the exercise of his irresistible masculine wiles. But old Frank stuck pretty well to his guns. The lawyer at length led Frank down to the final scene in Rosie's "badroom." Then he pointed his finger accusingly at old Frank and asked in a loud voice:

"Isn't it true that you finally went into the LaBeau bedroom because you wanted to go?"

Old Frank glanced at me and then at old Judge Belden. "Yes," he answered in a small voice. There was a squall of rustling and excited whispering among the LaBeau faction. Judge Belden glared them into silence.

"Isn't it true that you entered Mrs. LaBeau's bedroom with the intention of having sexual relations with her?" the lawyer intoned dramatically.

"No, Rosie she no relashaw wit' me," Frank promptly answered.

After Judge Belden had pounded his gavel and the laughter from both factions had died down, old Moriarity continued: "Now, Mr. Paquette, you don't understand me. Didn't you enter the bedroom with the intention of having sexual intercourse with Mrs. LaBeau?"

"Oh, dat—yes," old Frank glumly admitted, staring pensively down at the floor. "Ah," triumphantly breathed the LaBeau faction.

"And when Mr. LaBeau finally appeared were you not lying down on the bed with Mrs. LaBeau?"

"Yes," old Frank whispered.

"And you were lying there because you wanted to? No one forced you?" the lawyer continued.

Hanging his head: "Yes. I'm not force'."

"And weren't you then actually having sexual intercourse with her?" the lawyer pressed on. (While the actual guilt of the blackmail victim of the blackmail offense, adultery here, is no legal defense to the criminal charge of blackmail itself, it was plain that the LaBeaus' wily old lawyer was trying to arouse and inflame the jury against old Frank.) "Answer me," the lawyer barked. "Weren't you then having intercourse with her?"

Old Frank's chin sagged to his chest. He looked up shame-facedly from under his bushy gray eyebrows like a naughty boy, first at me, then at Judge Belden, then at a portrait of Abraham Lincoln, then fleetingly at Rosie herself, then down at the floor.

"No," he finally quavered in a small voice, still staring at the floor.

"Why not, why not?" loudly demanded the lawyer.

"Yes, why not?" Judge Belden demanded in a brusque and impatient voice. The jurors were sitting on the edge of their seats. I gulped a glass of water.

Finally old Frank raised his eyes and looked imploringly at old Judge Belden. He spoke slowly as every ear strained to hear.

"Some tam ol' feller lak me an' you 'e try 'is bes', 'e can do nossing."

A sigh ran through the courtroom. Judge Belden developed a sudden spasm of choking. The bailiff swiftly declared a recess. When the recess was over the trial continued and dragged through the day. Rosie did not even take the stand. The jury got the case by suppertime and in ten minutes returned a verdict of "Guilty as charged" against both defendants.

Judge Belden put Rosie on probation and Reechar' was sent to jail and also put on probation, one of the strict conditions of which was that the LaBeaus had to pay up every dime they owed on the "morgazhe" and had realized on the sale of the U. S. bon'.

The courtroom was nearly deserted. I sat at my table stashing papers away in my brief case. Someone shuffled up to me out of the shadows. It was old Frank Paquette.

"T'ank you, young fellaire," he said, patting me on the shoulder. "You pretty good 'torney for me. I'm ver' glad you get back de morgazhe an' de U. S. bon'." He paused and looked tragically sad. "But I feel hawful *baad* 'bout one t'ing w'at 'appen," he said.

"What's that?" I said, pausing in my stashing.

"I feel hawful *baad* I 'ave to confess on front all dem people on de court dat Frank Paquette 'e get so ol' now some tam 'e can't make propaire love to pretty woman."

I sat staring up at the magnificent old goat.

Chapter 8

BEAUTIFUL ST. ANDREWS BY THE SEA

WE HARBOR A PRISON in this county that resembles a ponderous and well-heeled country club. We also have a country club that looks like a prison. Doubtless both structures were conceived by the same school of soaring and eccentric genius that designs stoves to look like phonographs; phonographs to look like iceboxes; iceboxes that look like tombstones; and, to complete the dreary circuit, tombstones that look like stoves. But I wander and grow peevish. I started to dilate on prisons and must reluctantly get back to them.

The elected county D.A. handles all cases of crime occurring within the physical limits of his county (except federal offenses) and if fate plants a prison in his county it falls his unhappy lot to handle all of the criminal cases arising from these prolific incubators of crime. We have a prison in this county, a prison which is regarded by many prison administrators (not to mention the inmates) as one of the "hardest" in America, harboring as it does the most violent and desperate of convicted men spewn up from that teeming industrial maelstrom known as the Detroit area.

The main differences between our prison and Sing Sing is that ours has had a poorer press. None of its wardens has taken pen— or ghost—in hand and written books about it and I hasten to partially fill the breach. And, too, it stands so innocently on the shores of Lake Superior and looks, as I have said, like a slightly forbidding country club designed by a man who's grandfather was a brewer. All summer long tourists wearing those trick head visors drive into its beautiful grounds waving their greens fees and clamoring to play golf. At least up to a point—the point nearest the woods—they'd find plenty of willing caddies.

Every community that possesses a penitentiary has a time bomb planted in its midst which may explode any minute of any day. Our prisons are crowded with long-termers and lifers, most of whom are there because of some fatal social clash, some feverish inability to discipline themselves, to adjust themselves to the bewildering tempo of modern life. These long termers—many of them, not all—are men of wild impulses for good or bad, men of unbridled passion, incredibly courageous, cowardly, sentimental, ruthless, tender. They are the strayed, the wounded, the defeated and lost among all those intense individualists who wage a life-long war against the eternal and conflicting pressures of organized society. Their number is legion and my main feeling toward them is one of compassion for their lot and dismay over their blasted lives.

The failure of this swelling army of caged men to harmonize their restless natures with the common weal—the appalling waste of potential good—is one of the great tragedies of modern American life. "There, but for the grace of God. . . ." Suddenly these men who have brooked no discipline, heeded no halter, find themselves caught in the unyielding, iron regimentation of prison existence. Those that are not broken by it, utterly crushed, or those that do not become raving or quietly staring-eyed, spend their every waking moment planning, scheming, contriving to get out of there. *Freedom!* becomes their only prayer.

For all the profound official chatter to the contrary, our present theory of punishment and incarceration is still basically the Mad Dog theory: lock 'em up like a mad dog and let 'em fester—*but keep 'em locked up!* This dreadful waste of humanity (not to mention money) is appalling to contemplate, so most of us don't. We either feel a vague irritation that we have to support our convicts or we ignore them altogether. The thinking of most of those who are supposed to ponder the problem seems congealed into cautious patterns concerned mainly with how these men can be kept busy and out of mischief without their doing any work that competes with good old private enterprise and the labor unions. Despite tentative and hopeful advances here and there, prison rehabilitation is still dominated by the timid proctor approach, and for the most part is restricted to the dreary confines of a place called *prison*.

What a real challenge all this could be to someone aflame with a great dream! For a modest starting dream I have thought of recruiting selected inmate labor battalions for foreign service to implement our country's various foreign aid programs. Of course this would present serious problems but think of the appalling problems under the present system. The men could wear uniforms, be paid a fair wage, and win advances like any good soldier— on their own merit—with always the ultimate goal of winning complete freedom. The psychology of the thing is elementary. Get these men at last doing a *man's* work in human surroundings for a great cause, not crouching in squalid cages weaving children's baskets and endless plots to escape!

It is this consuming lust for freedom that fills our newspapers with fantastic tales of plots and riots and attempts at escape, stories of unbelievable burrowings and of actual prison breaks. A Dillinger fashions a wooden gun and escapes from a country jail—after first posing for a snapshot (later featured in all the newspapers) with his arm draped around the unhappy D.A.'s shoulder—and a nation follows a relentless, bloodstained, hounds-and-hare manhunt, winding up in the spattered gutter in front of an obscure Chicago movie house. The story is mild. Let me tell you just a few of the harrowing honeys that have happened at *my* prison.

Four lifers silently awaited their chance at the Saturday night movie in the darkened prison chapel—*"Now!"* one of them shouted—and when the smoke cleared away the warden was dead, his deputy and one of the escaping prisoners were fatally wounded. And the hapless prosecutor, who was probably out trout fishing at the time, had a new batch of murder cases to try. For, as I have suggested, it is the duty of the D.A. to handle all criminal offenses occurring in any prison located in his county. He helps gather away the debris, you see, whenever the bomb explodes.

My first experience with this relentless desire to escape of these men who often prefer death to confinement came near the end of my first term as D.A. These prison tales of sudden violence and death are like something taken out of a twenty-five cent shocker, so hold your hats.

2

The barred, guarded building where the state parole board heard its cases stood in the center of the main prison yard—a cage within a cage. The parole board was in session, hearing its last supplicant for freedom. The warden, his deputy, the chaplain, the prison physician were all there. The bored stenographer rapidly took his notes as the hearing neared its conclusion. The supplicant was unoriginally muttering: "Just give me one more chance and—and—"

There was a scuffle at the barred door, the door opened, and in rushed three gray-denim-clad inmates pushing a bound and helpless prison guard before them.

"This is a break, men!" Musto said, leveling a revolver at the assemblage. "Tie 'em up, boys."

Musto's two partners brandished long homemade knives. They carried coils of binder twine. In five minutes the job was done. Musto took one of the knives and held it at the warden's back.

"Warden," Musto said quietly, "I want you to make a telephone call for me."

"Yes?"

"I want you to phone outside for the fastest prison car—that's the big Cad—to drive up to the door of this building—and to open the main gates wide. Sorry, Warden, but we're going to leave you now. We want out."

"And if I don't?" the warden said.

"We'll kill every man in this room—starting with you." Musto laughed without mirth. "We've nothing to lose, Warden. No reflection on your hospitality but we'd sooner be dead than in here." He tested the sharp point of his knife with his finger. "Do you phone? I'm counting ten." Slowly, like a fight referee counting after a knockdown: *"One-two-three-four-five-six-seven—"*

"Phone, Warden," one of the others said. "It's our only chance."

"Shut up!" Musto barked.

The warden had a wife and three children just outside the wall. He had been the skipper on a submarine chaser during the First War. He knew no personal fear.

"Eight-nine," Musto counted and paused.

"Give it to 'em, Mus," Garrett said. Garrett was another inmate.

"Shut up, Garrett!" Musto said. "Warden, I like you—you've been good to us—as right as you slugs can ever be—but we've got to hurry. You've got to quit stallin'." He twisted the knife in the warden's back to mark his target and drew it back for the plunge. "We've got a blind date with freedom . . ."

The warden glanced at the others trussed in their chairs. They nodded their heads frantically. They could see something he couldn't: the wild fanatic gleam in Musto's eyes. "Your number's nearly up, Warden," Musto warned. "Here goes . . ." He drew his arm back.

"I'll give them your message," the warden said, speaking grimly into the phone held by another inmate.

When the big car rolled out the open prison gates an army of state, county, city and prison police and guards were lined up on both sides. They could have reached out and touched the purring car. Bristling with revolvers, rifles, sawed-off shotguns, tear gas bombs, submachine guns, they sat or stood there and silently watched their quarry ride away. For in the car with the inmates sitting packed in and around them like sardines, were the two trussed members of the parole board, the warden and his deputy. A third member of the parole board was driving.

As the big car rounded the curve on to the state highway, it shot into high, gathering speed. With a roar and clash of gears the army of officers rolled into pursuit. Except for the air of grimness it had all the aspects of a wild comedy chase in Hollywood.

Musto laughed and thrust his revolver under the warden's nose.

"Warden, now that we've got some *real* guns, what do you think of this job?" The warden grunted. Musto's original "gun" was made of painted wood. Dillinger was just a copycat. "I made it myself. Pretty good job, don't you think, Warden?"

The warden stared straight ahead. The big car sang and hummed down the road, rocking and plunging with its heavy load. The speedometer was passing eighty. The line of pursuers was drawing nearer.

"Stop the car!" Musto suddenly shouted.

The big car slid to a smoking stop and pulled up on the shoulder. The procession of police cars in the rear drew to a halt, the lead car but several hundred yards away. Musto quickly cut the bonds of the deputy warden, opened the car door, and pushed him out.

"Bill," Musto said, "you're the oldest member of this tea party—and not the worst screw in the world. Go back and tell the boys that if they even get in *sight* of us again, our next warning is going to be a dead body. *Get going!"*

Musto slammed the door shut and the big car again gathered speed. A half mile farther Musto ordered the car into a roadside gas station.

"But the indicator says the tank's full," Jerry, the parole board driver, said.

Musto pressed a knife at his back. "Drive in there, Chum. I want some fluid for my lighter. Got a heavy date tonight."

The gas tank of the big car took over nineteen gallons. It was nearly empty. It had been a prison trick and Musto had seen through it. "Keep the change!" Musto shouted as he flung a twenty-dollar bill at the goggle-eyed attendant. "Full hey!" he laughed at the driver as the car again gathered speed, taking the curves at seventy, passing Rapid River, Gladstone, Escanaba, approaching Menominee, where lay the Michigan state line. None of the inmates had thought to turn on the car radio, which would have warned them that the showdown would be at Menominee. Impatient, Musto brushed aside the driver and took over the wheel. "Faster, faster!" he shouted to nobody. It was growing dusk, a fine drizzle had started, and the big old car was careening along at over ninety as they approached the boundary bridge.

Musto shouted, "Look out ahead, men—*barricade!*"

As Musto swerved the big old car to the left, it leaned over like a sailboat, groaning and squealing, acrid with the smoke of burning rubber. It plunged over the shoulder, into the ditch. The right rear door sprung and flew open and Ross, the chairman of the parole board, leaped out and rolled away like a rubber ball. He had played football in his youth and still knew how to fall. As he stood up he saw the big car disappearing in a cloud of dust along a northbound gravel side road following the lake shore.

The lead pursuit car drove up and Ross leapt in and away they went. In two miles they sighted the prison car, drew nearer and nearer with their lights out, when suddenly at a sharp curve the tired old prison car left the road, pitched, tilted, and rolled over and over in the ditch, the rear wheels churning crazily.

"Are you hurt, men, Warden!" Ross shouted in the rainy darkness.

The warden raised the rear door of the car, lying on its side, submarine fashion, and climbed out.

"No, but we're hungrier than all hell!" he said.

The three inmates pleaded guilty, and another desperate prison break was ended.

3

One spring day four convicts, all lifers, by a strange coincidence found themselves sitting in the waiting room of the prison physician, each bearing a slip that the doctor should examine him for various minor ailments. By a further strange coincidence each of the four had a loaded revolver hidden in his clothing, this time real and not made of wood. The four prisoners did not talk with each other and sat there silently awaiting their turn. A male trusty nurse appeared at the door of the doctor's office.

"Alex Stasiak—next," he announced.

"What seems to be the trouble, Stasiak?" gray-haired Doctor Hornberger smiled as he read Stasiak's examination slip.

"A little cold, Doc, is all. Been sleepin' too close to a crack, I guess."

"Cold? On such a beautiful spring day? Here, open your shirt."

Old Doctor Hornberger advanced towards Stasiak with his stethoscope. "I'll listen to your chest."

"No, no, Doc." Stasiak quickly drew back. "It's—it's in my throat."

But Doctor Hornberger, laughing jovially, had pulled open Stasiak's shirt. There hung the hidden revolver. The two men stood watching each other for a frozen instant. The trusty nurse took one look and leapt down the open laundry chute.

"Doc," Stasiak said in a low voice. "Doc, I hate to do this. I didn't think—we didn't plan we'd have to do it to you."

Stasiak pointed the pistol at the doctor, and there were two shots. Old Doctor Hornberger fell dead with two bullets in his heart. Stasiak ran through the waiting room with the smoking pistol. "The bets are off, men! Follow me!"

At the main entrance to the hospital unit the four convicts overpowered and disarmed a guard and, lifting him before them like a football hero, they rushed across the open area to the tobacco factory, into the elevator, and up to the second floor. As they got to the second floor, an avalanche of tear gas bombs broke through the factory windows near the elevator. The guard and the four convicts began choking and blinking.

"Back into the elevator!" Stasiak shouted. "We'll shoot our way out at the bottom."

The elevator did not work. The power was shut off. Stasiak stood looking at his three companions and the guard.

To the guard: "Are you married?"

"Yes."

"Any kids?"

"Four."

"Get to hell into the factory by an open window. Keep out of my range!" Stasiak pushed him back into the factory and turned to the other three inmates.

"Men, we picked a loser this time. The game is up. There's only one way to fool these bastards." Stasiak leveled his gun at Bronski's temple. "Good-by, Bronk."

Bronski closed his eyes and nodded his head. Stasiak pulled the trigger. Bronski fell dead.

"Good-by, Gurney."

One more shot, and Gurney dropped dead in the elevator, falling over Bronski's body like a loose sack of potatoes.

"And you, Charlie—I'll see you in hell, too."

But Charlie, his eyes wide and gleaming with horror, leaped over the gushing bodies and tried to get back into the factory. Stasiak pulled the trigger, and Charlie fell with a bullet in the back of his head. He rose to his knees, bloody, walking like a man on amputated stumps.

"Stace! Stace! Oh God! No, no, no, no, no . . ."

Stasiak fired again and Charlie thumped on his ruined face. Just as the guards burst up the stairway and rounded the corner Stasiak finished reloading and, grinning, held the revolver to his own head and fired a last shot into his brain.

After the dead were buried, there was the question: Where and how did the men get the guns and ammunition? After months of ceaseless police work we found this to be the answer.

A convict called Barlowe was released from prison two months before the fatal shooting. Before his release he was told by Stasiak to go to a certain address in Detroit where he would receive two thousand dollars in cash. With the money he was to buy four pistols and ammunition and return to Iron Bay and hide them in a designated culvert outside the prison grounds. A trusty would smuggle them in. Barlowe was then to return at once to Detroit and keep the balance of the money.

Barlowe, released, went to Detroit, found the address, got the money—and proceeded to go on a wild binge. He was enjoying himself immensely when one day the bartender at the Blue Goose answered the phone and turned to Barlowe and said, "You're wanted on the telephone, Barlowe."

Barlowe answered the phone and an even voice said, "Get this, Barlowe! You're late. We give you just one more week. Do you understand?"

"Yes."

Barlowe understood. He went shopping immediately and took a plane back to the U. P. to deliver his promised firearms.

Barlowe's trial for his part in the attempted escape was a long and tedious affair involving stool pigeons and all manner of unpleasant things. His attorney was a crafty old fox who could always be depended upon to put on a good show for his fee. On behalf of his client he called, as was his right, a long list of inmate character witnesses from the prison. This struck me as dubious defense strategy, charged with obvious irony, but his case was desperate and perhaps he sought to ballast by sheer numbers what his defense lacked in conviction. (Believe it or not, jurors have been known to count noses and tip the scales of Justice to the side with the *heavier* array of witnesses! Aside from the exhaustion of counting witnesses it at least saves them wear and tear on the processes of cerebration.)

I did not question these character witnesses. It was their brief vacation; their extravagant answers were a foregone conclusion; and I did not want to spoil their fun or to dignify their testimony by bothering to cross-examine them. Also, it would have been churlish for me to have gone into their long criminal records and if I had we might have been there yet. One wondered how men who had spent so much time in prison ever found time to get into so much trouble in so short a time outside. Such devotion to mischief was impressive.

The defense called its last character witness, a giant Negro, who stalked panther-like to the stand, dwarfing his two guards beside him. He sat quietly facing the crowded room, somber and thoughtful, not unlike a benevolent emperor himself about to hold court for his subjects. In a resonant baritone voice this magnificent-looking man testified thoughtfully and with quiet restraint as to Barlowe's good character. I had his prison dossier before me and I wondered what drunken fate had trapped this man in a strange northern place, a place that lay closer to the Eskimos than it did to his native Louisiana.

"Any questions of this witness?" Judge Belden said, interrupting my morbid reverie.

"Yes, Your Honor," I said. The witness had been at once so gentle and majestic in his bearing, and also so persuasive, that I could not forbear questioning him. It afforded the only touch of humor, and something more, in a grim and prolonged courtroom struggle. I blessed the man.

To the witness: "When you speak of the good character of the defendant, Mr. Jones, do you mean good character *inside* the institution or *outside* the institution?" I did not mean the question wickedly; it was mostly a little friendly banter.

"Inside de prison walls, Mistah D.A. Suh," he answered in that melodious voice. The inherent humor of the situation struck him and he suddenly beamed at me, the judge, the jury, everyone. His smile was like a radiant light in a fog. I smiled back at him; he looked like such a *good* man. Perhaps it was well I was not on the parole board.

"Just what do you call good character inside the institution?" I asked, somehow beguiled by the entire notion.

The big Negro folded his powerful arms and grew thoughtful as a philosopher. Then slowly: "Even on de inside a man's got his 'pinions an' his pride, Suh." He paused and went on. "You ax what's good charactah in de 'stushun, Suh? Hm . . . Yassuh. An inmate what do a favah foh 'nother inmate, keep his mouf shut, an' pay his gamblin' debts—dat's what Ah calls good charactah, Suh. *Yassuh!*"

"Thank you, Mr. Jones," I said soberly. "I believe you've got something there."

But despite these glowing traits—which many of us on the outside might well emulate—Barlowe was convicted, sentenced, transferred to a down-state prison, and escaped while being held in medical detention. Two weeks later his bullet-riddled body was found in an alley—in an alley behind the Blue Goose, a chummy little tavern in the city of Detroit. Was it payment for late delivery? Was he suffering from a sudden excess of good character? Who knows? Anyway that was a headache for the Detroit D.A. to cope with. I shrugged and went trout fishing. I somehow wished Emperor Jones could have gone along.

4

The last prison case of scores I handled fell into the same bizarrely familiar pattern of all the others, with an added touch.

One day the prison Allah himself—the governor of the state—was inspecting the prison accompanied by his state police bodyguard and the warden and trailed by the usual buzzing knot of miscellaneous politicians that always swarm around a governor like bees around their queen. You see, inspection tours make good newspaper copy and the average politician would trail the Devil himself on an inspection tour through Hell to get his name in the newspapers. This trip must have charmed them: it made especially good copy.

By late afternoon the inspection group found itself in a sort of doubledoored pantry-corridor separating the main kitchen from the mess hall where hundreds of surly inmates sat eating their silent evening meal. Busy trayladen trusty waiters constantly passed and repassed the inspection group. Just as the governor was leaning over to taste some of the beans being served to the inmates—a nice democratic touch—two of the "waiters" lunged at the governor, one of them shouting, "Come on, Guv—you're goin' with us as hostage!"

Inmate Barnes brandished a kitchen knife at the governor as large as a Philippine bolo. "Come on, come on!" he shouted. Curwood, the state police bodyguard, ran over to protect the governor. The second inmate, Halter, then made for officer Curwood with a homemade ice pick and jabbed him in the back. The governor, young, powerful and full of guts, closed in and grappled with Barnes for possession of the knife. In the ensuing struggle the group pushed over into the main kitchen, and the wild waltz became visible to the 700 feeding inmates through a large separating window. This gravely increased the danger of a general riot during which a great many hideous things could happen.

Suddenly one of the dining convicts, Hamster, broke from the mess hall and darted through the pantry and into the kitchen, grabbing up a long-handled metal onion masher as he ran, a vicious weapon not unlike a branding iron that might be used on an elephant ranch. "He came zooming in at us like a madman," the governor said later. "He was waving the masher and screaming foul obscenities. I—I rather think he's not a member of my party."

The governor had a sense of humor, a quality not notable among political pros.

The warden then barred the kitchen door so that no further volunteer inmates could join the fray unless they broke through the separating window. That was a distinct possibility. In the mess hall a half-dozen sweating guards sought to keep 700 men from doing just that. The place was in an uproar of broken dishes, curses and hurled tableware.

By this time three guards arrived in the kitchen. They went after the still cursing and wildly swinging Hamster, who swung his onion masher viciously and broke both forearms of one of the advancing guards. He then turned and clipped the stalking civilian cook a glancing blow on the forehead, felling him. The other two guards closed in and grabbed him.

In the meantime the first two convicts kept trying to get at the governor. He was their man, their only hope of escape. Despite his back wound and a fresh hand wound from one of the knives, Officer Curwood whipped out a pistol. The warden barked: "Drop those knives or be shot!"

Barnes dropped his huge kitchen knife but Halter continued to lunge at the governor with his wicked ice pick. Curwood took careful aim and shot Halter in the belly—fatally, it later developed. This ended the melee and finally the mutinous rumbling stopped in the mess hall.

Score: One killed (inmate Halter) and three injured (the guard, the cook and officer Curwood).

Halter died the next morning. (Years before he had tried to escape through a sewer pipe; had nearly been scalded to death; and had to be cut out with an acetylene torch.) Barnes and Hamster were charged with felonious assault.

At their arraignment later in circuit court Barnes pleaded guilty. He took a better-luck-next-time attitude toward the whole thing. Hamster of the onion masher was brought in next, and as I read him the information I noticed that his eyes darted right and left like those of a trapped animal. I droned on reading my information: ". . . contrary to the form of the statute in such case made and provided and against the peace and dignity of the People of the State of Michigan," I concluded.

As the judge carefully explained the prisoner's rights and then took his plea of not guilty I still noticed Hamster's darting ferret eyes. He was unmanacled but surrounded by a cordon of armed flatfeet. Yet I felt in my bones that he was going to make a break. When, was the only question. Since my contribution to the tableau included only talents of the mind I stepped back to give him plenty of room. The group then moved slowly to a side door beyond which both Hamster and I knew that manacles and more flatfeet awaited him. The big mahogany door had scarcely breathed shut on them when there was a sudden scuffle, a thump on the door, and then the muffled sounds of shouts and running feet.

"What's happening?" the annoyed judge asked his D.A.

"I believe the defendant Hamster just took a powder, Your Honor," I said, running for the door. I had barely got out the door when I heard a shot. In the hollow corridors of the old courthouse it rang and echoed like a cannon. As I skidded around a corner I almost ran into a state policeman trudging up the marble stairs still holding his pistol.

"Get him?" I said, studying his sharpshooter ribbon.

"Right through the heart," he answered, not sadly, not gladly, but like a competent sharpshooter.

I felt like wiring the governor to build us a couple of additional prisons in the county. With them around there would never be a dull moment—and all of us found the work they gave us so goddam stimulating and exhilarating.

There were scores of cases like this and worse. I occasionally got one break: many of the cases never did come into court because there was no one left around for me to prosecute. Some of them the average layman would scarcely believe: wild stabbings and murders and suicides growing out of fetid and steaming prison "romances" and perversities and jealousies so fantastic that Freud himself would have doubtless gulped in bewildered astonishment and revised some of his earlier conclusions. We stoically buried the dead in the prison potter's field and piled another long sentence on top of a sentence on top of a sentence, like a gustatory Gertrude Stein cooking and piling up unneeded flapjacks in a restaurant window.

I sometimes felt it would have been an act of Christian charity to have put some of these poor devils of survivors out of their misery, but the opponents of capital punishment will have none of it. They have much on their side but sometimes I feel that the more emotional opponents of capital punishment don't know what gives. To avoid a specific cruelty they perhaps inflict graver cruelties. Their fallacious assumption may be that there is nothing worse than death. I don't know. Sobbing inmates have frequently begged and pleaded that they be mercifully shot (indeed some of them deliberately courted it) rather than return to a hopeless living death in that attractive prison that looks like a country club—from the *outside,* that is.

Chapter 9

MY FRIEND JAN TREGEMBO

MY CORNISH MINER FRIEND Jan Tregembo is quietly mad about
rabbit hunting and rabbit hounds. He has owned all varieties of
hounds, including beagles, bassets and fox hounds—not to mention various meditated and fortuitous combinations thereof. Every
fall come rabbit season he invited me to go rabbit hunting. This
had been going on for years, ever since I first met him at one of
the iron mines while campaigning for D.A.

"Johnnay," he would invariably say, collaring me, "why don't
you come 'untin' some Sunday with we? We'll let the 'aounds
loose in the swamp an' by an' by you'll 'ear the sweet music ave
'em givin' tongue—an' then along comes Mister Rabbit 'oppin'
an' jumpin' an' then we'll start a-shootin' ave 'em, a-missin' ave
'em, an' borrowin' shells . . . say, Johnnay, why don't you come
'untin' some Sunday with we?"

The prospect grew irresistible so one fall I accepted. After a
morning of good hunting we left the swamp and were sitting on
the running board of Jan's Model A Ford having lunch while the
squirming beagles tangled up their leashes and blew and rested
their feet.

"Damn good pasties, Jan," I said, between steaming bites of the
traditional Cornish meat, vegetable and suet pie.

"Pretty, partner," Jan chirped. "Ol' lady made 'em fresh just
for we."

"Lotsa meat, too," I added in a pasty muffled voice.

"Yes, Hi tole ol' lady says Hi, 'Lissen, dearie, be sure'n put'n
more meat an' less taters an' termits—a man ain't no rabbit an'
'is stummick ain't no blawdy root'ouse.' "

"Jan," I asked, when I had recovered, making talk so that I could listen to more of his beautiful Cornish brogue, "how long you been an iron miner now?"

"Twenty-hate years ave savage hamusement, partner," Jan replied promptly, holding his steamy pasty aloft from a leaping beagle. "Get daown, lover girl!"

"Didn't you ever aspire to be a boss?" I inquired slyly. "Shift-boss or even captain?"

"Naw, naw," Jan replied. "Bosses is too blawdy dumb. Hi haspire only to pay my bills, hown a few good beagles—an' 'unt rabbits ave a Sunday. Bosses is too blawdy dumb."

"How do you mean 'dumb,' Jan?" I said, coming swiftly to the defense of private enterprise, a fairly unfamiliar role. "They wouldn't be bosses if they were dumb."

Jan took a quick gulp of the bubbling lava he called tea. "Ow, they wudn't, wudn't they? Take our mine cap'n, Cap'n Dicker Kermode, say. 'E always prided 'isself big on 'ow smart 'e was. Wan day a bunch of us was daown hunderground a-workin' hup in a raise an' this 'ere Cap'n Dicker come daown the main drift an' stuck 'is 'ead an' 'ollered up'n the raise. ' 'Ow many men hup there, partner?' 'e 'ollered an' Hi 'ollered back respectful, 'Seven, Cap'n Dicker!' an' 'e 'ollered hup, 'Aff of you come on daown 'ere!' "

"Maybe he was only joking," I said.

"Jocking? Cap'n Dicker jocking? 'E wudn't laugh hif 'is mother'n-law stobbed 'er taw an' plunged 'ead first daown a bloomin' mine shaft. An' 'e poutin' an' pridin' 'isself on 'ow smart an' hintellectual 'e was!"

"A lot of serious and humorless men have been real smart," I ventured, rather piously.

Jan snorted and went on. "Wan day Hi asked Cap'n Dicker, 'Cap'n Dicker,' says Hi, ' 'ere's a deep problem: wot 'as three legs an' barks like a dog?'

"Cap'n Dicker 'e pondered for quite a bit an' then 'e give hup. 'Wot,' 'e says, 'wot is it 'as three legs an' barks like a dog?'

" 'Hanswer's easy, Cap'n,' Hi said, 'hit's a milkin' stool.'

"Cap'n Dicker 'e stood there blinkin' an' ponderin' real 'ard an' bitin' 'is hupper lip an' then 'e says, 'Gwan, Jan, no blawdy milkin' stool never lived wot barks like a dog.'

" 'Hi knaow that, Cap'n,' Hi replied. 'Hi just put'n in the bark to make'n 'ard.' "

In the meantime one of Jan's eager beagles had slipped his leash and escaped into the swamp. Just then he started bugling a rabbit.

"C'mon, Johnnay," Jan said, swallowing the last of his pasty and grabbing his shotgun. "Better you come 'untin' naow with we!"

This is the same Jan who used to pump the organ for many years in the loft of the Methodist Church—that is until he suddenly quit and instead took up hunting rabbits of a Sunday.

"How come you quit pumping the church organ so sudden, Jan?" I asked him one Sunday, the perfect straight man. I had heard the story but never from the lips of the master.

"It's this way, Johnnay," Jan replied, his eyes growing misty with recollection. " 'Ere I'm pumpin' the blawdy horgan for seventeen years steady as a clock an' wan Sunday they Church Boord hup an' hemployed a new horganist—without never consultin' me, mind you. This 'ere new horganist 'e's wan of they fancy, heducated fellows wot wears 'is heye-glasses on a shoestring. Very first Sunday 'e commence plyin' long rumbly tunes by this 'ere Bach an' 'Andel an' the likes of 'e an' me pumpin' an' 'e plyin' until I was close near to hexaustion back there pumpin' ave 'er so blawdy 'ard."

"What happened then, Jan?" I prodded.

"Hafter the hintermission, just before the new horganist cud get hunderway, Hi pops me 'ead araoun' the corner an' 'ollers aout real loud, 'Hi don't knaow wot *thee's* gonna ply, partner, but Hi's gonna blaw *Abide With Me!*"

One morning at nine Jan rushed into my office all out of breath. "I wants you to ketch the thief!" he panted. "I wants you to ketch the blawdy thief wot stole my Sarah Jane!"

"Sit down, Jan," I calmed him. "Sit down and tell me about it. Who the hell is Sarah Jane? Your wife?"

"Nao it weren't my ol' lady—'oo'd bother to steal fat she?

T'was a blue tick beagle she was, partner. Thirteen hinches of pure 'untin' 'eart. Jest got 'er las' night all the way from Kentucky. Hawful hexpensive, too. Hi 'ad to resign St. 'Uber's lodge an' quit drinkin' for a 'ole year to save hup the money to pay for 'er. An' me 'oo so dearly loves to drink. . . . Also Hi built a brand-new kennel for 'er an' hinsulated it with this 'ere naow rock wool. Don't even 'ave rock wool in aour own blawdy 'ouse. Ol' lady swears Hi love my rabbit 'aounds dearer'n she. Ol' lady is blawdy well right."

"But what happened to your new rabbit dog?" I asked my friend Jan Tregembo.

" T'was a case of love at first sight. She harrived from Kentucky last night on the midnight train. Me an' 'aff of my lodge brothers was daown there to depot to meet'n. 'Less you was drunk or sleepin' you shall recall las' night was terrible col' an' grizzly so Hi wraps 'er hup in my new hovercoat. She was a dear little whimperin' sweet'eart an' she tuck to me first off the bat."

"But what happened?" I pressed.

"Hi tucked 'er in 'er new kennel, still wrapped in my hovercoat. Tightened 'er collar a bit but not too 'ard. Was goin' to 'unt 'er today. Tried to catch a wink of sleep but just tossed an' turned an' thought like on my 'oneymoon. All night long was wonderin' fretful 'ow my little princess was farin'. Daybreak finally come an' Hi couldn't stand hit nao longer—so still clad in my nightshirt Hi snuck from the ol' lady's side—she snorin' an' 'eavin' there so pretty—an' tiptawed daown the creakin' stairs, daown off the back stoop an' stealthy like drew back the curtain of 'er new kennel." Jan paused dramatically.

"How was she?" I asked, getting my cue.

"There she was—*gone!*" Jan concluded dolefully. "An' John-nay, Hi wants you to ketch the blawdy thief wot stole 'er!"

I am glad to report that Sarah Jane beat Jan home from my office. The belle from Kentucky had merely slipped her leash and gone for a midnight exploratory stroll. I may add that the pups were part Airedale.

Chapter 10

"IT IS THE JUDGMENT OF THE COURT . . ."

THE PROSECUTION of a criminal case, to a convicted defendant at least, consists of a series of little public hangings, each a sort of death in miniature: arrest, preliminary examination, arraignment, trial, conviction, sentence, commitment to prison . . .

The most depressing time of all for most D.A.s—as certainly it was for this one—is the imposing of sentence on those who stand convicted of crime. This is the final pay-off, the time when the chips are really down. I shall never forget those gloomy sessions—the poor convicted devils sitting herded into the jury box and frequently overflowing onto the lawyers' chairs, all under guard, each glumly waiting for the judge to call him up and utter the few magic words that meant either freedom or prison. The rest of the courtroom would be filled with families and relatives. They always sat in little huddled islands of silent watchfulness. Unless some particular case had attracted wide notoriety the rest of the public stayed away. They were only interested in the drama and dirt of a trial, in the noisy clash of opposing lawyers; they wanted no part of the tears.

As the hour for sentencing approached the place would grow as hushed as the funeral of a bishop. There was nothing more to do or say. You could almost always pick out a mother or a wife in the crowd; she would sit there so terribly still with dread, so trance-like and dry-eyed, waiting and waiting for the law to take its course. Then—the crowd would stir electrically—the heavy door of the judge's chambers would breathe open and Judge Belden would slowly enter the courtroom and gravely take his seat on the bench. Then he would nod to the sheriff. "Hear ye, hear ye, hear ye," the sheriff would intone, as everyone stood up, "the Circuit Court for the County of Iron Cliffs is now in session!" Then he would bang his gavel and everyone would sit down but the D.A., who would remain standing. It was all part of a ritual older than the writings of Sir Thomas Malory.

"May it please the Court," the D.A. would say, slavishly following the quaint rigmarole, "the People now move for judgment of sentence on the convicted respondents."

"Very well," his honor would say, "the motion is granted." He would then open his notebook and consult his term docket and ascertain the first lucky name. Then: "James Jorick will come forward and stand before the Court for sentence."

One of the guarding jailers would frantically motion the defendant Jorick to stir off his dead butt—the *judge* had spoken—and Jorick would stride defiantly or shuffle up before the judge and stand there silently awaiting his fate.

The vast majority of these individuals, if they were first-timers and their offenses were not too grave, would be placed on probation; that is, they would be put on their good conduct for a definite period of time, say two years, conditioned upon their making restitution, where indicated, and supporting their families or refraining from beating their wives or writing phony checks or swiping cars or whatever else their offense happened to have been. And in general they were ordered not to break any other laws— a rather large order for any of us, these days. Most probationers were also ordered to lay off of drinking. (I am no blue nose, God knows—unless I acquired the hue from my *own* drinking—but I offhand estimate that at least 90 per cent of the defendants who passed before me got into trouble through drinking.)

Judge Belden, bless him, mercifully did not lecture the poor devils who came before him for sentence. He told them simply and plainly that they already knew why they were there and what they had done, and that he would at least spare them the final degradation of publicly reviewing their misdeeds. To the probationers he usually added: ". . . And, young man, if you are foolish enough to break this probation and again come before me for violation of its terms, be sure to bring your toothbrush along because I'm going to have to send you across the river." It was surprising how effective this homely little warning could be. Comparatively few ever returned. Those that did usually needed their toothbrushes.

As time went by I could nearly always tell when Judge Belden was going to send a man to prison. When he called the unlucky defendant's name he would lightly stroke his left cheek with the heel of his thumb. I don't think he ever realized it himself, but I had studied the grand old man under fire for many years. Then, when he asked the defendant if he had anything to say why the sentence of the court should not be passed upon him, I knew for sure that defendant's goose was cooked. The judge didn't ask that question of those he put on probation; it had no part in the ritual. And that particular ritual was older than Blackstone.

"Do you, James Jorick, now have anything to say why the sentence of the court should not be pronounced upon you?" Judge Belden would ask, his face grown suddenly as gray as a prison wall. I do not believe he ever liked the sentencing ceremony any more than I ever liked to watch it.

Ninety-nine times out of a hundred the doomed defendant would mumble "no" or merely shake his head. He had nothing to say. Instead he would stand there silent and numb and take it on the chin. I always marveled at the sort of bovine endurance and courage of these quiet ones who *knew* they were on their way to prison. How could they possibly stand it? The very lack of drama, in the Hollywood sense, invested these sentencing scenes with a stifled drama of their own. Sometimes I wondered why the poor bastards did not jump and rail and scream out at the trap that life was closing upon them. But no, these voiceless ones seemed finally stricken mute by the accumulated pressure of Society. Then one day, one of them did speak out. To me it was one of the saddest and most moving scenes I ever beheld in a courtroom. And I have thought about it a lot.

"Do you now have anything to say . . ." Judge Belden began, asking the usual fateful question of a confessed embezzler who stood before him for sentence.

"I do, Your Honor," he said quietly.

"Very well," Judge Belden said, not unkindly, "you may proceed."

The defendant, an intelligent, rather clean-cut looking man in his mid-thirties, began to speak in a low voice, rather diffidently at first. He had been, he said, an outstanding athlete in high school, which we knew was true. He had also been an honor student, which was also true. He told the court that following his graduation he had been approached by the athletic representatives of a number of colleges to attend their schools. They only loved him for his mind, of course, he said. (God, I thought, the man has a sense of humor.) The offers had been quite attractive.

"I didn't go to college," the defendant continued, his voice growing somewhat stronger. "I wanted desperately to go, but I couldn't. . . . You see, Your Honor, my mother was and is a widow—my father, a laborer, had been killed in an industrial accident when I was a boy. I had to stay home and support and take care of her. Then I had met a girl from a neighboring town. We fell in love. Then, to seal my decision, I was offered the job in the bank from which I have now stolen money.

"When I first got that job I thought I had the world by the tail. I was thrilled beyond words. Here I was, the son of poor immigrant parents, being offered a responsible job in one of the best banks in the Upper Peninsula. It seemed incredible. I took the job, as you know, and what happened? I worked there for five years before I got my first raise. I also got my first service chevron to sew on my sleeve. I knew from the checks that passed through my hands that I was being paid less than some of the young gum-chewing typists down the street. I also knew, from my work, the handsome dividends the stockholders were making on *their* stock in the bank where I worked. I shall not further embarrass them by mentioning their percentage of return.

"I kept going with my girl—we had been engaged for several years—begging her to wait, that I was sure that I'd get my break soon and then we could be married. She waited. You see, we were in love. . . . Another five years passed and I got my break, all right—I got a ten-dollar-a-month raise and another pretty felt chevron to wear so that no one could possibly forget the length of my servitude.

"Several more years passed and one day one of the older tellers suddenly died. I had been his understudy since I had come with the bank. I knew the job from A to Z. I asked for the job. What happened? I didn't get it—one of the stockholders had a faltering son-in-law downstate who was beginning to cost him money. The son-in-law was sent for and got the job over my head. It didn't take me ten minutes to discover that he didn't know a sight draft from a bale of hay. And I'm not blaming him; he was a nice guy who needed a job—and had the connections to land it. But it happened to be the job I was looking for and needed. It also happened to be the job which I was entitled to if there is any morality in business whatever. . . . I wound up doing most of the new man's work as well as my own.

"I grew desperate and despondent. I grew cynical and didn't care much what happened. I told my girl that I didn't quite land the new job but that I had got a substantial raise and we could be married soon. I lied to her. I didn't get a substantial raise—or any raise; instead I got another chevron to add to the others. These chevrons, by the way, cost the bank thirty-seven cents each in job lots—I looked up the bill. It somehow fascinated me to learn. . . . I grew embittered and wanted to quit. But there was my mother to think of, and the girl I loved—and by then about all I knew to do was my particular little niche in banking. I was a has-been at thirty-three—and yet I felt I couldn't quit. I'd lost what little pride and spirit I had left."

His voice, rising now, began to shake a little with emotion. "Then I began to steal. It was easy. I knew my business well and I found the way that you now know about to cover up my tracks indefinitely. As all embezzlers feel, I thought I would pay it back some day. But I felt no particular sense of wrongdoing, nor do I now. I think I should tell you that. I felt and still feel that I was taking no more than my due. I bought my girl an engagement ring and began making payments on a lot. We planned to be married just about now. Instead she has gone away to take up nursing. She says she'll wait for me. . . .

"Then came that small error, the auditors were called in, and I was caught. I confessed to my employers and told them every penny I had taken. I can't resist saying that it was more than the auditors had found missing. That somehow pleases me. . . . As for my shortages, I could not pay them back—I had no wealthy connections or fathers-in-law who were important stockholders in the bank. So I was prosecuted. As you know, I came in here and pleaded guilty.

"You have asked me if I had anything to say. This, Your Honor, is what I had to say, and I have said it not in any mitigation of my guilt nor to seek any sympathy at your hands. I'm smart enough to know that I'm through. The reason I have spoken as I have is so that some other eager young men going into similar banks might perhaps know what they may be getting into; and so that possibly, and less likely, the eyes of the boards of directors of some of our banks might at last be opened to the wizened fruits of their quiet and urbane greed. That is all I have to say. Thank you, sir, for the opportunity to get all this off my chest."

The courtroom had grown as still as a church. The sudden electric time click of the courtroom clock sounded like a knell. I moistened my lips. Judge Belden sat looking at the eloquent and pallid defendant. His own drawn face had turned an ashen gray. His voice was weary and old when he finally spoke.

"Young man," he began, and his voice broke with pent emotion. He cleared his throat. "Young man, there are times when the weight of responsibility resting upon a judge is almost more than he can bear. This is one such occasion. . . . I want you to know that I have reviewed your case carefully. Most of the things you have told me I already know. Some of them indeed come as a surprise. I am moved, and deeply so, and I wish it were possible for me, under the law, to take a different course. But a judge, alas, must be ruled by his head as well as his heart.

"Other less articulate men will presently stand where you now stand. They will stand there when you and I are gone. Their stories, if they could speak, would also wrench the heart. It is nearly always so at a time like this. Few of us are compounded solely of evil, just as few men are made up only of good. It is one of the awful dilemmas of crime and punishment—indeed, of life itself. I can only give you the cold comfort that what I am about to do I shall do reluctantly and with a heavy heart, but with the sad conviction that under the scheme of things I must."

Judge Belden sighed and turned slightly toward the silently busy automaton, the court stenographer. This would be the sentence, it was coming, I knew all the signs. "It is the judgment of the court that you be confined to the state prison situated in this county there to remain for a period of not less than one year nor more than twenty years. I recommend that you be made to serve no more than the minimum term."

There was a faint sighing whistle in the tall chamber, like a jet of escaping steam. Someone sobbed behind me and spoke softly in a foreign language. I looked around and saw an old woman leaving the courtroom. I never learned for sure who she was. An attendant came up and touched the arm of the defendant and motioned him to follow him. Judge Belden again consulted his court docket. He cleared his throat.

"Ralph Ashlund will come forward and stand before the court for sentence," Judge Belden said, softly stroking his cheek with the heel of his thumb, his voice still weary and old.

I arose suddenly and went swiftly out to my office. I closed the door and stood looking far out across Lake Superior. The vast lake glittered and heaved in the cheerful sunlight. The gulls endlessly wheeled and tacked over the harbor, far below. They looked so obscenely *free*. . . . I stood there looking and thinking for a long time. What an incredibly lovely world it was without men. . . . Somehow into my brooding thoughts crept the name of a book; a book by a man called Dreiser. *An American Tragedy* it was called. As I stood there I wondered just who in hell I thought I was, to be part of the monstrous machinery that presumed to pass judgment on my fellow men.

Chapter 11

THE BITE

STOUT IS MY BELIEF that I shall never go to Hell; I've helped shingle too many churches. The only reason I lack a share in a synagogue or a mosque is that we hadn't any to shingle. This circumstance bothered me for a time because it struck me as smart theology to parlay my chances for reaching Heaven. But then I remembered that churches were against gambling, and I was comforted. For during my time as prosecutor I must surely have shingled my way to salvation and won a permanent life membership.

My situation fills me with wild delight; I can now fish every Sunday without a pang. It is something like getting credit for viewing a church service over television clad in one's pajama tops and clutching a Scotch. For I logically reflect that since St. Peter must long ago have stamped "complimentary" on my passport, going to church now would only be showing off and loading the dice—and would doubtless offend the old gentleman.

All politicians are vulnerable to fund raisers, and prosecutors, being much in the public eye, are a prime target. And there is no more zealous group of fund raisers in the world than a church congregation on the make. Every time they put on a new roof, or install a new grate in the furnace, or hack away the pigeon guano and hang a new bell, the congregation fans out among the politicians like a swarm of locusts and administers The Bite. They prefer to call it asking for a "donation." Donation hell; it's sheer blackmail. "We voted for you, Traver," they would leer significantly. So you sighed and reluctantly put another ten spot on the number marked Paradise.

I have suggested that churches are against gambling. That is not precisely true. Never shall I forget the look of religious ecstasy I once saw on the intent faces of an entire church congregation watching a money wheel at a church bazaar. It was a revelation and I was deeply touched. And by whom have entire state legislatures been coerced to lift the ban on Bingo for charitable and benevolent purposes? Who wrought this miracle? The hoodlums and gangsters? But then, of course, churches are against gambling . . .

I am not being fair. Many churches, especially endowed ones, are against gambling, in or out of church. They can afford to be. Others are against it on principle. Yet, for the poorer ones, there is no more painless way in the world to give the pastor a raise or buy him a new Chev than to let his flock fight it out over the Bingo tables. I'm all for it. It also serves to protect the poor politicians from The Bite.

Wherever you see widespread public commercial gambling, there you will find corruption and bribery among public officials. It is as simple as that. And I don't know which is the worse evil. Church gambling does not pitch in that league. It is largely a "family" enterprise; it is an innocent vent for the gambling instinct in all of us; public corruption does not follow in its wake; and the ultimate results are good. Amen.

I must confess that while all during my time as prosecutor I had cracked down hard on all forms of public commercial gambling, at the same time I deliberately closed my eyes to "church" gambling. There is no warrant in the law for making this distinction and it is a beautiful example of the prosecutor as legislator. But I reflected that the ways of the Lord were indeed mysterious, and if His work could occasionally be advanced by a whirling raffle wheel or by aligning kernels of corn just so on a numbered card—then *Bingo!* so might it be. The Devil occasionally has to be beaten with his own tail.

Naturally this made me a hypocrite and I loved it. When the righteous of non-gambling faiths grumbled to me about it I smiled and invited them to sign a criminal complaint. None ever dared tie a bell to the cat's tail, which perhaps made them hypocrites, too. At any rate I could have shingled Notre Dame Cathedral with the church raffle tickets I purchased during my time as D.A. Once I had the singular misfortune to win an electric broiler containing an inert and plucked turkey, and I had to act pretty fast to shunt the broiler and turkey back in time for a reraffle. The possibility that one might ever *win* one of these raffles had simply never occurred to me. I was amazed. Prosecutors may perhaps safely wink at church lotteries but they can scarcely afford to win one. Thenceforth, coward that I was, I bought all my raffle tickets in the name of my daughter Julie. But the charm was broken; she never won.

Like all politicians the prosecutor has many other benevolences. The churches can't hog all the limelight. There are ragged soft ball teams to be clothed; winning basketball teams to be feted; losing teams to be consoled by a trip to the finals in Flint; testimonial dinners to be run out. The list is endless and all of it is a form of public blackmail. "Turn us down, Buddy, and you're through!" is the tacit threat in all these appeals. I was weak. I had to support the myth that Traver was a right guy. Wrong guys in politics have a tendency to get licked.

But my private benevolences charmed and pleased me most. Especially Willie Mulrooney. Willie had been stalking me for quarters for years. He had dedicated his life to it—and filling his rotund belly with whiskey. He lay in wait for me at the back gate. He waited patiently at my office stairway for hours in a blizzard. He sometimes followed me out fishing. Once in his extremity he tracked me clean down to circuit court. I was trying a mere murder case but I swiftly recessed it to minister to my Willie.

"I'm sick, Johnny," was the sesame from which all quarters flowed. He seemed to sense when I was in a benevolent mood. Presto, there was little Willie. There was no escape. He also seemed to sense when I was not in a benevolent mood. I've seen his chubby form evaporate into thin air when he spied me coming along in a dark mood. The man was clairvoyant and could have made a fortune without so much as a cracked crystal ball. Instead, alas, he preferred to trail me for quarters.

No one took it harder than Willie when I ceased to be prosecutor. His little world tumbled all around him. It was so bad he stayed sober for three days. Things grew so critical that I hunted him up and forced a quarter on him. It was like an intravenous shot of bar whiskey. Since we're all creatures of habit, Willie slipped right back in the groove—and the stalk was resumed. Johnny was still good for quarters, D.A. or ex-D.A. Everything had turned out all right.

During the War the boys at his favorite tavern kidded Willie into believing he had been drafted. Willie was only sixty-four, but everybody had to register in those days, drunk or sober, and when Willie got his registration card the boys told him he had been drafted. "You've got to leave for Milwaukee tonight for your physical," they solemnly told him. So they staged an impromptu farewell party. "Skoal!" Poor Willie Mulrooney had to go to War.

An inflamed Willie presented himself at my office late that afternoon somewhat the worse for wear. He carried his luggage safely corked in his pocket. It was a little gift from the boys. I was surprised, not at his condition, but that he had stalked me right into my office. It was the first time.

"Willie," I frowned, "what are you doing here?"

Willie hung his head and surveyed me furtively with his red little eyes. He was sore troubled. "Came to say goo'bye, Johnny. Leavin' fer the War tonight on the 6:20." I could not help smiling and Willie suddenly pounded my desk. "I'm Ir'sh I am an' I ain't afraid to fight! But what'n hell are they draftin' a drunken ol' son-of-a-bitch like me with all them healthy young bashterds runnin' aroun' doin' nawthin'?" Willie waved his arm vaguely to embrace the tavern district of Chippewa. It was a pretty sweeping gesture, as it had to be.

"Let me see your card, Willie," I said. I looked at it. The joke had gone far enough. I explained the situation to Willie and returned him his registration card along with a shiny new half dollar. This was a new high and Willie rose to the occasion.

He offered me his hand and I took it. "Thanksh, Johnny—an' God bless you," he said with quiet dignity. I watched General

Mulrooney turn and carefully weave his way out of my office. I watched him with almost paternal concern.

"God bless you, Willie," I murmured. You see, I love that man. His was one bite that never irked me. Perhaps St. Peter will forgive me.

Chapter 12

THE TRUTH IS A THIN WOMAN

THE TRIAL of young Donald Blair was nearing the end of its third day. It was a drab, drizzly afternoon in the fall. In the coppery glow of the clustered old-fashioned brass courtroom lights, foaming out of the high ceiling, Judge Belden sat on the bench quietly preparing his instructions to the jury. I sat at my table with the People's files and exhibits spread out before me looking, I hoped, professional and mean as hell. Tall young Blair, the defendant, his long legs crossed, sat opposite my table beside his lawyer. I glanced over at him. He was rubbing the soft down on his cheek, staring dully at the big sheriff who sat on the witness stand. The rank steaming odor of rain-soaked clothing pervaded the crowded courtroom, which smelled as gamy as the washroom of a kindergarten. The sheriff was the People's last witness and I was nearly done with him.

All during the trial, which had been uneventful enough, I had had a feeling that something unusual was going to happen. Perhaps it was sheer mysticism. Perhaps it was merely the fact that this was my first kidnaping case in all my time as prosecutor. The feeling of impending surprise persisted. I tried to dismiss it from my mind by telling myself that—as any D.A. knows—all criminal trials have a faculty of taking unexpected turns, sometimes exploding in the very faces of the astounded judge, counsel, and mystified jurors.

It is this mercurial quality, I thought, and the unpredictable emotional factors which induce it, that make criminal trials the fascinating duels that they are. Potential drama is inherent in

127

even the most obscure criminal trial. Maybe you're getting jittery, Johnny, I thought. I decided I had better get on with the People's witness. Enough of this phony premonition business.

"Sheriff," I resumed, "after the bloodhound stopped before this young man in the jail corridor did you learn his identity?"

"Yes, *sir,* Mr. Prosecutor," the sheriff answered, as briskly as an insurance agent. The sheriff was a smart operator and there were lots of voters in the crowded courtroom.

"Who was the young man?" I asked.

"Donald Blair, the defendant in this case," the sheriff answered with finality, pointing at young Blair. Donald Blair quickly hung his head and stared at the courtroom floor.

"That's all, Sheriff," I concluded. "No questions," the defense attorney surprisingly said. I turned to Judge Belden. "The People rest," I said, puzzled by the failure of the defense to question the sheriff. I sighed and shrugged. At any rate the People's case was in. It was now up to the defense to put in its testimony.

Judge Belden looked up at the courtroom clock. It was nearing four-thirty. Court ordinarily adjourned at five. But it was a nasty fall day and everybody was tired and Judge Belden was plainly debating whether to proceed until five or adjourn until the next morning. The judge glanced at the jury. Twelve fidgety citizens, anxious to get home, looked hopefully back at the judge.

"The defense will proceed," Judge Belden dryly said. His decision was more eventful than any of us knew. The jurors sighed and sat back reluctantly.

Young Blair's lawyer arose and, as we lawyers are prone to do, announced pontifically: "The defense will waive its opening statement and call the defendant, Donald Blair, as its first witness!"

Donald Blair's quavering, youthful falsetto, as he said "I do" to the oath, scarcely went with the tremendous height he had unwound as he had walked up to the witness stand. He was inches over six feet tall. He sat in the witness chair, facing his lawyer, his dark eyes watchfully unblinking, his boyish cowlick falling over one eye.

To put it mildly I was curious to learn what young Blair's defense would be. The People had already shown that just at dusk on the day of the crime someone had snatched a sleeping child out of its parents' parked Ford sedan; had run with it into a field towards the woods on the outskirts of Princeville, the little mining town which was the scene of the crime; that shortly after that the parents discovered that their child was missing; that a search was made; that the dead body of the child was finally discovered lying in the driver's seat of a Chevrolet truck parked by the side of a tavern; that the diaphragm of the child had been crushed.

We had also shown that the driver of the Chevrolet truck was in the tavern during all these events; that strange fingerprints, not the driver's, were discovered on the handle of the truck door; that the bootprints of the apparent abductor were unusual in this locality in that they were made by high-heeled boots similar to riding boots; that the marks of these boots were traced from the parked Ford sedan through the field near the edge of the woods, where the abductor had knelt or fallen, thence back to the parked truck where the baby's body was found, thence to the paved main road, where they abruptly disappeared.

During the past three days of the trial I had painstakingly developed before the jury that the sheriff had finally obtained a bloodhound to aid in the search (a nice Uncle Tom's Cabin touch); that this horrendous, slavering beast had repeatedly taken the searchers over the same trail, always ending at the paved road where the bootprints ended; that several days of frenzied search to pick up the tracks had proven fruitless; that one evening as the tired searchers were returning to the little Princeville jail, which was their headquarters, they encountered the usual knot of curious persons in the jail-house corridor; that as the sheriff was leading the bloodhound down the long corridor the big dog suddenly bristled and growled deep in its throat and strained at its leash to reach a young man who was standing far back in the crowd, a young man who was wearing low oxfords on his feet; and, finally, that this young man was the defendant, Donald Blair.

I had shown that the officers had warned and then questioned young Blair; that after some questioning he had finally admitted he owned high-heeled riding boots; that, in company with the officers, he had produced the boots; that they exactly matched and fitted certain of the preserved footprints at the scene of the crime; that young Blair had then put on the boots at the officers' request and had walked home, in company with an officer, from the paved road; that the bloodhound was again started from the site of the parked sedan and led the officers unerringly over the entire course, not stopping on the main road this time but going right up to Blair's home, about a mile from town. Finally I had shown that the fingerprints on the door of the truck (where the body was found) were those of Donald Blair.

But through all the pre-trial investigation the defendant had steadfastly and sullenly denied that he had seen or touched the little girl. It is true that the People's case was based largely on circumstantial evidence, yet contrary to the popular notion, this is often the most reliable kind of evidence that can possibly be produced. Witnesses on both sides of a case may lie or disappear or die or forget. But physical facts like finger- and boot-prints—and, I am informed, bloodhounds—never lie.

So I sat there wondering just what young Blair's story would be. His attorney, a capable lawyer of many years' experience, had started to question his client. I leaned forward.

"You are Donald Blair, the defendant in this case?" his lawyer was asking.

"I am," Donald replied in his incongruous high-pitched voice.

"How old are you?"

"Seventeen," Donald answered.

The jurors glanced quickly at one another and a few of them clucked their tongues and shook their heads sadly. I mentally marked down a three-bagger for the defense.

"Where do you live, Donald?"

"I've been working on a farm near Princeville. Two years ago I came there from Chicago."

"Are you living with your parents?" his lawyer asked.

"No." Donald hesitated and then went on. "My mother and father are divorced. I don't know where my father is."

"And your mother? Where is she?"

Donald's lawyer was doing all right. Naturally he knew all

about Donald's mother and father, but he was shrewdly bringing it all out in a way best calculated to arouse the sympathy of the jury.

"Where is your mother, Donald?" his attorney repeated.

Donald Blair gulped and his eyes glistened. His speech was halting. "She's working. She—she's a thin lady with a circus. I—I wish she was here."

I glanced at the jury. A home run for the defense. Donald's attorney paused to let all this sink in. This is known in the trade as the pause pregnant. He was an old smoothie.

"When did you last see your mother, Donald?" his attorney resumed.

"Not since way last winter. She doesn't work then. I'll see her again this winter—I mean, I hope I will." He turned and looked at the jury and then down at his hands.

The pitifully forlorn quality of this statement from this pathetic marital waif had even me swallowing a lump in my throat. This was no calculated show; it was the real McCoy, a lonely homesick kid longing for his mama.

"Isn't she coming up here for the trial?" his attorney went on. He was piling it on a little thick and I could have objected but didn't dare.

"She wrote she was going to try to. I—I hope so. We don't have much money. I want to see her so bad." Tears were in his eyes.

Donald's attorney walked up close to Donald. I sat up. This was the part, here it was coming. The members of the jury leaned tensely forward.

"Donald, did you take this little girl from her parents' sedan?"

Donald sat up straight and looked squarely at his attorney. "No, sir," he answered, confidently, almost defiantly. There was a subtle change in his demeanor that puzzled me. I sat studying the boy carefully.

"Did you touch her or hurt her in any way?"

"No, sir."

"Did you enter or reach in her parents' car?"

"No, sir."

"Were you in Princeville that night?"

"Yes, sir. I had been in town a couple of hours. I shot a game of pool and started home. It was just getting dark. I saw this Ford sedan parked there by the main highway and I walked over to it to see if I could get a ride toward home, but there was no one in it."

"What did you do then?"

"I then decided to walk across the field towards home and take a short cut through the woods. Halfway through the field it got pretty dark and I stumbled and fell, so I decided to go back to the main road. Passing the side of the tavern I saw this parked Chevrolet truck. I grabbed the door and looked in, still looking for a ride, but only saw what I thought was a sleeping child."

"Did you touch her?"

"No, sir. Not at all."

"Then what did you do?"

"Then I walked out to the main road, waited a while for a ride, couldn't get one, so then I walked home."

"Is that all there is to it, Donald?"

"That's all, sir."

"Did you cooperate with the police in every way to help them find out who did this thing, Donald?"

"Yes, sir, I did, sir. I even went to the jail to tell them I had seen the little girl in the truck. Then—before I could—that dog smelled me. If I had really done it I would of stayed away from the jail."

"That is all, Donald." His attorney turned to me with a slight private smile. "How'm I doin', Johnny?" his mocking smile seemed to say. I smiled ruefully back. "You may take the witness," he announced.

The jury leaned back and sighed in unison, darting quick glances of wide-eyed surprise at each other. Being an involuntary student of jury psychology I guessed they were revising a previous settled conviction of guilt. It was a bad sign for my case.

So that was it! Donald's attorney had used one of the simplest and yet most effective criminal defense practices: that of admitting as much of the truth as possible short of admitting guilt. Aside from any question of ethics it is the wisest defense strategy of all. He had accounted neatly for everything. And there was always the haunting possibility that it was *true;* that Donald hadn't abducted the girl or touched her in any way; that it had really happened that way. D.A.'s had always to bear that in mind. (In fact our inability to show clearly just *how* the child met her death or *who* was responsible for it was one of the reasons I had chosen the kidnaping charge rather than one of homicide.) I cleared my throat to speak, pausing, feeling my way for an approach. I was in a tight box and knew it.

Just then the big mahogany courtroom door breathed open. Framed in it stood the tallest, palest, thinnest woman I have ever seen. Certainly she was the homeliest. She looked like a grotesque female Abraham Lincoln. She saw her son on the witness stand. "Mama!" he murmured. Her lips silently formed his name. The bailiff came forward and led her to the other lawyer's table. Wordlessly she sat down, still staring at her son. Her son buried his face in his hands. His shoulders shook silently. Everyone in the courtroom, including the D.A., was visibly affected.

Judge Belden looked down at me. It was quarter of five. Young Blair's entire direct examination had taken but fifteen minutes. Fifteen minutes and my case was going up the flue! Perhaps this was the surprise I had been waiting for.

"Under the circumstances, Mr. Prosecutor, perhaps we had better adjourn until the morning, hadn't we?" Judge Belden suggested.

Ordinarily a judge's slightest whim is a command. But in a flash my hunch came to me. It was a dangerous, daring hunch, and I had missed my share of them in the past, but after all, I was seeking only the truth, wherever it lay, and the quicker I found it the better. The thing that bothered me was that Donald had claimed he had finally *walked* home. For it was obvious that he must have caught a ride from the paved road, else the bloodhound would have tracked him home—as it did later. Why then had Donald lied about such a minor point? Or was it a minor point?

"Your Honor," I said, "the People would like to continue until five o'clock. I think I can be through with this witness in less than fifteen minutes."

The jury collectively glared at me. That was one of the danger- ous parts of the hunch, further prejudicing the People's wavering case with the jury for my heartlessness in keeping this sorely stricken mother from her son, not to mention further delaying the jurors' homeward trek.

Judge Belden glanced at the clock and frowned and debated my request. "Very well. You may proceed," he finally ruled.

"Thank you, Your Honor," I said. I turned to Donald. His face was still buried in his hands. I walked over so that I stood close to and slightly behind his mother. It was not a trick. If Donald was innocent—and by then I hoped he was—I wanted to show it and show it fast.

"Donald, please look at me. I want to ask you a few questions," I said.

Donald slowly looked up, saw his mother, and then quickly stared straight in my eyes. His eyes were crowded with tears.

There was a number of approaches I could have made. I could have put on my D.A. wig of bland innocence and given the boy a bad time. I could have asked him *why*—if he came to the jail to tell about seeing the little girl in the parked truck—why hadn't he later told us just that, dog or no dog? Why had he instead denied ever seeing the little girl? Why hadn't he *then* told us the whole story just as he had now told it from the stand? I considered all this and scrapped it. That approach was a good treatment for tripping up crafty liars but here I was dealing with a confused child. I felt that this was not the time to set out brilliant D.A. traps; traps that could boomerang shut on the trapper. The chips were down and I felt it was time instead for some simple ques- tions, some simple truths.

"Donald," I said quietly, "your mother always taught you to tell the truth, didn't she?"

Quickly glancing at his mother, then back at me. "Oh yes, sir."

"And always to thank people for helping you; for any courtesies they might accord you?" I felt like a Boy Scout leader drilling a tenderfoot.

"Yes, sir. She always did, yes, sir."

"And you are going to tell us only the truth here now, are you not?"

Donald glanced at his mother, searching her eyes. I glanced down at this gaunt stricken woman. She had shut her eyes and sat convulsively gripping and gripping the arms of her chair. Her head nodded forward imperceptibly.

"Oh yes, sir," Donald replied.

"All right, then, Donald," I said, and then I paused for perhaps thirty seconds. I could pause pregnantly, too. Then quickly: "Tell us, Donald, did you thank the person who gave you the ride home from the paved road in Princeville to the farm the night the little girl was killed?"

Quickly, quietly. "Yes, sir." There was no time for falsehood, for his attorney to make a warning diversionary objection or anything.

There it was. Just like that. It had to be. "Yes, sir," he had said.

"And it isn't true that you *walked* home that night as you had just claimed here before your mother arrived?"

"No, sir." In a small, wan voice.

"Why did you tell the police and now the jury that you had walked home, Donald?"

Slowly. "I—I was mad at that bloodhound and I—I wanted to show him up."

"Why were you mad at the bloodhound, Donald?"

"B-because he got me in trouble."

"You mean at the jail?"

"Yes."

"When you came to the jail did you think the dog wouldn't discover you if you weren't wearing the riding boots, was that it, Donald?"

"Yes, sir."

"And yet you were curious to see this animal, and find out if it could really detect a guilty person by scent alone?"

Quietly. "Yes, sir."

There was one final question that had to be asked. "Now,

Donald, will you tell us—your mother and all of us—why you didn't want to be discovered?"

Donald's mother opened her eyes and looked at her son. Her tragic eyes were tearless, her face was bloodless and drawn. It was one of the saddest, most moving scenes I have ever witnessed in or out of a courtroom. Though I sought only the truth I felt like a monstrous heel. Again the mother nodded her head, ever so slightly. Her lips began to move, she was speaking. "Tell Mother, Donald," she said. "Tell Mother the *truth*—just like she always taught her baby." Her voice was curiously flat and tone-less.

Wide-eyed, Donald began speaking to his mother, rapidly, in a high, piping voice. It was a confessional made in a childish gush of words. "Yes, Mama, I did it. I—I don't know why. . . . I had read lots about kidnapings and ransoms. So I opened the car door with my handkerchief, to hide the fingerprints, just like I read. I grabbed her, Mama. . . . She started to cry. . . . I didn't mean to hurt her, Mama. Honest I didn't. . . . I ran away in the dark and tripped and I guess I fell on her. She didn't make a sound after that. . . . She grew so limp and quiet. . . . I—I got scared and ran back and saw this other truck and put her in it. I forgot all about my fingerprints. . . . I ran out to the highway. Just then a logging truck was going by. I thumbed a ride and went home. . . . And—and I thanked the driver, Mama. . . ."

"My *baby!*" Donald's mother said. The words seemed wrenched from her very soul.

"I—I only did it for you, Mama—so I could make some money so you wouldn't always have to be a—a thin lady in a circus. . . . If—if you'd only been here I'd have told them guilty long ago. They scared me with all their questions."

I had indeed discovered the truth, and the taste turned to bitter ashes in my mouth.

"That's all, Donald. You may go to your mother now," I said.

I glanced up wearily at the courtroom clock. It was two minutes to five. The impatient jury could go home now. We'd gather up the broken pieces in the morning.

Chapter 13

THE ALL-AMERICAN BULL

MOST AMERICANS regard their police officers with an ill-disguised contempt. Cops to them are a necessary evil, like congressmen, tax collectors and baseball umpires, but the people really don't begin to like them or trust them as, for example, our Canadian neighbors look up to their Mounties or the British look up to their Bobbies or we look up, say, to our own Marines.

It would take a profounder student of psychology or native folkways than I to account for this national distaste, but any schoolboy can recognize its presence. Certainly a trial-battered ex-D.A. can. . . . Perhaps it has partly to do with our revolutionary beginnings and normal frontier attitudes and the fact that the sturdy migrants to our shores were for the most part presumably just those who sought most fiercely to throw off the restraints at home—invariably imposed by stern men in uniform. There seemed to be a studied irreverence for tradition, a tacit and perhaps defensive desire to banish and forget the past. To hell with *verboten* swiftly became a national attitude; an attitude that has persisted to this day. The shock to these immigrants to discover that America was filled with strolling Irish cops—a strange new breed of tormentors—at once posed a new dread and conjured up a sort of dark, half-remembered hurt. *Now* was their chance to pay them back. . . .

Despite our elaborate criminal codes (the most complex in the world) Americans will stand only as many laws and cops as they think they need. Beyond that they buck like wild mustangs. The ignoble experiment of Prohibition was the classic proof. My guess is that this feeling against cops is gradually relaxing, though far from disappearing; and I ascribe this partly to the twentieth century flowering of such highly trained and effective corps of cops as the F.B.I. and most of the various state constabulary, and also to the enormous and generally favorable publicity given their activities by the glamorizing detective stories, radio, television and the movies.

But after all most of our cops are still unromantic and buniony patrolmen; men who work long hours for relatively little pay; weary men who shuffle and trudge the midnight streets of your town and mine in creaking leather shoes, trying doors here, snagging a free cup of coffee there, all the while sagging under the weight of a .38 special which they pray they will never have to use. They are the real day-to-day keepers-of-the-peace and their role has changed but little since the Middle Ages.

Many efforts have been made to improve our police training by various schools, courses and seminars, and some of these have been quite successful. And we have prettied up their uniforms so much that it's getting hard to tell the average cop from the retired admirals that guide Greyhound busses. But for the most part the common cop remains a plodding and disillusioned man who stands by and watches kids and nifty pimps, whores and dope peddlers, touts and gamblers and grafters, enjoy infinitely more money and fun than he; and yet who is constantly fearful that he may offend some wheel in the city hall and lose his job; or, worse yet, that his clique in the hall will lose out come next election and he will have to go back to his lathe or his truck. Is it any wonder that an occasional cop decides to get in on the racket, to climb aboard the gravy train? The wonder is that more of them don't.

All this might be mildly amusing if it were not for the serious effects on law enforcement. Distrust and disrespect for cops causes many jurors to disregard their testimony and free the obviously guilty, while the frequent lack of respect of the cops for their own jobs in turn often discourages them from doing the heads up job they might otherwise be capable of—a vicious circle constricting the very heart of sound law enforcement, and therefore, of sound government itself.

In my county the cops were generally pretty good. Some were incredibly inept and stupid, of course, and many times in court I would have preferred to confront a dripping trained seal in the witness chair than some of these stout garrulous fellows who ran on at such great lengths, speaking so authoritatively from such a vast fund of ignorance. One could at least silence a seal with a herring. . . . But there are fumblers in every walk of life and most of my cops were damn good and still are. (I always felt that Big Mac down at Iron Bay was a much better D.A. than I, he was that smart.) What it must be elsewhere I shudder to contemplate when I read in a report of the National Commission on Law Enforcement that "over 75 per cent of the members of the police force of this country are not mentally endowed to perform the duty assigned."

Sometimes I think that our modern cops, for all their training and laboratory facilities, are not nearly as resourceful and effective law enforcement officers as were many of the old-time flatfeet of yesteryear. In the old days a community frequently picked a man as a cop because nobody else could lick him; the town bullies and rascals quailed before him; and he earned the grudging respect of the community because he was the strongest and bravest man in town. If there was a riot his sole question was: "Where is it at?" He wasn't much on these fingerprints or ballistics but, goddamitt, he nailed his man.

Old Judge Belden, a prosecutor long before me, has told me tales of the heroism of some of these old-time cops that make the blood run cold. There was the payday when a saloonful of drunken iron miners in Hematite suddenly turned on the proprietor, who'd shut off their drinks (believe it or not, saloonkeepers really used to do that), and threatened to dispatch him along with any cop that dared to interfere. Gleaming hunting knives began to appear. The proprietor stashed away his bottles and said his rusty prayers. The word got out and in five minutes Big Tom Gribble, the town constable, quietly entered the saloon, unarmed, grabbed up a stout chair and walked the length of the bar swinging his chair right and left, strewing acute submission and concussion in his wake. He brought the quaking saloonkeeper out alive.

When I first became prosecutor one of these legendary cops was still acting down in Princeville. His name was Con Kennedy, a towering great, red-wristed Irishman. He must have been a fumbling adolescent of eighty when I first met him outside the county jail in Iron Bay. He sat hunched over the wheel of a throbbing Model T Ford nearly as ancient as himself. The sheriff introduced us.

"Pleased to meet you, Mr. Kennedy," I said, shaking his calloused paw.

"Glad to meet ye, bye," he boomed, beetling his gray Airedale brows at me. "So you're the new D.A., are ye? Hm. . . . Say, I've got a little legal quistion to ast you—jist wan quistion."

"Well, I'll try to answer it—that's if I can," I replied, modestly fluttering my eyelashes.

"Hm . . ." old Kennedy dubiously began. It was plain he was not too impressed with this beardless youth. "O.K. thin. Here's me quistion: Kin the same man act as village night watch and arrist the goddam defindint fer window peepin', lock the laverick up fer the night as township jailer, hawl the 'hore into justice coort the next mawrnin' an' sign the complaint ag'inst him as township constable, issue the warrant as justice of peace, swear hisself and take the stand and tistify as the State's sthar witness, find the defindint guilty and sintince him to the county jail as justice of peace, and, after havin' done all that, fetch the bastard over here to the jail as diputy sheriff? Is all that there legal, bye, can you be after tellin' me?"

"Oh no, Mr. Kennedy!" I shrilled, aghast at such appalling irregularity. "You simply can't *do* such a thing!"

"To hell I can't, young man," he snorted, jerking his thumb over his shoulder. *"Look!* I've got the son-of-a-bitch handcuffed right here in the back seat!"

Perhaps my favorite cop of all was old Felix Gerochino. Old Felix used to be an iron miner until, many years ago, a chunk of ore fell on his head and opened his eyes to the delights of being a cop. Poor addled Felix joined the Chippewa police force by the simple expedient of sending away for a mail order star and shoulder holster and reporting one night for duty.

"Looka here, Chief," he told the astounded chief of police, patting his rusty .45. "I'm a new a man ona police a force. I like worka da nighta sheeft. Whoodyou wanta me to peench a firs'?"

The chief didn't have the heart to fire such a zealous volunteer without a fair trial, and, after determining that the .45 was unloaded, sent Felix out to check door locks.

"Hockay, Chief," Felix saluted, and away he went, subsequently enjoying the questionable distinction of finding more unlocked doors than any cop west of Southhold, Long Island. One night he found a railroad flag shanty unlocked and, investigating, flushed out a nude brakeman and his girl friend before he could engage the lock with the hasp. The brakeman lost three days' work with quinsy sore throat. Felix simply marked "Arson" on his report of the incident.

As Felix became a fixture on the police force, everybody naturally contributed his mite to making him look more and more like a cop to end all cops. By-and-by he got to resemble something out of a Gilbert and Sullivan opera, what with his donated leather puttees, Sam Browne belts (he wore *two*), epaulets, gold braid, a four-foot trench knife, three gelded hand grenades, and his alarming array of antique pistols. A carload of unwitting tourists once hailed Felix to inquire directions and, after five minutes of witnessing Felix and his gesticulations, turned and fled horrified across the Canadian border. "Wronga way, folks, wronga way!" Felix shouted after them.

Fortunately for Felix the Chamber of Commerce never heard of the incident. They would surely have stripped him of all his medals. Felix finally wore more badges and stars and decorations than any diplomat from Graustark. He was proudest of a big star that someone unearthed labeled "Chicken Inspector"—can anyone remember when *they* were the rage?—and he carried a bottle of silver polish around on his beat to keep it forever bright and gleaming. "Mist' Chicken Inspec'," he began calling himself.

One night I was walking home late from Sunday school or some place when Felix clanked out of an alley and waylaid me under a street lamp. Trussed up in his two Sam Browne belts and all the rest of the loot he carried he looked like an invader from Mars. He peered up into my face.

"Ah, Mist' District Attorn'," he breathed at me, evidently fresh from a successful bout with a bushel of garlic. "Look—whatsa mat', Mist' Trave', you never give me da job catcha da crook?"

I quickly got up wind from Felix and leaned groggily against the lamppost until the pain went away. "Will very first chance I get, Felix," I panted. "Been watching your good work. Keep it up. Good night, Felix." I turned to escape.

Felix winked a beady eye at me and again leaned over close to give me a farewell blast. "Goodanight, Mist' Trave'," he breathed, glancing furtively up and down the empty street. He put his finger over his lips and leaned even closer. Then in a knowing stage whisper: "Keepa da eye ope', Mist' District Attorn', keepa da eye ope'!"

I turned and reeled blindly off into the night.

By-and-by the burden of Felix's equipment began to outweigh his responsibilities. One morning the poor man was found dead of a heart attack evidently suffered while trying to lock a boxcar that had no door—an understandably frustrating experience. Felix was accorded full honors: eulogized by the mayor, escorted to the cemetery by the Boy Scouts and Chippewa's finest, and buried with all the pomp and circumstance that befitted the one and only "Mist' Chicken Inspec'."

Chapter 14

THE CORONER AND I

WHEN I WAS a young dewy-eyed D.A. still full of idealism and zeal, I used to take a morbid delight in following one or the other of the two county coroners on their macabre rounds, restlessly sniffing the death-laden air for signs of criminal skulduggery. I had been reading too much Dashiel Hammett, I guess. The gesture was a laudable one for which I shall doubtless be rewarded in an appropriate sulphurous subterranean niche reserved for ex-ex-D.A.'s. While the coroner and I occasionally stumbled onto evidence of foul play, more often we didn't. And in the few cases that we did we had to call in the police anyway, to do a thorough job; so by-and-by it percolated my consciousness that the coroners might better prowl their lonely death rounds alone—if only they would promise to call in the cops in case of the slightest doubt. They promised and I retired from being a volunteer unpaid assistant-coroner. I never felt any urge to emerge from that retirement. I shortly got so that I'd much rather try a murder case than view one.

So while the coroners and I, during our brief beautiful friendship, uncovered no grisly murders (though the cops did later in at least one case that I recall), I saw a hell of a lot of wizened dead people: results of suicides, drownings, burnings and accidental and self-inflicted deaths of all kinds. Some, by far the most, were simply people that had died respectably in bed. But I played no favorites and peered cautiously at all of them. (I am not here counting the obviously criminal death cases where I occasionally accompanied the cops.) At any rate, some luckless undertaker lost a likely soft-shoe assistant when Traver stuck to the law. At one time I had all the makings of a fine professional ghoul.

Speaking of undertakers, one of these gentry once found the opening clue that lead to the discovery of a murder. This is how it happened: A young married woman, separated from her husband, had died suddenly in bed. She was quite naked when found, and the blushing coroner had called a doctor to act as chaperon; the doctor had examined the woman and, himself puzzled, had pronounced her death as one caused by that old puzzle-solvent, a heart attack. Then the undertaker during the embalming had observed a tiny bloodless wound under her left breast, the merest bluish bruise. How he happened to be looking there deponent knoweth not. . . .

The subsequent autopsy disclosed the lead pellet of a .22 caliber shot lodged neatly in the woman's heart. During the following investigation and before any arrest was made the estranged husband quietly shot himself with the same gun. He left a note behind relating how he had dispatched his wife in a fit of jealousy. The observant undertaker duly received his just reward: he had *two* cases to embalm instead of one. One wonders how many murders thus go not only unsolved but, perhaps more frightening, entirely undiscovered. I rather suspect that the number would stagger the imagination. The old saying should be amended: Murder will *sometimes* out—if you dig it out.

At any rate, if trailing the coroners did not make me an appreciably better D.A. it at least furnished me with considerable creepy story material, scads of it, in fact. If coroners could only talk. . . . Two death cases that stand out in my memory involved, oddly enough, two tired old people who died quietly in their beds. Offhand rather dubious material, one would think. But you be the judge. The first one was "The Sucker King."

Old Rolf Ohming had a weepy mustache long enough to tie under his chin. People called him "The Sucker King" because almost any time of the day or night, during the spring spawning run on the Sucker River, one could see him patiently fishing for suckers in that turgid river, his drooping blond mustaches wafting gently in the spring breezes. Old Rolf's two-room, tar-paper shack stood on a bald lonely hill above the river and commanded a splendid and totally unobstructed view of the confluence of the Chippewa sewage canal with the Sucker River. This propinquity understandably assured him an exclusive franchise on all suckers for miles around.

Old Rolf was poor. He was so poor that passing motorists pitied him when they saw him sitting huddled on the riverbank fishing for the greedy suckers. He was so poor he even used a burlap potato sack for a creel. He dug his bait in his garden and cut a sapling for a fish pole—"government poles," the natives call them. Total investment: one fish line and the hooks he used. . . . After many hours, when the sack was full of slippery fish, he would arise stiffly and shoulder his slithery load, and plod across the road and up the hill to his shack—where he proceeded to clean his fish and preserve them in tin containers of salt brine. For it was known that old Ohming *ate* these loathsome-looking fish, which was cause enough for pity considering the abject poverty it disclosed, not to mention brooding about the *place* where he caught them.

When he first came to Chippewa from Denmark, many years before, old Ohming had been married. For a number of years he worked in the carpenter and repair shop of one of the iron mines and lived in a little rented company-owned house on a treeless street appropriately called Elm. (The real elms were on Pine Street.) He was an expert sharpener of saws—filer, I think, is the technical name. The Ohmings were childless and when his wife died during the flu epidemic of the First War old Rolf suddenly quit his job in town, packed his saw-sharpening tools, and built his tar-paper shack on the outskirts of town overlooking the Sucker River. There he dwelt, hauling wood, catching and preserving suckers, sharpening saws, and cultivating his potato patch and his long flowing mustaches. A prevailing west wind coupled with the presence of the sewage canal also assured him that he would never have any neighbors. The Sucker King's domain was broad, malodorous and empty.

Like the pilgrims to Emerson's artisan of better mousetraps, people continued to beat a path to old Rolf's door to get their saws sharpened. For one thing, while he charged more than most saw sharpeners, he did a much better job than any. And the saws would be ready when he promised them. And loggers and carpenters and others who sought his services could nearly always find him in. Most saw-filers, it appears, are occupationally allergic to sobriety and continued toil, but old Rolf never drank and rarely left his shack except to fish or forage for firewood or to make an infrequent trip to town for his meager supplies. He was a queer, secretive one. . . . When he left his shack, even to fish in the river in plain sight of his place, he always drew the blinds and elaborately locked the stout door with two large padlocks. The windows were screened and barred like a rural jail or some forest fortification against the assaults of raiding bears. An eccentric man was old Rolf Ohming of the flowing mustaches, but a hell of a good man with a dull saw.

Another of his drolleries was never to invite any of his customers—he had no friends—into his shack. A charming welcome sign on the door read "KEEP OUT." A logger might appear at his door in the midst of a crackling thunder shower and be obliged to wait outside in the naked deluge while old Rolf clanked and rattled his series of chains and bolts, cautiously opened the door a few inches, thrust out a grimy arm to take or deliver the saw in question—and then slammed the door in his visitor's face. But still they came back, because no one could set and sharpen saws quite like old Rolf Ohming.

Couples who occasionally parked on the hill near his shack to wrestle and make love were known to have claimed later that they heard wild strains of violin music coming from his darkened shack late at night. It could have been the radio, of course, but it was like no radio music *they* had ever heard. (We later learned that old Rolf didn't possess a radio.) Always these lovers avoided repeat performances and parked elsewhere. Somehow this eerie midnight music proved a greater deterrent to casual trespassers than a slavering dog. The nocturnal wrestlers quickly found other hills upon which to conduct their love bouts undisturbed.

Then one autumn evening shortly before the last war, Makinen, the Finn logger, brought two saws to be sharpened. Repeated knocks on old Rolf's door brought no answer so Makinen went away. Before he left he observed through a crack in a tightly drawn curtain that a light was burning. The next morning Makinen came back and still no answer. The outside hasp locks were still dangling the same way, unlocked. Since this was the longest time old Ohming had ever been known to fail to appear at his shack, Makinen proceeded to town and reported the incident to the chief of police.

"Somet'ing he be damn funny up dat ol' man Ohming's tarpaper s'ack," Makinen concluded.

The chief got the coroner and the coroner got me and we headed out there. We also brought along some heavy tools to make sure we could get in. We needed all of them. . . . We found old Ohming dead in his shack, sitting up in bed, hugging an old family Bible. People had never suspected such piety on his part. There were no signs of violence or struggle. "Heart attack," the coroner observed sagely as he drew a blanket over the body. Always coroners draw a blanket over the body. There was a kerosene lantern suspended from a rafter above the body, still lighted. We shrugged and looked around.

The shack was a fantastic litter of filth and dirt and odds and ends: balls of salvaged string and rope suspended from the rafters, endless piles of old newspapers and paper bags, a little work bench littered with files and saws and other marks of his trade. And that fearful stench! What caused it? Ah, yes—a score or more old metal carbide cans sitting around the room, loaded and festering with salt brine and the bloated floating bodies of deceased suckers.

"Open that damn door!" I called to the prowling coroner, being driven at the same time to light a defensive Italian cigar. What a sty in which to die.

In one corner we saw a homemade music stand from the side of which hung suspended a violin and a bow. A table near the music rack was covered with piles of sheets of ruled brown wrapping paper. It was musical manuscript. I looked closer. Even with my stunted musical education, I perceived that the sheets were serious musical compositions, mostly for violin—solos, concertos, string quartets, trios, duets—all composed, dated and signed by Rolf Ohming. I recall that one composition was called *The Ghosts of Horseus.* I still half recall a few haunting measures, which soar and sigh like the wind. . . . I discovered later that Horseus was a town in central Denmark. Was this some of the strange music that chased stray lovers from the hillside late at night?

"Look here!" the chief spoke, rummaging in a tall, old-fashioned writing desk. He drew out a canvas bound bookkeeping ledger. In it, in old Rolf's careful handwriting, appeared to be noted every penny old Rolf had spent since he had moved to his shack years before. Most of the purchases were for preserving salt and flour and kerosene and more salt, a few for sugar and coffee, a very few for clothing, and a small amount for annual taxes on his plot of ground. Nothing more. What did he live on? The answer was obvious: potatoes and suckers. . . . Here was a man whose adventures in penury made a spendthrift out of Thoreau and elevated his historic stay at Walden Pond into the realm of a prolonged bacchanalian orgy.

"What'n hell are these?" the coroner said, taking a sheaf of brown wrapping paper from a pile on a wooden shelf. What were they indeed! Perhaps an Einstein or Oppenheimer could have given us the answer. The sheets were covered with involved mathematical equations, some so long that old Rolf had had to paste two or more sheets together to accommodate his figures. We stared at one another. Old Rolf Ohming—saw-sharpener, composer, mathematician. . . . Was he a madman or a genius or both? Alas, we shall never know for later on the lard-headed administrator of old Rolf's estate had all the old newspapers—along with the musical composition and equations—burned before anyone could raise a finger to shoot him. I've never ceased wondering. . . .

"What estate?" You ask? Let me tell you. Before we left—the day we found the body—we rummaged around to try to find the names of some relatives. "I'll get the family Bible," the chief said, removing the blanket from the dead man. I looked away as he and the coroner wrestled the volume from the death-clutch of old Rolf. "Here!" he finally said, flipping the pages of the old leather-bound book. "Hell, it's written in Arabic!" he said.

"Let's see," I said. "It's probably Danish." I reached for the heavy book. "Whoops!" I exclaimed as the Bible slipped from my hands, the pages fluttering idly as the volume thudded to the floor.

"My Gawd!" the chief said, kneeling and recovering a hundred dollar bill which had wafted from its pages. It fell in delicate eccentric swoops, like a maple leaf in autumn. I must try it some day.

All of us reverently knelt and, for slightly ambiguous reasons, suddenly became devoted students of the Bible—Rolf's Bible. Our conversion was touching to behold. Before we left we found slightly over three thousand dollars in currency in the old Bible. Old Rolf had apparently used hundred-dollar bills to mark his favorite passages. Personally I am inclined to use old unpaid water bills.

After the funeral, when the administrator's men came to clean out the filthy shack, preparatory to selling it, they finally had to get rid of the revolting carbide cans full of dead fish. So they dug a deep hole, averted their eyes, and poured the ghastly suckers down the hole. On a last-minute hunch I had suggested that the coroner and I should be present at this ceremony. They'd already witlessly burned the music. . . . We'd see the rest of the thing through. After dismally watching them pour out Niagaras of dead suckers I swore to keep my future hunches to myself. Then on the seventh dumped can a metal object scraped and thudded as it tumbled out. It surely couldn't be a sucker; bad as they were they scarcely clanked.

"Fish it out!" I yelled. The men scowled and reluctantly fished the object out of the fetid hole. It was an airtight metal container which yielded over four thousand dollars in cash and government securities. The rest of the suckers were sifted with loving care—it made such a pretty picture that I wished and wished I had brought my Brownie—and yielded nearly fifteen thousand dollars additional in two separate metal containers. Fishing was indeed good that day. Number 12 Coachman was the fly.

Where did old Rolf get all the dough? I don't know. Filing saws and starving, I suppose. I guess all of his life he must have been one of that strange breed of men: a miser. We could never find out his background—his apparent education and all the rest. After the lawyers and tax hounds hacked out their shares, the bulk of the estate went to two lucky nephews in Nebraska. They'd scarcely ever heard of Denmark let alone their miserly uncle.

Old Rolf was a true miser, of course, although his preoccupation with music and mathematics, however primitive, was most unusual. Most misers find no time for anything but acquiring more money and then gloating over it, like a trout fisherman over a new beaver dam. Old Rolf Ohming, "The Sucker King," was a trifle different—a sort of poetic Grandpa Moses among misers. I've never forgotten him nor ceased to wonder over those mysterious reams of wild music. Sometimes I even imagine I hear it late at night. Perhaps I'd better change my brand of whisky.

2

"Johnny," the coroner phoned, "I just got word some old retired schoolteacher's been marooned in her smokeless house for three days"—it was the dead of winter—"and me an' the chief's going up there to take a look see. Wanna come along?"

"Pick me up," I said, fleeing the phone and lighting up my curved bulldog pipe and donning my checkered front-and-aft peaked deer-stalker's cap. Damn those kids!—where was my pet magnifying glass?

Mary Jane Emery was her name. She was the last survivor of an old pioneer mining family. She'd taught elementary school for heaven knows how many years and had retired even before my grade-school days. By then she must have been as old as G. B. S. himself. She lived alone in a fabulous old rambling house on the outskirts of town—the kind with ugly square cupolas adrape with droopy lace curtains and filled with boxes of dead geraniums; the kind overlaid with a tangled maze of sagging lightning rods like the home of a TV fiend; the kind with an iron deer tethered out on the lawn.

The coroner and chief and I met and drove immediately to the "old Emery place." Night had fallen, the wind had risen, and it was already considerably below zero. As we drove up the incline of the drifted driveway our car lights searched through the naked wind-tossed elms and gleamed bluely on the darkened windows of the old house. As we waded through the drifted snow to the front door, occasional tufts of long-neglected grass rose above the snow like prairie hay.

The burly chief tried the door, which refused to budge. "Locked," he said, nodding wisely. It appeared to be bolted from the inside. The mailbox bulged with neglected mail, which the coroner removed and put in his inevitable brief case. The chief stood morosely rattling the knob of the heavy door. We looked at one another. The chief shrugged. There was nothing to do but break in the door, so with a rhythmic one-two-three we lunged against the door and catapulted into the front hall, all grim and breathless—just like in the movies. We closed the door behind us and the chief played his flashlight, looking for a light switch. He found one by the hall door, the old button kind. It clicked noisily but no light came on.

"Don't work," the chief observed.

We moved into a larger carpeted hall at the foot of a wide winding stair. The hands of a tall silent clock stood frozen at midnight, a nicely appropriate hour. High noon would certainly have broken the spell. . . . Our breath steamed and we left tracks in the heavy dust which lay over everything. The chief found another light switch, but it also failed to work. Mary Jane had been without electric lights. The chief cast the beam of his flashlight into the large living room. Drooping family photographs adorned the top of an old upright piano, some sprung from their folders. A solitary piece of sheet music stood open on the music rack. For some obscure reason I recall that the selection was a glutinous thing called *Hearts and Flowers*. Mary Jane's musical tastes were evidently as elementary as the grades she taught. I shivered. It seemed much colder inside than out.

"Cold," the chief said. He was the observing one.

By common accord we walked to the stairway and started up, single file. The wavering beam of the flashlight cast weird leaping shadows on the high walls. At the top of the creaking stairs we came to a long corridor off of which appeared a number of tall white doors with closed transoms, like those in an old country hotel. All of the doors stood closed. We approached the nearest door. The chief stared uneasily at us. Who'd go first? We stared back at him and shrugged. After all, *he* was the strong working arm of the law; we were simply along for the ride. The chief gulped and then resolutely squared his shoulders and tried the first door. It was locked. It looked like we'd have to huddle and play on the line again.

But the chief fooled us and moved down to the next door, the coroner and I crowding close behind him like frighteend children. He turned the knob and the door creaked open. In the light of the flashlight we saw a furnished bedroom. A large canopied double bed was completely made up, spread and all. Lying on top of the spread, on one side, was a man's old-fashioned long flannel nightgown; and on the other side rested a woman's lacy nightgown. Over all this troubled Faulknerian scene lay the accumulated grime of many years. It was like visiting some sort of haunted and deserted museum. We felt like midnight interlopers at Mount Vernon. We glanced at each other and hurriedly backed from the clammy room. The chief softly closed the door. "Jesus," he whispered. We had disturbed the bedroom of Mary Jane's long-dead mother and father. We huddled even more closely as we proceeded down the creaking hall.

The next room appeared to be a sewing room. There was an ancient handcranked sewing machine, a collector's item in anybody's antique shop. There was a busty old dress form with a frilly dress still on it. There were sheaves of scattered paper dress patterns, piles of dusty dress material and rows of bulging and begrimed cardboard boxes. We turned away and closed the door softly. The chief, getting into the spirit of the thing, carelessly flung open the next door. It was a completely furnished child's playroom—undoubtedly Mary Jane's, since she was an only child.

There was an orderly array of dolls staring unblinking at each other, sitting stiffly around a doll table and a set of tiny dust-covered dishes. One doll had fallen from its place; I carefully replaced it. There was even a dusty rocking horse—I hadn't seen one of *those* in years. We withdrew silently.

"Gloomy," the chief said.

The next room was a storeroom; the next appeared to be a guest room—while the last room was an upstairs sitting room, complete with a fireplace, a big chair with an under-sliding foot-stool and—of all things—a stereopticon viewer and a set of Venetian views (I looked) resting on a dusty table by the chair. A tall whatnot full of sea shells and similar curios stood in a corner. There was one of those back to back love seats. There was also—but why go on? This is not an estate inventory. It is enough to say that an antique shop lady would have taken one look, whooped, and then blown her top. The chief played his flashlight about—but still no sign of Mary Jane. We hurriedly backed out of this Victorian tomb and closed the door. "Kind of old-fashioned," the chief observed keenly as we clattered down the bitterly cold corridor and huddled about the first locked door at the top of the landing. We glanced at each other. The chief again tried the door.

"Still locked," the chief said. He was a sharp sharp fellow to have around.

It was the chief's turn to shrug. He leaned against the door and beckoned us to join him. With another huddled one-two-three, we lunged and burst into the locked chamber. It took the chief a few seconds to recover his balance and focus his flash-light. *"Jesus!"*—this time from all three of us.

Mary Jane Emery was sitting up in bed. She was clasping a book or something in her skinny arms, which were folded in a singularly prayerful attitude across her withered breast. Mary Jane was quite dead, of course, but her eyes were open and she was staring across the room with an expression that I can only call horribly beatific. We edged closer. An old-fashioned kerosene lamp rested on a table beside her. Playing Sherlock Holmes, I shook it. It was empty, burned out. Hm. . . . She had evidently died while the lamp was still lit. Heavy deduction Number One. The chief shifted his light beam. On one side of the room was a small Franklin stove upon which stood a teakettle. Its contents were frozen solid. There was a frying pan containing, one hoped, a sort of frozen stew. Deduction Number Two: Mary Jane had prepared her last meals in her bedroom. We turned back to the body.

There were a half-dozen cheap wooden tables on either side of the bed. On these tables, and on a series of rough wooden shelves over the head of the bed, were piled countless hundreds of magazines. Wherever we looked there were magazines. There must have been thousands of them in the room, even reposing under the bed, resting on every chair and piled so high on her large dresser, opposite the bed, that we could not see the tall square mirror behind them. Arrayed on top of this mountain of magazines on her dresser was a series of photographs. "Hold the light still," I whispered to the chief. "I—I can't believe it . . ."

Yes, it was true. They were all photographs—photographs of old-time movie stars. There must have been several dozen of them, all under glass, all in elaborate silver frames. I am not precisely a fumbling adolescent, but there were only a few that I could even faintly recognize. I guessed that two of them might have been William Farnum and Maurice Costello, both leading "matinee idols" of their bygone day. The juveniles of the group, and the only ones I surely recognized, were Milton Sills, Wallace Reid and Francis X. Bushman. "Francis the Lion," we kids used to call him. . . .

"The magazines, the magazines!" the coroner whispered. "Why'n hell are all the magazines?" Out of sheer relief in action we pawed over the mounds of begrimed and dusty magazines. All of them were movie magazines, old and new, thousands of them, with the faces of long-forgotten stars grinning and smirking at us from dusty covers. John Bunny, Flora Finch, Musty Suffer, Theda Bara the "vamp"—the list was endless. Mary Jane's bedrom had become the Library of Congress of the movie magazine, a sort of grim Hollywoodian heaven. The coroner fumbled in his brief case and drew out the neglected mail he had found on the porch. Yes, more movie magazines. At the time it seemed entirely natural that he should move to the bed and reverently place them alongside her body. He stood staring down at her.

"Look!" the awed coroner whispered, pointing at the body.

For the first time we observed that old Mary Jane was made up like a dancehall girl in an early Western movie. She wore large gold earrings and her face was adorned with powder, heavy lipstick and rouge—with frozen globules of illy-applied mascara dripping from her eyelashes like great back tears. There was a bright red ribbon tied in her sparse gray hair. And that rapt, beatific expression. . . . Then I noticed, without making comment, that she had died staring up at the array of photographs across the room. These were her heroes; her obedient regiment of lovers. It was indecent to look any longer. I looked away.

"What *is* it?" the chief whispered. It somehow seemed a sin to talk out loud.

"What is what?" the coroner whispered back.

"That—that book or something she's hangin' on to?"

It took both of them to make her surrender the object from the avid clutch of her frozen, skinny arms. It wasn't a book at all. It was a large photograph—framed in sterling silver, we discovered later. The chief played his flashlight. There was writing on the photograph; small, cramped, feminine, teacher-like writing. "To my own beloved Mary Jane Emery," the inscription read. The chief studied the signature. " 'Bronco Billy' Anderson," the chief whispered hoarsely, naming one of the earliest of early movie stars. "Gentle Jesus," he repeated, this time like a benediction.

"Amen," I whispered. The coroner said huskily: "Let's get out of here!" and all of us turned and tiptoed hurriedly from the room, carefully closing the door.

That was the last time I went along with a coroner on his deathly rounds. Too often one blundered in and saw what other prying eyes were never meant to see—haunting evidence of the awful loneliness, the ultimate solitude, of each one of us, here, upon this empty whirling earth.

Chapter 15

PAULSON, PAULSON, EVERYWHERE

UP MY WAY old township politicians never die; they merely look that way. Instead they become justices of the peace. It is a special Valhalla townships reserve for their political cripples and has the following invariable rules of admission: the justice of the peace must be over seventy; he must be deaf; he must be entirely ignorant of any law but never admit it; and, during the course of each trial, he must chew—and violently expel the juice of— at least one full package of Peerless tobacco. It is preferable that he speak practically no English, and that with an accent, but in emergencies an occasional exception is permitted to slip by. Sometimes I preferred the former.

I could write a lament as thick as this book about the grotesque experiences I have had trying justice court cases out before some of these rural legal giants. It is a depressing thought. Instead I shall tell you about the trial of Ole Paulson before Justice of the Peace Ole Paulson.

Ole Paulson of Nestoria township was charged with catching forty-seven brook trout out of season with a net. Ole Paulson was in rather a bad way because it is never legal to take or possess forty-seven brook trout in one day; to fish for them in any manner out of season; or ever to take brook trout with a net, in or out of season. Ole Paulson promptly pleaded not guilty and the case was set for trial before His Honor, Justice of the Peace Ole Paulson, also of Nestoria. I drove up there to try the case rather than send one of my assistants, not because I panted to sit at the feet of

157

Justice Paulson, heaven knows, but largely because I was dying to find out precisely where a man could ever find forty-seven brook trout in one place, regardless of how he took them. It was also a riotously beautiful September day, and afforded the D.A. a chance to escape from that personal prison he inhabits called his office.

"Vell, hayloo, Yonny!" His Honor greeted me as I entered his crowded courtroom, a high-ceilinged, plaster-falling, permanently gloomy establishment from which he ordinarily dispensed insurance of all kinds, assorted tourist supplies, game and fish licenses, live bait, not to mention various and sundry bottled goods and rubber accessories. "Ve vas yoost satting here vaiting for yew!"

"Was you, Your Honor?" I cackled gleefully, warming up disgracefully to this local political sachem, pumping his limp hand, inquiring about his rheumatism—or was it his flaring ulcers?—respectfully solicitous over his interminable replies, making all the fuss and bother over him that both he and the villagers demanded whenever the District Attorney came to town to attend court. It was understood that we two initiates into the subtle mysteries of the law had to put on a show for the groundlings. The courtroom was crowded, every adult male in the community having somehow gathered enough energy to forsake the village tavern for a few hours and move across the street for the trial.

I turned to the People's star witness, the eager young game warden who had arrested the defendant. "Is the jury chosen yet?" I asked him in a stage whisper that must have been audible to a farmer doing his fall plowing in the next township. There could be no sneaky professional secrets in Judge Paulson's court—the penalty was swift and sure defeat.

"Yes," the game warden answered, "I struck the jury this morning. The list of jurors was prepared by Deputy Sheriff Paulson here. The six jurors are all here now."

It had not escaped my notice that I seemed to be getting fairly well hemmed in by Paulsons, but it was a trifle late to get into that now. I'd have to trust to the Lord and a fast outfield. I turned to Justice Paulson and said: "Very well, Your Honor, the People are ready to proceed with the trial."

"Okay den," His Honor said, rapping his desk with a gavel ingeniously contrived from a hammer wrapped in an old sock. He pointed to six empty chairs against a far wall. "Yantlemen of da yury," he announced, "yew vill now go sat over dare." Six assorted local characters scrambled for their seats, relaxed with a sigh, and were duly sworn by Justice Paulson. Allowing the jurors to sit for the oath was only one of his minor judicial innovations.

Justice Paulson, exhausted by administering the oath, opened a fresh package of Peerless and stowed away an enormous chew in his cheek. There was a prolonged judicial pause while he slowly worked up this charge. He spat a preliminary stream against a tall brass cuspidor. *"Spa-n-n-n-g!"* rang this beacon, clanging and quivering like an oriental summons to evening prayer. "Okay," His Honor said in a Peerless-muffled voice.

"The People will call Conservation Officer Clark," I announced, and the eager young game warden arose, was sworn, took the stand—and told how he had come upon the defendant, Ole Paulson, lifting the net from Nestoria Creek just below the second beaver dam in Section 9. "I caught him red-handed," he added.

"Do you have the trout and the net?" I asked the young warden, slyly noting the latitude and longitude of this fabulous spot.

"Oh, yes," he answered. "The net is in my car outside—and the trout are temporarily in the icebox in the tavern across the street. Is it okay if I go over and get them now?"

I turned to His Honor. "Your Honor, the People request a five minute recess," I said.

Judge Paulson, moon-faced and entirely mute now from his expanding chew of Peerless, whanged another ringer, banged his homemade gavel on his desk and, thus unpouched, managed to make his ruling. "Yantlemen, Ay declare fi' minoot intermissin so dat dis hare young conversation feller kin go gat his fish." He turned to a purple and bladdery bystander. "Sharley," he said, "go along vit him over an' unlock da tavern."

I gnawed restlessly on an Italian cigar while Charlie the tavern owner and my sole witness went across the street to fetch the evidence. The jury sat and stared at me in stolid silence. His Honor replenished his chew, like a starved Italian hand-stoking spaghetti. *"Whing!"* went the judge, every minute on the minute. A passing dog barked. The bark possessed a curious Swedish accent, not "woof!" but *"weuf!"* I wondered idly whether "Sharley" and my man had got locked in a pinochle match. Lo! they were back, the flushed tavern keeper appreciatively licking his moist chops over the unexpected alcoholic dividend he had been able to spear. The jury watched him closely, corroded with envy to a man. The young officer placed the confiscated net and a dishpanfull of beautiful frozen brook trout on the judge's desk and resumed the witness chair.

"Officer, you may state whether or not this is the net you found the defendant lifting from Nestoria Creek on the day in question?" I asked, pointing.

"It is," the officer testified.

Pointing at the fish: "And were all these fish the brook trout you removed from the net?"

"They were."

"Were the fish then living?"

"About half. But they were nearly done in. None would have survived."

"How many are there in the pan?"

"Forty-seven."

I introduced the exhibits into evidence and turned to Judge Paulson. "The People rest," I said.

"Plink!" acknowledged Judge Paulson, turning to the defendant. "Da defandant vill now race his right han' an' tell da yury *hiss* side of da story." It was not a request.

Ole Paulson was sworn and testified that it was indeed he who had been caught lifting the writhing net; that he had merely been patrolling the creek looking for beaver signs for the next trapping season when he had come across the illegal net; that the net was not his and was not set by him; and that he was just lifting the net to free the unfortunate trout and destroy the net when, small world, the conservation officer had come along and arrested him for his humanitarian pains. "Dat's all dare vere to it!" he concluded.

I badgered and toyed with the witness for several minutes, but it was an unseasonably hot September day and I could see that the fans were anxious to get back across the street to their hot pinochle games and cool beer, so I cut my cross-examination short. In my brief jury argument I pointed out the absurdity of the defendant's story that he was out prowling a trout stream in mid-September looking for beaver signs for a trapping season that opened the following March. I also briefly gave my standard argument that every time a game violator did things like this he was really no different than a thief stealing the people's tax money—that the fish and game belonged to *all* the people. The members of the jury blinked impassively over such strange political heresy.

"*S-splank!*" went Judge Paulson, scoring another bull's-eye. Had any man moved carelessly into the cross fire he would have risked inundation and possible drowning.

The defendant's argument was even briefer than mine. "Yantleman of da yury," he said, rising and pointing scornfully at the fish net. "Who da hecks ever caught a gude Svede using vun of dem goldang homemade Finlander nets? *Ay tank you!*" He sat down.

"*B-blink!*" went the judge, banishing the jury to the back room to consider their verdict.

The jury was thirstier than I thought. "Ve find da defandant *note gueelty!*" the foreman gleefully announced, two minutes later.

"*Whang!*" rang the cuspidor, accepting and celebrating the verdict.

After the crowd had surged tavernward, remarkably without casualty, I glanced over the six-man jury list, moved by sheer morbid curiosity. This was the list:

> Ragnar Paulson
> Swan Paulson
> Luther Paulson
> Eskil Paulson
> Incher Paulson
> Magnus Carl Magnuson

I turned to Deputy Sheriff Paulson. "How," I asked sternly, "how did this ringer Magnuson ever get on this jury list?"

Deputy Paulson shrugged. "Ve yust samply ran out of Paulsons," he apologized. "Anyvay, Magnuson dare vere my son's brudder-in-law. My son vere da defandant, yew know!"

"Spang!" gonged His Honor, like a benediction. "Dat vere true, Yonny," he said. "My nephew dare—da daputy sheriff—he nefer tell a lie!"

I lurched foggily across the street and banged on the bar. "Drinks fer da house!" I ordered, suddenly going native. "Giff all da Paulsons in da place vatever dey vant!"

Chapter 16

TRAMP, TRAMP, TRAMP

CONTRARY TO the folk mythology prevailing in Hollywood and points east, it is not in the courtroom that a D.A. really gets to know his people. It is in his office. In court his relations with his constituents are apt to be a trifle strained. But in his office. . . . Day after day, week after month after year, an unending line of people tramp their way to the office of every D.A. in America. Sad people, mad people, but rarely ever glad people. Tramp, tramp, tramp. . . . "Is the D.A. in?" they inquire hopefully, composing themselves and rehearsing their laments. And ninety-nine out of a hundred of them bring nothing but *Trouble*. The long shot will be a lawbook salesman called McQuire. Mr. Parnell McQuire. Let me give you just a brief sampling of the thousands of times it wasn't McQuire.

One day an old Finn logger came in with his own special brand of *trouble*—like patterns in trout flies or mixed drinks, the possibilities are endless. He was cutting several "forties" of pulpwood out near North Greenwood and had bought a fine big horse from his Finnish neighbor to skid his logs with. Now he wanted his neighbor arrested for cheating. "Yessir, Mister County Lawyer, dat neighbor man he c'eat me on dat horse."

"How did he cheat you, Matti?" I said, wondering from the sudden pervasive aroma whether the horse might not be out in the waiting room.

"Dat horse he's 'lind."

"How do you know he's blind, Matti?"

163

" 'Cause he can't see," Matti answered, reasonably enough. "Ven I try skid dose log, vun minoot dat horse he step in hole an' 'tub his toe, next minoot he all time bump his head on tree an' bush. Vun day he bump hisself an' fall down *boom* like 'runk man. Yesterday morning he bump hisself so godtam hard he knock hisself out for *ten* minoot! Dat horse he can't *see!*"

"Hm. . . . Didn't you try out the horse before you bought him?" I said, trying to sort out the legal issues. If the complaint amounted to anything, which I doubted, it would be a "false pretense" case, I tentatively concluded. "Did you try the horse first, Matti?" I repeated and sank back. D.A.'s must early learn to compose themselves and listen, sometimes a trying exercise in self-discipline.

"No siree, I never try him. Dat ain't da vay man buy horse." Matti scowled at my ignorance of the dark ways of horse traders. "No free trials. Anyvay, dat neighbor man he fool me. When I go buy horse I go wisit his place and he take me out to one big son-a-bits field an' dere's dat fine big horse running aroun' da field, holding his head up like big s'ot, all time farting an' snorting like million bucks. He sound like good bargain so I pay da money an' take dat horse."

"Maybe you'd better first go talk things over with your neighbor before you ask to have him pinched," I suggested, seeking a way out of this horsy dilemma.

"I do dat yesterday," Matti countered. "On vay to town yesterday I go first t'ing an tell dat crook man neighbor dat horse he's 'lind—he all time bump his noodle on 'tumps an' trees—an' even little bushes. I say, 'Look, you foxy 'rook man, I vant my money back!' "

"What'd he say, Matti?"

"Hm . . . He fold his arm big s'ot vay like dis an' say, 'Matti, you go peddle you pulp-voods before I kick'n you nass. Dat fine big horse I sell you he's not 'lind—only reason he bump into stuff he's lotsa guts an' real tough—*dat horse he yust don't give a s'it!*' "

I called in Matti's neighbor and somehow negotiated an uneasy truce.

On another occasion the judge had jailed a man for theft and I heard his wife was gunning for me. It seemed that she claimed I had it in for her husband and had helped railroad him. I shrugged. If all the people who had threatened to shoot me had done so I would have long since been displayed in the Field Museum, mummified in a wall of lead a foot thick. "Traver the Just," one hoped the display card would have read. . . . I dismissed the threats from my mind.

Several weeks passed during which I remained intact, and suddenly a woman was arrested and brought in by the game wardens for shooting a deer without a license. The game wardens consulted me.

"Who is the woman?" I asked, for it was still rather novel to find ladies out violating the game laws. Too many men were usually there ahead of them.

"Mrs. Jennie Dawson," they said. I sat up. It was the same woman who was rumored to have threatened to plug me. What a small world, I mused, bewitched by the prospect. Anyway, it was comforting to learn that my Calamity Jane could shoot straight; there'd at least be no lingering pain.

"Whose rifle did she use?" I casually asked the wardens. Here was my chance to learn her arsenal.

"Rifle hell, Johnny," one of them replied. "She shot this deer from over a hundred feet away with her own .38 pistol—right through the heart. She's an expert shot—has been ever since she was a kid. Won prizes and all."

"You don't say?" I murmured, loosening my collar. "My, my—d-did she plead guilty?"

"Yup."

I wondered in that event why they were over torturing me about her marksmanship. "How much was her fine?"

"That's what we came to see you about, Johnny. There's a new game law just out that reads that anyone found guilty of killing a deer unlawfully must receive at least a five-day mandatory sentence in the county jail. That's what's got us and the justice of the peace up a stump." They produced the brand-new statute.

I read it. There it was all right—at least five days in the jug for all rascally deer-slayers, no sexes barred.

"Good God, men," I said, "the woman's got three kids—small ones. And her husband's in the clink. We just can't send her there to be his roommate. People would grumble. And who'd take care of the kids?" I paused and shook my head. "But why did she kill the damn deer in the first place?" I was growing afraid it was for target practice.

"She told us her husband had been railroaded to jail by you and she couldn't live on the public relief she was getting—so she killed it to eat it, I guess."

I grabbed my hat and accompanied the wardens back to justice court. Mrs. Dawson—an unusually pretty little spitfire of a woman —scowled when she spied the villainous D.A. The judge and I huddled privately and concluded that, law or no law, no over-zealous legislature was going to tie our hands and *make* us send this woman to jail. What did the lofty legislative giants in Lansing know about three lonely kids? No deer was quite worth that. Instead the judge imposed a small fine, suspended its payment, returned the woman her .38 pistol, and sent her home to her children. She thanked the judge and left the courtroom without another word. When it was over all of us postured around feeling very charitable and gallant. D.A.'s are obliged to do so many inescapably harsh things that they are inclined to grow maudlin when they are able to give people a break. I returned to my office where I sat wrapped in a warm benevolent glow. "Poor little Mrs. Dawson," I ruminated. "And so pretty, too."

Donna popped her head in the door. "Mrs. Jennie Dawson is outside," she announced. Instead of going home the little woman had apparently followed me back to the office.

"S-show her in," I gulped, composing myself for the end as I rapidly reviewed the tag ends of a dissolute life. And here I'd tried to *help* her. At least I'd just paid my insurance premiums. . . . But who'd get my fly rods?

Mrs. Dawson came in blazing—not with twin .38's, but with a radiant smile. "Mr. Traver," she said, offering me her tiny trigger hand, "I want to apologize to you. I've had you all wrong,

I guess. Frankly I thought you were a heartless wretch over my husband's deal. Now I know you've really got a heart. Thank you for what you've done for us today. You're not half as bad as you look."

"It's nothing, Ma'm," I said, pondering her last remark. The quaking D.A. had won a last-minute reprieve. "Nothing at all," I muttered, seeing her warily to the door.

One day a husky Finn miner came in and shook a clenched ham first dangerously close to my craggy nose. "My missus he be two-timing me."

"Sit down, Matti," I placated him, swiftly pleading not guilty and recoiling out of range. "Who's the other man?"

"He be truck driver for my groceries store. I 'spect him long long time. Las' veek I vork night s'ift at mine—but I no go vork." Matti paused and his eyes gleamed craftily. " 'Stead I sneak back my house an' sure 'nough dere is fresh tracks numper nine goulashes in da snow—going in, coming out."

"What'd you do, Matti?" I sparred, wondering where the fateful tracks would lead to in this flaming triangle.

"I goin' in house an' my missus he holler out from bedroom real lovy, "Oh, Nestor, you come back?' an' I holler back real mad, 'Dis ain't Nestor—dis you husband Matti' an' I goin' in bedroom an' dere's my missus laying on bed reading dose real true love stories an' she's all dolled up like Hurley Gertie, rouge an' lips stick all mussed up, hair all tangled, an' room he's full cigarette smoke—me an' her don't never never smoke—an' on top bed dere's all kinds *red voolen yarns* an' my missus he vear da silky 'tockings an' I don't never never vear da red socks mine whole life!"

I explained to this rural Sherlock—still keeping carefully out of range—that I was afraid he hadn't yet sufficiently identified the termite in his family bed to warrant a criminal prosecution; but that when he actually saw the red-socked man with "numper nine goulashes" tarrying upon his premises *without* groceries we might be able to help him out.

Three nights later a man called Nestor, the delivery man for

Bateman's Grocery, got the living hell beat out of him. The state police interviewed him in the hospital, where he lay writhing around clad in mounds of adhesive tape and his trusty red woolen socks. His number nine galoshes stood neatly under the bed. For some odd reason Nestor couldn't or wouldn't identify his assailant so, alas, not having the vaguest notion who it might be, we reluctantly closed the case.

One Monday morning the breathless and unshaven manager of the Superior Arms rushed in to see me. The Superior Arms was a swank resort hotel on the shore of Lake Superior. In the subsequent excited gush of words I pieced out this story:

A distinguished-looking and apparently wealthy male guest had arrived the month before at the height of the hay-fever season. Jaguar roadster and matched luggage and all that sort of thing. Man about forty called J. Dudley Washburn III. Hailed from a distant state. Very quiet and polite; kind of shy in fact. Did not mingle much with the other guests—dames didn't seem to interest him—but occasionally in the evenings would play a game or two of bridge with other male guests who needed a fourth. Insisted on paying his hotel bill each week. Paid all his bills by checks drawn on a Chicago bank. The checks had cleared without question.

"Yes?" I said, wondering only what *form* the bad news would take.

Each summer, the manager rushed on, a reputable jewelry firm from Chicago sent up a representative who opened a temporary store in a spare room off the lobby. Seasonal sort of thing. "All high-class, expensive luxury merchandise for our wealthy fall hay fever clientele from the cities," he explained. He spoke like an ad in the *New Yorker*. And it charmed me to learn that both lawyers and hay-fever havens now called their customers clients. It somehow instantly established a brotherly bond between us.

"Yes?" I prompted, wondering if the mysterious Washburn had dropped his shyness and stuck up the high-class jeweler.

"Well, it now seems that Mr. Washburn had bought a few small things from the jeweler during his stay, paying him by check. These checks also cleared promptly."

"Good," I applauded. At least it wasn't another lousy bad check case. My pending files were nicely loaded with those. I craved a little variety.

"Then Saturday morning just three days ago—just before noon as I learned later—he visited the jewelry shop and bought a rather expensive ladies' jeweled wrist watch. As usual he paid by check. From the shop he appears to have come directly to the lobby desk and checked out. I happened to be on duty. Again he paid by check, this time in an amount considerably larger than his bill. This is not unusual with departing guests. I paid him the difference and gave him his receipted bill. Washburn told me he had enjoyed his stay. He was still very shy and courteous. He remarked that he was going upstairs to pack and would leave shortly after he had eaten lunch."

"Go on," I said, speculating where all this shyness lead.

"In a few minutes old George, our elevator man, rushed up to tell me that Mr. Washburn had just tried to sell him an expensive watch for fifty dollars; that Mr. Washburn had said it was brand-new but that he had somehow suddenly concluded that he didn't like it. Old George had looked at the watch and then put him off . . . We checked at once with the jewelry shop and discovered that he had just purchased the very same watch for five hundred dollars." He paused. "I naturally began to smell a rat."

"Not in the Superior Arms?" I exclaimed, aghast.

The distraught manager was in no mood for raillery. "Figuratively," he snapped.

"Oh, I see—like smelling something rotten in Denmark or something?"

"Precisely."

"Well, what did you do after you smelled whatever you smelled wherever you smelled it?" I was sorry I had mentioned it, but Mondays were sometimes my bad days.

"The jeweler and I huddled in my office. What to do? First I thought of phoning the Chicago bank about the checks but it was past noon and I knew it was too late—the banks would be closed. I even tried to phone you—but I was told you had gone fishing for the rest of the day." He paused and looked somewhat peevish and distressed. His predicament was plainly somehow all my fault. "They tell me you like to fish," he added petulantly.

"Like?" I said slowly. "Do I *like* to fish? Look, my friend, fishing is my secret lust—I am its slave. As a drunkard does not merely like his bottle nor a lecher merely like his mistress, so I do not merely *like* to fish—I *love* to fish." I was delivering an impassioned lecture and the poor manager stirred uneasily. I reeled in my line reluctantly. "What did you do after you couldn't find me?"

"Well," the manager went on more calmly, as though he were placating an addled hay-fever guest, "I didn't know just what in hell to do. We couldn't let this guy Washburn walk out of there with the watch and the balance of our dough and leave us with the two rubber checks, could we?"

"What did you do?" I repeated, reluctantly a D.A. again.

"When he came out from lunch I had the house dick arrest him."

"Then what?"

"He protested his innocence but we had him held in the county jail over the week end until this morning."

"The *county* jail!" I said. "I see. And what happened then?"

The manager looked very unhappy. "This morning, at his suggestion, we phoned the Chicago bank about the two checks he had given us."

"Yes?" I said.

"The checks are good—in fact, at Washburn's request the bank man told me his account could cover a considerably larger amount."

"Go on," I said. "What happened?"

"The guest is sorer than all hell and threatens to sue the hotel for slander, false arrest, false imprisonment, false teeth, and false everything under the sun—unless we pay him five thousand dollars —on the line!"

"I see," I said, and what I saw wasn't good. "And where does my office come into this rosy picture?"

"Well, you're the D.A. aren't you?—and I smell a—I mean,

something looks fishy here—and I wonder if we couldn't *really* have him arrested?"

"For what?" I asked, because I really wanted to know.

"I dunno. Illegally luring us into pinching him or something. The whole setup looks fishy as hell. It—it's like a sort of a reverse confidence game or something."

The thing certainly did look screwy all right. Even weird. Fishy as a rat in Denmark, in fact. But on the manager's own story I could see no reason whatever to arrest Mr. J. Dudley Washburn III. However eccentric, the guy was paying his way. He could have heaved the damn "high-class" watch in Lake Superior if he had wanted. I explained all this to the manager. He grew more and more despondent. I could have sent him away to consult his own lawyers, but just then I had a sudden wry little thought. The *county* could have a big stake in this mess, too. After all Washburn had languished in the *county* jail over the week end. I grabbed the phone and called the jail.

"Look," I said, when I got the sheriff, "did your men happen to fingerprint that Washburn character the Superior Arms parked with you over the week end?"

"Yup, Johnny. Routine, you know. Just like you ordered."

"Well, in the future don't ever accept casual prisoners from private dicks or hotels or any private agency without proper police sanction or proper commitment papers. Don't forget this, and be sure to tell your men. The county could get in an awful jam. And by county I mean *you*. You still might on this deal. . . . Yes, I mean false imprisonment. In the meantime please clear Washburn's prints with the local state police files and call me back. Yes, I'll wait here. Solong."

"Do you think—" the manager began, worriedly stroking his unshaven chin.

"I don't think anything right now. Suppose while we're waiting you try slumming in a mining town and go out and get yourself a drink or a shave. You look like you need both. I'm going to write a sonnet on hay-fever clients. I think I'll have some word for you when you get back. Might even show you the sonnet."

"Thanks awfully."

The worried manager was back in half an hour, still unshaven. He had followed one of my suggestions, however, and he smelled good. He leaned close. "Any word?" he breathed, spraying me gently with the fine fumes of bourbon whisky.

I rallied and consulted the notes on my desk. "Mr. J. Dudley Washburn III has seven aliases besides the name he registered with you. He is a nationally known confidence man—one of the best; he stays out of jail. He has served but one term in prison, that out in California. You should preserve his autograph under glass. He is not presently wanted anywhere as far as we now can tell. But our local records are not up to date."

"Is all that good?" the manager said dubiously.

"I would be inclined to think so," I answered dryly. "If it weren't good I'd guess you and your hotel—and possibly the county sheriff—would be up to your necks in one hell of a lovely damage suit."

"What do I do now?"

"I suggest that you hightail back to your hotel and shave. I want you to look suave as Menjou for your task. Once anointed I suggest you go have a quiet little talk with your ruffled guest. Alone. Tell him you don't want any trouble, but that if he doesn't blow quietly by nightfall you're afraid you'll have to visit the D.A. and maybe have his fingerprints checked. Tell him you smell a rat."

"Yes?"

"Don't tell him what we already know, however. Be courteous and firm—and a little stupid. And phone me tomorrow what happens."

"Thanks awfully," the manager said, pumping my hand. "You've been swell."

"One more thing," I said. "Hereafter don't jump the gun on arresting your shy guests—especially after the banks are closed and the D.A.'s gone fishing."

"Don't worry, chum."

"And don't forget to shave! No Washburn has ever been routed by a character with a three-day beard."

The manager phoned the next morning. First he had shaved.

Honest he had. . . . Then he had visited Mr. Washburn in his suite and spoken his piece. It had worked like a charm. The guest had cooled off rapidly, paid up in cash, picked up his uncashed checks, and had left immediately. "Thanks awfully," the manager concluded.

That was the last we ever heard of the shy J. Dudley Washburn III and his reverse confidence game. The timing was perfect—banks closed, the D.A. gone fishing and all—but the little thing that had spoiled it was the clumsy accident of the fingerprints. Just a little stupid mischance. Everything else had gone according to schedule. . . . I often wonder where he is. But a man with his shy talents will doubtless pop up one of these days before a Congressional committee or something. I'll just watch the newspapers.

One day a buxom widow of about forty came in and wanted to have her neighbor, a widower, arrested for begetting her last child, then two months old.

"Tell me the story," I sighed. It was one of the oldest and most frequently told office stories to come before any D.A.

"Vell," began Mrs. Kellstrom, "I vere vidow for sexteen year, vit t'ree small boys by my firs' husband. Den 'bout two year ago along come dis hare neighbor man, Holmquist, an' me an' him began keeping company. He vere a vidow, too. An' he vere certainly looking hard for a voman, all right."

"How do you mean? What happened?"

"Vell, vun nice summer night he parked his car out by da gulf club—near da firs' green. Den he quvick began making violent love an' monkeying an' all dat taffy—you know—an' I vas veak—sexteen year vitout a man—and dare vere a big moon. . . . Den before I could say Yackie Robinson he up an' yazzed me! Den what happen? Hm. . . . Now I got brand-new baby. Girl dis trip. I vant him arrested."

Holmquist was indeed a fast worker. Good men like that were getting hard to find, I suggested. Would she marry him? Blushing prettily she allowed that, oh yes, she certainly would. "He vere quite a man." I then suggested that perhaps I'd better have Mr.

Holmquist in for a talk before any discouraging bastardy warrants were popped. Arrest frequently tended to chill romance. Maybe I could persuade him to walk up the altar instead. I'd be glad to write him to come in and talk it over.

"Oo, dat vould be dandy," she said, already planning her trousseau.

Mr. Holmquist, a dour specimen, had other ideas. "No siree!" He didn't want to marry any woman who brought him a dowry of three hungry growing boys—besides the new child. "Vould cost vay tew much money to support dem all," he said. "Ever'ting's so high dese days." He was one of those gay dogs, you see, a loose spender from hell.

"Very well," I said, abandoning my uneasy role as cupid and again becoming the tough D.A. "Then, my friend, you'll either have to pay the welfare authorities five hundred dollars for the child's support or be pinched." That amount was then the modest going rate to settle such a case out of court.

"Oo no, I don't haff to pay notting!" he said, smiling triumphantly. "I've got a *receipt!*" He'd evidently taken—and failed—a correspondence course in law.

"Wha'dya mean, a receipt?" I asked, incredulous.

"Vait, I show you." He dug out a bulging purse and rummaged around in his various licenses and permits and social security cards and dog-eared snapshots and finally fished out a soiled paper and smoothed it out on my desk. "Dare!" he said complacently, still holding on to it. No slick D.A. was going to grab and destroy *his* evidence.

It was a plain printed form of receipt for the payment of money, the kind one can get in pads at any drugstore and fill in for the payment of rent or a load of wood or the purchase of an old sow. *Anything,* it developed, for this is what it said:

> 10:27 P.M.   Aug. 5, 1946.
> Received of Mr. August Holmquist
> Ten and no/100 . . . . Dollars
> Saxal Entercorse in return
> $10.00   (signed) Mrs. Olga Kellstrom

Unhinged, I swayed in my chair. Now I had seen everything! "Did Mrs. Kellstrom really sign this?" I whispered weakly, my mind reeling.

"You bet!" he said, carefully folding away the precious evidence. "Dat vere certainly true!"

"Who filled it out?"

"Me."

"When?"

"At home, before I tuck her out. All but her signature and the time. I couldn't tell exactly *ven* ve vould, you know. You know how it is . . ." I ignored his effort to establish a camaraderie of the hunt.

"When did *she* sign?" I asked, gnawed by a morbid curiosity. "At what stage in the proceedings?—before, during or after?" Evilly enough, I just had to know.

"Before, of course!" Mr. Holmquist would have me know that *he* was a man of the world; that here was a man who paid his way right on the barrelhead.

I swayed again. Here at last was wild Romance, hot love pulsing and untrammeled, the kind celebrated by the bards of old! I sat staring at my great lover; the fiery swain who carelessly bestowed his love in budgeted sprees of ten dollars. The giant economy size.

"Look, chum," I said, when I felt I could again speak. "Let me give you a friendly tip . . ." I told him that paying for his little back-seat collision with Mrs. Kellstrom and taking a receipt was no defense to a bastardy charge; that this was not a rape case (to which consent was a defense), as he seemed determined to think, but a case involving mainly the public's keen financial interest in the support of an illegitimate child. "Far from your receipt being a defense," I told him, "it would only serve as conclusive proof that you laid her on the very night she claimed. On the very minute, in fact," I added, recalling the deathless "10:27 P.M."

It was as though I had stuck him with a sockful of night soil. His long face grew even longer. "Oo, I din't know dat, I din't know," he kept repeating dolefully. Then: "Are you sure?" His shrewd El Brendel eyes grew slit with craft; I was setting a sly lawyer trap.

"Look," I said, counting ten, "supposing you dredge up five bucks out of that leather vault you're carrying around and go down the street and consult a lawyer—any attorney of your choice. In your ledger call it, say, an investment in peace of mind. I want you to be sure I'm not kididng you." The thought would have haunted me. "Then come back and see me tomorrow."

"T'anks," he said, and he and his receipt for "saxal entercorse" fled like a flash.

The next morning the great lover was waiting for me on the bottom stairway. He looked as though he hadn't slept very well. "Mr. Holmquist, I presume," I grunted. We trudged silently up the creaking stairs together. "Mornin', Donna," I grunted again.

"Well?" I said, as we sat across from each other at my desk. "What do you say?" I was in no mood to fool. "Do you marry her—or pay up—or do we pinch you?"

"I vas just t'inkin' las' night layin' home dare in bed," he began, smiling craftily. "I vas yust t'inkin' what a really nice vidow lady dat Missus Kellstrom vere, after all, an' what t'ree nice strong boys she got—pretty soon dey big enough to go vork in da mine. Hm . . . I t'ink maybe I change my mind an' marry her."

This winning prodigal had figured every angle. He'd also obviously spent five bucks on a lawyer, which must have hurt him cruelly. I arose and pumped the prospective groom's hand. "Let me be the first to congratulate you," I said to this romantic spendthrift. "Maybe she'll even go fifty-fifty on the price of the marriage license."

"Oo, you really t'ink so?" he brightened, serious as an owl.

"If she doesn't, I will," I said, somehow determined that I'd help the Widow Kellstrom land her man—such as he was—even if I had to chip in on an initial wedding present. "All I want in return is a copy of that receipt."

Late another afternoon Donna popped her head in my door. It had been a particular trying day. "Who in hell is out there now?" I blurted petulantly.

"Mr. McQuire, the lawbook salesman."

"McQuire, McQuire, come in!" I shouted, delirious with joy, rushing gaily out to greet him. "Come in, man—come in and sit down and let me tell you my troubles!"

Chapter 17

THE SAD PASSING OF HURLEY GERTIE

THERE IS A SPECIES of womankind loose in the land that resembles a female impersonator more than she does a woman. While she doubtless possesses a heart of gold and the soul of a swooping angel, her sole outward badge of femininity, and one that does not invite further exploration, is her hair: she *always* keeps it done up in little metallic ringlets of damp pin curls, so tight, so precise, as though she were a belle forever preparing for a ball never to be held. Thus coiffured, she sails confidently through life—confident at least, I swear, that *I* shall never molest her. Such a charmer was Mrs. Shepard.

"I want," she said, settling herself firmly in the office chair across from me, "I want you to run that awful Gertie woman and her prostitutes out of town." She glared and nodded her forbidding battery of bobby pins at me so hard that they rattled like porcupine quills.

"Hm . . ." I said. I did not dare pretend that I didn't know all about Gertie and her prostitutes—she would surely have assassinated me in my chair. *Everybody* knew of Hurley Gertie, the madam of the oldest whorehouse in Iron Cliffs County. Gertie was more than an aging whore; she had become a hallowed institution, albeit one rather more covered with greenbacks than ivy. She had been in business since I was in grammar school. Veterans of three wars sought solace in her old iron beds. "Hm," I repeated uncertainly. This was a grave crisis: as though I had suddenly been asked to banish the Civil War cannon from the city square. "What happened?" I ventured, groping for an opening.

179

"She sent my man home with a—a social disease. One of her new girls fixed him up—but good. I tell you I won't stand for it!" Mrs. Shepard was hopping mad. The agitated bobby pins began faintly to clank.

"My, my," I said. I could not blame the woman any more than—after viewing her—I could quite blame her husband for fleeing her to seek Romance in other quarters, however squalid. More disturbing, it was the first complaint I'd ever had against circumspect old Gertie. "I'll look into it at once," I promised.

"Mind you do," Mrs. Shepard warned grimly, arising and clutching her purse. "If you don't do something *I* will! And mine isn't the first man her girls have fixed up. *It's got to stop!*"

"I've given you my word," I said petulantly, grabbing the phone. "The moment you leave I'll call the chief of police."

"Good-by!" she snapped, her lips a thin line of distaste for all prostitutes—and prosecutors. "And remember—*if you don't* . . ." She shook her head at me so hard I thought she would dislodge her last vestiges of femininity.

Lo! they held. "Good-by, Mrs. Shepard," I said, fascinated by the rigid geometric design of her still intact pin curls. By then I felt it would have been a distinct act of charity for the D.A. and police to rescue Hurley Gertie from the personal attentions of this forbidding creature.

"And how much was your cut, Traver, for letting this brazen prostitute operate illegally?" you may fairly ask. The answer was nothing, not a dime—not even in trade—just nothing at all. But why let her run? Because I happened to share with Cicero the belief that the best law derives from considering the true nature of man, not a lot of lofty theories about him. Stated more bluntly I felt that Hurley Gertie and her toilers were a real safety valve in our boisterous mining and logging community; indeed, were themselves an important if unwitting factor in preserving law and order. All law enforcement everywhere is merely relative, and I confess I would rather have seen Gertie and her gang violating one set of laws than, by virtuously banishing her, see a whole new crop of ugly abortion, rape, bastardy and attendant criminal cases springing up during—and largely because of—her absence. But Gertie was not playing the game according to the unspoken rules. Personal hygiene was one of them. Something had to be done.

"The Chief is here," Donna announced.

"Chief," I said, after telling him about Mrs. Shepard's complaint, "I want you to go tell Gertie to get rid of that diseased girl till she's fixed up or I'll close her joint and run her out of town. In this age of penicillin there's no rhyme or reason for such carelessness."

"That won't be easy, Johnny," the chief warned.

"Whadyou mean, not easy?—not easy to give her my message? Why, Chief," I teased slyly, "I didn't know you cared . . . Perhaps you worship at old Gertie's shrine, too? You naughty boy . . ."

"I mean it won't be easy to run her out of town, damn it. She— she's pretty well connected in these parts, you know." The chief was blushing prettily.

"Chief," I said, my temperature rising, "you deliver the word to Gertie—and I'll worry about her big shot friends." Violators who claimed real or alleged "connections" had always waved a red flag at me.

The chief was back the next day. He smiled sheepishly as he sat across from me. "I delivered your message to Gertie," he said.

"What did she say?"

"I can't remember all she said—the explosion was terrific— but I remember the important part."

"Let's have it, Chief."

"You won't like it, Johnny."

"Let's have it," I repeated.

"She said, 'You go back and tell that goddam lean, hatchet-faced, pussy-footin' Traver to go pittle up a limp hemp rope. You tell him he ain't dry behind the ears yet, and if he don't look out I'll tell all my clients to go out and vote and work against him!' " The chief paused. "She said a lot more, and swore in five languages, but it all added up to the same thing. She won't do a thing."

"Did the old blister really say all that?" I said, wishing I had been present to witness the magnificent explosion. Windows must have been shattered as far west as Las Vegas.

"That's what she said, Johnny."

"Well I'll be damned—I really thought old Gertie had more brains." I shrugged. "Well, now she's asked for it. We've got to call her bluff."

"And something more," the chief continued soberly. "I learned last night that the same new girl has set up two more men—both young miners—and another one of 'em rolled a drunken lumberjack last Saturday night. Gertie must be losing her mind. Either that or she's making a last minute cleanup for a quick departure. Either way it looks like war."

"It is war, Chief," I said. "And Gertie's by way of hampering the defense effort."

"What do we do now?"

"I don't know yet—give me time to think. One thing is sure: we've got to get her and get her fast. I'll phone you in the morning."

"Okay, Johnny," the chief said.

We could simply have bulled things and tipped her over in a police raid, but I wanted Hurley Gertie to *stay* tipped. The Civil War cannon had to be carted away permanently. I did not want her to come galloping into court, with her expensive attorneys running intereference for her, presenting valid motions to suppress the evidence and quash the proceedings because of our illegal raid. We could also have sent some hardy male "plants" in there each armed with five dollars (under the new ceiling) and then made a formal pinch on their evidence. But I never pandered to stool pigeons, in or out of whorehouses, and anyway all that that would accomplish would be to make Gertie more careful and give her a breathing spell until the next term of circuit court. A lot of miners could develop "whooping cough" in that time. That night I went fishing and, as I fished, wrestled with Gertie—figuratively that is, for I had always shunned prostitutes, not on moral grounds, the Lord knows, but largely on esthetic ones.

"What do you say, Johnny?" the chief inquired the next morning.

"When is the next big mine payday, Chief?" I asked. "There's one soon isn't there?"

"Friday—two days from now. Why?"

"Okay—this is what I want you to do. Station an officer at the bottom of Gertie's back stairway twenty-four hours a day starting at six tonight. Better make it three eight-hour shifts. Don't give her any rest from this vigil. Have each cop hold a notebook and pencil in his hand. Tell the officers not to speak to anyone or bother anyone or make any explanations whatever. That is important. Tell your men to simply do this: whenever any person enters or leaves Gertie's, have the officer at that moment write his *own* name and address in the notebook. No more, no less. Do this through Sunday night and report to me Monday."

I had stolen a leaf from old Judge Belden's book: while fishing I had recalled that he had successfully followed the same strategy as prosecutor many years before. (Perhaps it was Gertie's own grandmother.) But would it still work? The chief was back Monday morning.

"It worked, Johnny," he grinned. "Boy oh boy, it worked like a charm! Eight men went in the first night two the next day, one drunk payday night, and none all week end. Every other man in town is scared green he'll be pinched or subpoenaed as a witness or something. Worried husbands have pestered hell out of me all week end. . . . Then Gertie phoned me last night and threw in the sponge—she's leaving town tonight."

"For good?" I asked.

"For good," the chief replied.

"Didn't old Gertie send her favorite D.A. any farewell message, Chief?" I pouted.

"She sure did," the chief replied grimly.

"What did she say?"

"She said: 'Tell that psalm-singin' s.o.b. to go pittle up *two* hemp ropes!' "

I shook my head and clucked my tongue pensively. "Too bad," I sighed. Poor old Gertie simply didn't know her own D.A.

Chapter 18

THE GREAT URANIUM HOAX

ONE BEAUTIFUL October day I was sitting disconsolately in my office way up on the second floor of the local Woolworth tower working on a trial brief. I confess an acute allergy to the preparation of trial briefs. I paused and sighed and wished I were out partridge hunting. Then Donna came in and interrupted my reverie.

"Walter Holbrook's outside," she said. "In person—not a movie."

I sat up. Walter Holbrook was the big wheel of the Peninsula Land and Timber Company, one of the biggest owners of mining and timber lands in the entire Lake Superior district. What could *he* possibly want with the local D.A.? Maybe, I thought, his company was at last coming to its senses and was about to retain me. I grew as fluttery and expectant as a debutante facing her first stag line.

"If he's sober, Donna, show him in," I said. Donna and I are always full of little private jokes. Our days are one dizzy round of gaiety and fun.

Mr. Holbrook was an efficient operator. He wasted no time. "Mr. Traver," he said, briefly pumping my hand and sitting across the desk from me, "our company has a problem that our attorneys advise us may require the attention of your office."

"Oh, yes," I answered rather inanely, ruefully admiring the swift smoothness with which he had got across the idea that he was consulting me purely in my capacity as D.A. "What is your problem?"

As Walter Holbrook paused to light a cigarette I studied him with considerable interest. I had never moved extensively in the rarefied atmosphere inhabited by big business executives, and this was my first traffic with one as D.A. I was rather curious to observe a member of the species at work. When Walter Holbrook finally went on speaking I quickly found myself recognizing the type: brisk, dominant, self-assured, persuasive—the kind heavily favored by the dream merchants of Hollywood. Yes, here was a man who knew precisely what he wanted to say— and said it like a Scotchman dictating a cablegram. A prepaid cablegram, I should perhaps add, to labor my little joke.

"Ah . . ." he breathed, exhaling a thin cloud of cigarette smoke. "Well . . ." He seemed to be mentally assuming the role I was giving him. "It's this way, Mr. Traver," he began. "It all started last month. Stranger called at our main local office. Man by the name of Robbins—Kurt Robbins. Insisted on seeing me. Refused to state his business to the receptionist. Accordingly refused to see him." He shrugged. "Got to do it, you know. All manner of creeps and crackpots call on me every day. Couldn't ever get anything done otherwise."

"Yes," I said, recalling that *he* had not stated *his* business to Donna. (But then I also recalled that D.A.'s were elected to sit there and take it.) "Then what happened?"

Walter Holbrook resumed the composition of his cablegram. "The next day he was back. Same result. Then he left and telephoned from a pay station. Mysterious as hell. Told my secretary that he had to see me. Matter of the utmost importance to my company. Something about a mineral discovery. Had to discuss it on the highest local level. Said I would readily appreciate the necessity for secrecy and strict confidence when I talked with him."

"You saw him?" I said, pondering the qualities—and lack of them—that apparently made up a successful executive.

He smiled briefly. "Yes," he said. "Guess my curiosity got the best of me. That phrase 'mineral discovery' threw me, I guess. He was back at my office in five minutes. Ellen—that's my secretary —showed him in. He was a tall, lean, outdoor-type sort of man of about 38-40. Kind of resembled what's-his-name—hm—that strong, silent, hard-riding Western movie actor, I forget his name. Anyway, he introduced himself.

" 'My name's Kurt Robbins,' he said. 'I'm a prospector. I've prospected everywhere for everything, I guess. Practically all over the world. This past summer I've been doing a little prospecting in this Lake Superior area. Very interesting country.' Then he glanced over his shoulder. 'May I close your office door?'

" 'As you wish,' I said, as he went and stealthily shut my door. I half expected him to suddenly wheel on me with an old six-shooter—the kind with the cadaver score nicked on the handle. 'But just how do your interesting international prospecting activities affect our company?' I sparred.

" 'I'll try to show you,' he said. He was carrying a bulging and battered leather case—more like an old saddlebag. He must have lugged it along on his first prospecting trip. He now opened it and produced not a six-shooter but several rock samples—all about the size of my fist—and plumped them down on my desk blotter. 'These grab samples came from land owned by your company,' he announced, giving me one of those piercing, far-away, open-range looks of his. 'Beautiful, aren't they?'

" 'What are they?' I asked Robbins, growing a trifle impatient with his juvenile air of mystery. 'The damned stuff looks like a poor grade of coal to me. We're exclusively in the business of handling timber and iron and copper mining rights, in case you didn't know.'

"He laughed coolly and said, 'You're also primarily in the business of making money, Mr. Holbrook. If the stuff in these samples is what I think it is, perhaps both of us can make a bundle of money—that is, if the idea doesn't cause you excessive pain.' [The trapped and listening D.A. was beginning to develop a sneaking regard for Prospector Robbins. Walter Holbrook went on with his story.]

" 'What do you think it is?' I asked Robbins.

" 'Well, I haven't run an assay on it yet,' Robbins said, 'but from the way it kicks hell out of my Geiger counter, I know that these rock samples are pieces of a highly radioactive mineral. I'm sure of that. However, if it's radioactive thorium it's commercially valueless, as even a slave to iron and copper doubtless knows.' He was quite a sarcastic dude, you see. 'But if it's uranium—' He paused and shrugged.

" 'But whichever it is, thorium or uranium, it would still be on *our* land,' I told Robbins, thinking it was time to remind him of this minor detail.

" 'Precisely. That's why I came to see you,' he replied dryly. 'If it's uranium I want to make a deal with your company.'

" 'What's your proposition?' I asked.

" 'Fifty per cent of the net profit,' he answered, as cool as a cucumber. He even smiled. Yes, Mr. Traver, this—this common trespasser sat there in my office, never batting an eye—and demanded half of the profits on our own stuff." Walter Holbrook paused and shook his head in wonder. He finally composed himself following the contemplation of such heresy and went on with his story. "At that point I also told him that I did not believe my company would agree to pay such a high percentage for the mining of its own minerals from its own land. 'In fact,' I told him, 'I'm not sure that they will be willing to make any "deal," as you call it, in any event.'

"Here Robbins rose abruptly, still smiling, ready to leave. 'Well, will you at least put it up to your company?' he said. Then he added, with that mocking smile of his: 'Only Uncle Joe and his Russian rangers would be apt to reward you for flatly turning down a possible new American uranium mine. Will you put my proposition up to your company's top brass, Mr. Holbrook?'

" 'Even that is a question,' I frankly answered him. 'You admit you're not sure yourself what the stuff is. Before I can be bothering our head office at Wilmington with a slim prospect like this I'll have to know that it's uranium; and, equally important, that it is of sufficiently high grade and quantity to be worth mining. The only way we can determine this last point is for you to tell me where on our land you found the stuff—so that our consulting geologist and his staff can go out and look it over. How about it?'

"Robbins walked to my office door and put his hand on the knob and turned to me, smiling. 'Relax, my generous friend. *That* will come after you boys have signed on the dotted line—50 per cent.'

" 'Suppose—just suppose, of course—that we get a little greedy and go out and find it ourselves—without you?' I suggested, testing him out a little.

"He continued to smile; a lofty, superior sort of smirk. 'Greed is of course every man's privilege,' he said. 'And I have lived long enough never to discount its possible presence in others. But I'll take a chance on that. I guess I like the look in your steady little gray eyes. And after all, you've only got about one— or is it two?—hundred thousand odd acres of land to comb over. My guess is that in about, say, thirty years your geologist might stumble onto it. Both you and I would be a little on the ripe side by then.' Then he opened my door, ready to leave.

" 'Aren't you going to take your precious samples?' I said, pointing to the rocks on my desk. I really had no intention of giving them up. . . . 'Or perhaps I should keep them, since you admit that you trespassed on our land to get them.'

"He quickly closed the door and stood facing me. 'You're welcome to the samples, Mr. Holbrook. Take them with the blessings of the copyright infringer. There're a lot more where they came from. Really quite an unusual outcrop. As for our "deal," as you seem not to like to call it, I'll be back in two weeks for my answer. Right now I must take a little business flight to New York. Remember, 50 per cent is my proposition. No less. If the stuff's thorium I apologize for wasting your time—and for trespassing on your property. In the meantime, you will of course understand that it is to our mutual advantage to keep this discovery in the utmost confidence. But, as I have said, I trust you to keep my secret. Good day, sir'—and he was gone."

Walter Holbrook paused and lit another cigarette. First he carefully rolled it and tapped it and fitted it into a long amber holder. During this elaborate ritual I packed and lit my pipe, glanced furtively at my watch, and saw my evening's partridge hunt flying out the window. But at least I'd still try for it.

"Did he ever come back?" I gently prodded.

"In two weeks to the hour he was back at our office," Walter Holbrook went on. 'Well,' he said after he had again carefully closed my door, shook my hand, and sat down, 'Well, do I get the 50 per cent?'

"I told him that our consulting geologist had run an assay of his samples locally and that the stuff indeed showed some small uranium content, all right; that I'd communicated this fact to the Wilmington office and that it had somewhat reluctantly agreed to enter into a preliminary contract to pay him 10 per cent of the net, providing that the extent of the deposit, in our sole judgment, warranted mining it. 'We're only doing it because the country needs the uranium,' I added."

"What was his reaction to that?" I said, deciding to put up a last fight for my partridge hunt.

"As I told you, this Robbins was a cool one. 'Mr. Holbrook' he said, 'I assure you it's a tremendous comfort to know I'm dealing with such blazing patriots.' He smiled and even chuckled a little over his joke. Then he took a letter from his pocket and tossed it over to me. 'Read that and weep,' he said. It was addressed to him at a New York hotel—dated within the week—from a reputable New York assay laboratory reporting that the mineral samples he had recently left with them contained pitch-blende assaying 78 per cent U_3O_8. That's uranium oxide, Mr. Traver. You see, pitchblende is the richest known ore of uranium. 'There's your "some small uranium content," ' Robbins said, smiling cynically at me. 'Perhaps you consulted a soothsayer about my samples rather than your assayer.' "

An excited D.A. interrupted at this point. "Seventy-eight per cent," I murmured. I tried vaguely to recall my high-school chemistry. The effort was not fruitful. "Is that good?"

"*Good!*" Walter Holbrook said, rolling his eyes up in his head. "Good Lord, son—it rivals the richest known uranium ores in the world—the Katanga region in the Belgian Congo and the fabulous El Dorado in Canada. Uncle Joe Stalin'd give his—his favorite curved pipe to lay his peace-loving hands on stuff half as hot."

It was my turn to do some eye rolling. "You—you mean, Mr.

Holbrook, we've got deposits of rich uranium ore like that—right here in this county?" The partridge were forgotten. Instead my mind buzzed and sang with the sweet whine of Geiger counters.

"I don't know whether or not it's in this county. That's the trouble. You see, we own scattered tracts of land all over this blessed state—not to mention Minnesota and Wisconsin—assuming that the damned stuff ever came from our land."

"Then you didn't learn where it came from?—you and Robbins didn't make any deal?" I asked.

"Hell, no," Walter Holbrook answered. "My smiling friend, Robbins, calmly picked up his assay letter and walked to the door. He turned and spoke. 'Sorry we can't make a deal on my terms. Get in touch with me when you change your mind—providing I haven't changed mine. It's been nice knowing you. And in the meantime I hope you'll continue to so splendidly keep the secret I told you in strict confidence.'

" 'Thanks,' I said, and I hope just as sarcastically.

"Then Robbins paused, his hand on the doorknob, and slyly added: 'I know that you're not apt to forget my terms, Holbrook, because I'm fully aware that you've recorded on wire our conversations of two weeks ago and again today. Or was it on tape? Tape generally has higher fidelity. And all of us appreciate a high degree of fidelity, don't we, Mr. Holbrook?' Then he *winked* at me. 'But you really shouldn't lean so far over your hidden microphone. It gives the thing away, you know, and also causes annoying distortion and voice blast. Good day, sir.' Then he and his mocking smile disappeared."

"Was he right, Mr. Holbrook?" I asked, smiling a little myself. "I mean about the hidden recorder?"

Walter Holbrook flushed, grimaced, and took the bit in his teeth. It appeared hard for him to be divulging such, should I say, intimate company strategy to a mere backwoods district attorney. "Yes, damn it," he answered, swallowing hard. "We have to deal with all sorts of people, you know, and sometimes on damned important deals—transactions, I mean. A verbatim recording often avoids misunderstandings later on, you know."

"Of course," I said, reflecting on how pleasant it was that the expanding marvels of science had kept so nicely abreast of the expanding distrust of men, one for the other.

"But mainly I keep a recorder for night dictation," he added, rather lamely and belatedly, I thought. "At any rate our attorneys and I have played this damned recording over so often that I know it by heart. And then," he continued more brightly, "it should help a lot in court when we press the criminal prosecution against Robbins. Don't you think so?"

I heaved a sigh and decided that it was time for the D.A. to do a little talking. "Mr. Holbrook . . ." I began. I explained to him that in my opinion he had so far failed to even remotely make out any criminal case against Robbins or anyone else; that all he had shown was that Robbins had claimed to have discovered some valuable minerals on the company's land; that he had tried to make a *transaction* regarding it and, having failed, had simply gone about his affairs.

"However eccentric or mysterious Robbins' conduct may have been," I went on, "he does not appear to have committed any crime. No one can compel him to show or prove where he found the uranium. And his conduct does not strike me as being particularly unnatural or suspicious. Try putting yourself in his place and him in yours. Would you honestly have shown *him* where you found the stuff before you—pardon me—had made a deal?"

Walter Holbrook grinned, almost boyishly I thought. "No," he slowly admitted, tamping a new cigarette. "No, I guess not." The high-powered, staccato-talking executive was breaking down a little, relaxing a trifle. He might not, I thought, really be such a bad companion on a fishing trip.

"Perhaps," I gently suggested, "there are some things you haven't yet told me—things that might be relevant to this most interesting story." I felt in my bones that there were. Walter Holbrook and his battery of suave Eastern lawyers were too smart to have let me in on this much without there being more. "Isn't there something else?" I repeated. I was not wrong.

"Yes," Walter Holbrook said. "I hadn't quite finished. Was just taking a little breather. Been doing a lot of talking today."

He sighed. "Damn that man, Robbins! Wish I'd never laid eyes on him."

"I'm sorry if I interrupted you," I said. "Now suppose you proceed in you own words and tell me *all* the story, right to the end. I'll fire any necessary questions as you go along."

This, then, is the rest of the story that Walter Holbrook told me—and not, I may add, without considerable personal embarrassment—concerning the strange case of Kurt Robbins, prospector.

The moment Robbins had left Holbrook's office, following his first visit when he had left the uranium samples, apparently quite a scamper had taken place. Walter Holbrook had hastily summoned the company's chief consulting geologist and told him the startling story, played over for him the tape recording—indeed it *was* tape —and showed him the samples. The geologist had been impressed. They had then airmailed several of the samples to the same "Robbins" laboratory in New York and the geologist had assayed the rest locally. Results: Contents 77 and 79 per cent U_3O_8, respectively.

They had then rounded up virtually every geologist they could beg, borrow or steal—not to mention a flock of hurriedly mustered young student geologists from a neighboring mining college— and armed them with Geiger counters, and even a few new Canadian scintillometers, and sent them swarming out over the company's far-flung land holdings in search of Robbins' uranium. All this ostensibly, Walter Holbrook carefully explained, the result of a suddenly conceived program on the part of the company to patriotically determine if it had uranium on its lands.

"Did you find any?" I asked Walter Holbrook.

"Hell, no," he answered glumly. "A few low grade whispers but nothing like *his* stuff. And we've still got 'em out prowling all over the damned state. Costing us thousands of dollars." He shrugged. "But what are we going to do? The stuff runs nearly 80 per cent. We've simply got to find it—providing it's there."

"This is all very interesting, Mr. Holbrook, but I'm still afraid there's no provable crime," I said, refilling my pipe. "There must be something more you've neglected to mention." My complainant seemed oddly reluctant to tell me something important about his case. "Let's have it, Mr. Holbrook," I said quietly.

Walter Holbrook suddenly grasped hard at his side of the top of my desk, with both hands, fingers up, and sat staring at me. His knuckles whitened under the pressure. "Yes," he said slowly, "unfortunately there is more to tell. A hell of a lot more." He was flushing deeply. "I'll tell you . . . You see, when I learned that there appeared to be such a rich uranium deposit on our company's lands I felt obliged to confide this important knowledge to my superiors in Wilmington. Sense of company duty, you know. In fact, I had to, to let them pass on his proposed 'deal.' And who was this Robbins to be saddling me with his unsought confidences?"

"Yes," I said, beginning to see daylight. "And what else? There must be something else."

"Well, we felt that such valuable new mineral discoveries on our lands would in the normal course naturally increase the value of our company's stock, when the news broke." He hesitated and then took the plunge. "We also felt that—er—we might just as well profit, so to speak, from our inside knowledge, by in the meantime sort of naturally enlarging our own personal holdings of company stock." Ah, the real story was finally coming out. Walter Holbrook's face had assumed the radiant hue of a red brick schoolhouse.

"Naturally," I agreed, embarrassed at witnessing his embarrassment, suddenly studying the elaborate whirls and flourishes on my law school diploma hanging on the far wall. "Then what happened?"

"So we—well, we went into the market and tried to buy up all the company stock we could lay our hands on. The word got out, as these things do, that *something* was cooking—they knew not what—and the more stock we bought up the higher the price went." He paused and sighed. "It was then that we learned that a certain individual had beaten us to the punch. Singlehanded, he'd damn near cornered all the readily available stock on the market."

"And the name of this certain individual?" I asked, knowing.

"Kurt Robbins, of course," he replied harshly. "Always Robbins, Robbins, Robbins . . ." He fumbled and lit a cigarette, ignoring his amber holder.

"Then what?" I said, wondering how this battle of the foxes would turn out.

"Though the news of the supposed uranium strike on our lands didn't break publicly—it hasn't to this day, as a matter of fact—naturally, with all the inevitable rumors of our heavy prospecting for uranium and the unusual demand and market activity over our stock, the price kept going up and up. And we—meaning me, our chief consulting geologist, a few cronies, yes, even my poor wife, and our associates in Wilmington—kept right on buying it. And paying, I may add, right through the nose. Knowing that Robbins was loaded only spurred us on. We were sure, then, that he had found the uranium on our land." He stopped and sighed deeply. "Then it happened."

"Yes?" I said.

"Kurt Robbins suddenly unloaded all of his holdings of our stock—at top prices. It started the very next day after he last left my office. Naturally the damned stock went down immediately. As a matter of fact, even today it's a few points lower than when Robbins first saw me. He must have made a fortune. And our losses are way up in the thousands. I haven't even tried to count 'em." Walter Holbrook, the harried executive, was perspiring freely now. "And naturally I'm in a devil of a hole with my superiors back in Wilmington—not to even *mention* my wife. I really don't know which way to turn. That's why I've come to you. Our Wilmington attorneys felt I should lay all the facts before you."

Walter Holbrook sighed, lit a new cigarette from his last one, and gloomily crushed out the butt in the growing mound in my ash tray. "What can be done?" he said.

I lit my pipe, sparring for time. I was already pretty well convinced what it was I had to tell him, but I wanted to make sure. I also thought I might at least let the poor man down easy. He'd had a pretty rough day of it. So I told him I wanted time to clarify my thinking about the situation and possibly to look up some law. I arranged to meet him at my office the next morning. For, uranium or no uranium, I was surely going partridge hunting the next afternoon. Perhaps, I thought, I'd even take along a battery of Geiger counters, too.

A rumpled, red-eyed, and unshaven Walter Holbrook was at my office the next morning promptly at nine. As we shook hands I thought I detected the faint smell of whisky, but as I'd consumed a few "onions" myself the night before perhaps I was mistaken.

"What's the verdict?" he asked, slumping into his chair across from me. His fingers were stained from smoking cigarettes. "Insomnia—couldn't sleep." He laughed briefly and without mirth. "My wife also abetted the insomnia," he wryly added.

Of all the victims of possible fraud a public prosecutuor is ever obliged to listen to, none is at once more distasteful or more pathetic than one who is the victim of his own greed and cupidity. So, in as kindly a manner as I could manage, I explained to Mr. Holbrook that as matters then stood he had not in my opinion produced any proof that Kurt Robbins had defrauded him, his company, or anyone, or that he had been guilty of committing any other criminal offense.

"Assuming that Robbins did find valuable uranium deposits on your land," I went on, "—which is something he need not prove and which you people can scarcely ever be able to finally disprove —wasn't it entirely natural and businesslike that he should act to protect his discovery by buying up your company's stock? All he needed to be able to do that was money. Wouldn't you have done the same thing? In fact he could point to his heavy stock purchases as rather persuasive evidence that he *did* discover uranium on your land. Also, when you flatly turned down his proposition, wasn't it equally natural—or at least legal—for him to take his profit and run?"

"Perhaps," Walter Holbrook grudgingly admitted, shifting uneasily in his chair.

The relentless D.A. closed in. "After all, it was *you* men who tried to short-circuit Robbins by finding his uranium without him,"

I pressed on. "To call a spade a spade, weren't you trying to freeze him out of his discovery? Weren't you men trying to profit, and exclusively, from important information he had confided to you? Let's face it. These are all questions any competent defense attorney would throw at you, and throw at you hard, if Robbins were ever prosecuted."

"Oh, Lord," Walter Holbrook said, mopping his brow.

"If I may say so, Mr. Holbrook, your main complaint seems to be that he outsmarted you at your own game." I paused to let this sink in. "As a matter of fact, Robbins seems rather to have banked shrewdly on your doing just what you did. Quite a plan, quite a plan. . . . If this is a fraud, it is one of the most subtle and airtight ones I have ever seen or heard of. And I've run into a few."

"But look at the *money* we've lost!" Walter Holbrook said, hunching his shoulders and spreading out both hands, palms up, in a most un-executive-like gesture.

I quickly slammed the door on that. "Your losses strike me as being largely paper losses. I assume that you people still have your stock. Surely you have enough faith in the future of your own company to hang on and weather the storm. Or would you men prefer to publicly testify in effect that you lack this faith? Your stock might really nose-dive if you did such a thing." I paused. "But perhaps I'd better not be suggesting things that are more properly matters of company policy—your own resourceful staff of lawyers is fully capable of that." (I could not resist this little professional shaft.) "After all, you came here with a criminal complaint to lay before me as D.A. so I'll try to stick to analyzing that."

Walter Holbrook slumped lower in his chair. It was rough, giving it to him that way, but it had to be done. I felt like a gruff old country doctor removing a mustard plaster from the chest of a quaking child. It was easier in the long run if you just ripped it off.

"Generally speaking, Mr. Holbrook, an indictable criminal fraud requires the combined presence of three elements: an actual fraud or misrepresentation of an existing fact or situation; a reliance on this fraud by the victim to his injury; and an enrichment of the suspected villian as a natural result of his fraud." I guess I am something of a pedagogue at heart. I was enjoying my little lecture on the subject of fraud. But Walter Holbrook was not sharing it.

"You mean," he said huskily, "I don't make out a criminal case because we can't prove the first and third elements, regardless of our losses?"

"You should have been a lawyer, Mr. Holbrook," I said, grading him an A. "You've put your finger on the two basic weaknesses of your case. Especially the first."

"Humph . . ." he grunted. "I wasn't such a hot lawyer with that snake Robbins. I flunked that test."

"Perhaps you met a better lawyer," I ventured.

"Perhaps!" he flared. "You're damned right I did!"

"The only possible way I can see to begin to hold Robbins for fraud is to show that his uranium samples came from somewhere else," I continued. "But that is something which, under our American law, the People would first have to prove—not something that Robbins would first have to disprove. It might even help some, as a starter, if you could show he'd ever worked at or visited one of the big Canadian or African uranium mines; or, better yet, that his hot uranium samples came from one of them. . ."

Walter Holbrook nodded glumly. "Our attorneys warned me about this proof business. But they made me come here, anyway. No, we can't prove where the lousy stuff came from. Like peroxide blondes, pitchblende is pitchblende, wherever you find it. As I've already suggested, all of it looks like a damn poor grade of coal. And we've already worked the African and Canadian angles. Even sent his leering, smiling picture around. Nobody ever saw him before. The guy must've crept out at night from under a damp plank." He brightened a little and sat up. "But couldn't our Atomic Energy Commission or Congress or *someone* force him to tell them where he got his damned uranium? God, our country needs the stuff, man!"

"Not under any present law or procedure in this country of which I am aware," I said. "And in any event, that would be a matter for the federal authorities, not me." I paused, feeling a wave of pity for the man. "And may I say this, Mr. Holbrook," I went on, "before you carry your complaint any further, might you not pause and reflect how you and your Wilmington associates would appear to the public, the business world, your competitors—not to even mention your own small stockholders—if you men were to take the witness stand and testify to such a story as you have told me?" I paused. "I think you'll agree that certain aspects of it would scarcely tend to glorify the loftiest aspirations of our free enterprise system."

I had plunged the needle pretty far. He nodded his head glumly. "I wish I had a stiff drink," he said.

"But I've got an idea," I went on. "You might bury your pride and try meeting Robbins' own terms—that's if you know where he is. *Give* him his 50 per cent. If he now refuses to accept you might possibly have the opening wedge of a fraud case—though I doubt it. And if he should accept, then—when he showed you the uranium deposit and the big word got headlined around the country, as these things do—this should pull your stock out of its slump and you, Robbins and everyone should live happily ever after. Perhaps even your wife might rally. Remember, the stock went up before on a mere market hunch that something was cooking."

Walter Holbrook shook his head dolefully. "Hell, we've tried that. Guess I forgot to tell you—we've had detectives trailing Robbins ever since his last visit. He now calls 'em by their first names and invites them to drink with him. And I'm beginning to suspect they're accepting. And guess where the great Robbins is holed up? Over in Paris shacked up with some foreign movie actress, the lucky devil, wading up to his hips in vintage champagnes—and all on our dough! Two days ago we cabled our acceptance of his original terms."

"Did he answer?"

"*Answer!*" Walter Holbrook shouted, suddenly pounding my desk with his fist. "He cabled back collect. This was his answer: 'Dear Holbrook: We're in bed. Wish you were here. This place is expensive so my terms have jumped to 75 per cent. Next time higher. Confidentially yours, Robbins.' " Walter Holbrook paused. "It—it's diabolical. The man is stark, raving mad."

"Like a fox," I said. "But I'm afraid that as things stand there's nothing my office can do about it. I'm sorry."

Walter Holbrook slumped back in his chair, a beaten man. "I'm in hot water from here clean to Wilmington." He wagged his head. "You're sure you've got nothing more to suggest?"

I was sorry to see any man in such a jam. "Well," I smiled, "possibly two things. Both are long shots."

"Name 'em," Walter Holbrook muttered.

"Keep looking for Robbins' uranium till you find it."

"And if I don't?"

"Then—heaven help you—turn author and write a bang-up mystery movie scenario for Hollywood."

"Movie scenario!" he bridled. "About what?"

"About your strange adventures with Prospector Robbins. You've already got most of the dialogue on your tape recorder. And I've already got a title for you: *The Great Uranium Hoax*." I reached into my phone stand and quickly dredged up a bottle and a glass. "But before you embark upon the hideous travail of authorship I suggest that you try a slug of this cooking whisky— for years the favorite of many peasants of extinction. You asked for it."

Walter Holbrook reddened and glared hard at me for several moments. Then he broke into a broad grin. With a shaking hand he poured himself a stiff drink. He raised his glass aloft and smiled at me gamely.

"Skoal, pal," he said. "I don't like your diagnosis but I like your medicine. Here's uranium in your eye."

"Drink hearty, Chum," I replied, vowing that someday we two really *would* go fishing.

Chapter 19

BUTTON, BUTTON, LITTLE MAN

It was a hot moonlit Saturday night in July—so hot that a hardy northern people, conditioned to eternal cold, did not even try to sleep; instead they perversely crowded the hot and fly-blown taverns to hear Bing and Gary on the juke box or, more sensibly, went driving among the Norway pines along the shore of cold Lake Superior or lay on the cool beaches or else just sat perspiring on their porches and lawns.

Doris Smith, aged fifteen, lay uncovered and sleepless in the bedroom of her home on L'Anse Avenue waiting for her parents to come home. She heard the neighboring schoolhouse clock endlessly boom midnight, she went to the bathroom and got a drink, then she dozed a little, then she heard the clock strike one. She lay there in a half doze sleepily listening to the drowsy slow creak of the neighboring porch swings and the fitful chirp of the crickets. She glanced at her alarm clock, lit by the moonlight streaming through her open bedroom window. One-fifteen. Mama and Daddy should be home soon. Did she just hear them downstairs? No, they always called to her. Anyway, the doors were locked; there was nothing to be afraid of. . . . Again she fell into an uneasy doze.

"*Psst!*"

Doris awoke and froze in her bed. There stood a strange man— a naked man—approaching her bed, a warning finger to his lips. "Sh-h-h," he whispered.

"What do you want?" she whispered tensely.

The man remained silent and continued slowly to approach her bed. Doris lay there watching him in terror. As he neared the

201

edge of her bed he passed through a shaft of moonlight exposing himself in all his male splendor. Realizing this he suddenly crouched down against the edge of her bed. "Don't be afraid," he whispered. "I won't hurt you."

Just then there was the roar of a car motor outside and the bedroom was suddenly lit up by car headlights reflected from the garage doors below.

"Who's that!" the man whispered.

"Mama and Daddy," Doris managed to reply.

The man silently scrambled from the bedside and disappeared through the bedroom door. Doris could hear him hurriedly padding down the carpeted stairs. In a few minutes the Smiths came into their house.

"Mama! Daddy!" Doris shouted.

Doris' parents came running to her room and found her sitting up in bed, half hysterical with fear and shock.

"What happened?"

Between her sobs Doris blurted out her brief story.

"Did he—did he touch you?" the mother asked.

"N-no," Doris said. "You came just in time."

"Did you know him? Could you tell who it was?" the father asked.

"Y-yes," Doris answered.

"Who was it?"

"It was Toody. I saw him in the moonlight."

"Toody Breck?"

"Yes."

In ten minutes the police arrived and got the story. Toody Breck was the unmarried brother of a next door neighbor of the Smiths. He worked and lived in a neighboring town and occasionally spent the week end with his brother. The police and the father went to the darkened Breck house. The married brother finally appeared sleepily at the door.

"Where's Toody?" the police asked.

"Who? Oh, Toody . . ." The brother pointed to his garage in

the side yard. "He's in there sleeping on a spare cot. Why? What's wrong?"

Grimly: "That's what we came to find out."

The police approached the garage carefully with drawn pistols. One of them rapped on the window. No reply. Another rap.

"Who's there?" came a sleepy voice from the garage.

"The police," came the answer. "We want to see you."

After a pause: "Come on in, then," answered the sleepy voice.

"Turn on the light and open the door!"

"Okay," the voice answered, stifling a yawn.

The lights went on and the garage door swung open. There stood a yawning Toody Breck—quite naked—holding in his hands, of all things, a stuffed rabbit and a sewing basket full of buttons and odds and ends.

"Glad you came," he said, thrusting these strange objects at the police. "Was lying here. Couldn't sleep. Heard a car come in. Right after that heard some noise and the sound of running—so I went out and found these things lying by that open window." He pointed at the Smith house and a police flashlight lit up an open window in the basement. "Decided to bring these things in till morning. Guess I must have dozed just before you came."

One of the police turned to Mr. Smith. "Do you recognize these things?"

"Yes. The rabbit belonged to Doris as a child. I believe the other is an old sewing basket of my wife's—we kept them stored by that basement window."

"Was your basement window closed when you left tonight?"

"Yes, and locked. We never open it."

Toody Breck stretched and yawned elaborately and looked at Doris' father. "What happened, Smitty?" he coolly inquired. "Someone try to rob your house?"

The father stood staring at Toody Breck. "Why you dirty bastard!" he cried, lunging at him.

The police pulled them apart and took Toody Breck to the county jail. They booked him on a charge of suspicion of assault with intent to rape. Questioned further he refused to budge from his original story. On Monday morning the busy D.A. cleaned up the accumulated minor woe of the weekend—drunk drivers, wife beaters, etc.—and finally huddled with the Iron Bay police to determine what if any criminal charge should be placed against Toody Breck.

There was no doubt that whoever entered the Smith house that night was bent on no good; his actions and his few spoken words and his, should I say, general appearance clearly showed that he had some sort of sexual designs on Doris. If that person was Toody Breck he also knew that her parents were out because they remembered seeing him downtown about midnight. But the fact was, whoever it was, he had not laid a hand on her. True, he had not had time to, but to constitute a foolproof case of attempted rape or assault with intent to rape it would have been much better had there been some overt act, some offensive touching, and here there was none. The fact was that it was rather difficult to predict just *what* sort of sexual designs he entertained. (The possibilities are more extensive than the average sheltered citizen might think.) On the other hand there was no doubt that our man was Toody Breck—Doris had seen and recognized him in the moonlight and again in the reflected car lights.

What to do? What to do? Here was a cool, bold, crafty character that richly needed disciplining. We couldn't have a man like that wandering the midnight streets. But I did not want him to possibly slip away from us by bringing a rape-type or other sexual charge against him that we could not back up by adequate proof. Almost any jury might and probably would convict him of whatever we charged. That was not my worry. But speculation on the man's intent did not take the place of proof. Would a careful judge let the case go to a jury on this evidence, and letting it, would an appellate court sustain a guilty verdict on appeal? I explained my doubts to the police.

"But we can't just let the bastard go," the chief boomed in his deep bass voice.

"I know, I know, Mac," I said, pondering. "That's just what I *don't* want to do."

"I wonder why he took those damned buttons and that old stuffed rabbit?" mused the chief.

"I dunno—probably to cover up," I said. "By the way—could you pick up any fingerprints off the stuff?"

"Naw—the rabbit showed nothing at all and the sewing basket and cellar window and sill were all smudged and dusty—" The chief paused. "Say, Johnny, what're you smiling at?" he asked me.

I slapped my leg. "Mac, I think we've got it," I answered. "I think we've got a felony charge we can make stick against 'Bare Ass' Breck." (By that time we had a pet name for him.)

"What's that, Johnny?" the chief inquired.

"Look," I said. "Whoever took that junk from the Smith basement probably did it to try to cover up his real reason for entering the Smith house. Right?"

Dubiously: "Yes, I guess that's right."

"But the stuff belonged to the Smiths and, however old and junky, was their property and therefore the subject of larceny, wasn't it?"

"Right," the chief answered, breaking into a slow smile of comprehension.

"So when Bare Ass hurriedly grabbed up this junk as he scrambled out the Smith window—to try to cover up his *real* reason for entering—wasn't he thereby providing us with a beautiful airtight charge against him, namely, the felony of breaking and entering in the nighttime with intent to commit larceny?"

"Boy oh boy," said the giant chief, joyfully hugging the little rabbit. "If we crack this one, Johnny, I'll present this rabbit to you—with all *four* feet—as a goodluck charm."

The trial took a day. Little Doris came through beautifully on direct examination. But on cross-examination by the defendant's lawyer she really nailed down the lid. Breck's lawyer had been carefully purring along, toying with her gently, trying with kid gloves to shake her story—especially her identification of Toody Breck.

"Are you *sure* it was the defendant you saw that night in your bedroom?" he asked her for the umpteenth time. (Evidence of the bedroom scene was admissible as part of the *res gestae* and to identify and show the defendant's unlawful presence in the house.)

"Positively," Doris answered.

"But if you recognized the defendant in your bedroom, why didn't you tell him so then?" Breck's attorney asked her suavely, taking a new tack.

Doris glanced fearfully at Toody Breck who sat at his table glaring defiantly at the far wall. "I was afraid," Doris answered in her small, little-girl voice.

"Afraid of what?" pressed the lawyer, falling neatly into his own trap. I held my breath for the boomerang.

"Afraid of what *else* he might do with me after he raped me— if he thought that I knew him," Doris answered.

"I object to that answer as unresponsive and prejudicial, and move that it be stricken!" Breck's lawyer shouted, sore wounded.

"Objection overruled," the judge wryly said. Breck's lawyer had asked for it.

I glanced at the jury. Each member was sitting stiffly erect, a grim smile on his face—accompanied by an expression that read "Guilty as Charged" as clearly as though it were printed there in neon lights.

After I had finished putting in the People's case the defendant took the stand and, skillfully led by his attorney, repeated his original story that he had not entered the Smith house but had merely found the rabbit and the sewing basket outside. If he could sell this to the jury it was a complete defense. On cross-examination I could not shake him from this story. It was his defense and he stuck to it. I hoped that he was also stuck with it. So I put in his criminal record—which consisted mostly of disorderly conduct and other misdemeanor offenses, with no sex offenses—and reluctantly let him go.

"The defense rests," his lawyer said.

During my opening argument the jury remained stiff and grimfaced—and very attentive—a bad sign for Toody Breck. They did not even smile when, always the wag, I tried to make a ponderous joke about the basket of buttons: something about hoping that he meant to use them to properly clothe himself on any future nocturnal forays. The defense lawyer then took over and struggled manfully, talking about the law of reasonable doubt, the hot weather, orating beautifully about the sacred safeguards of the Constitution, waving the American flag—talking about everything but the naked facts in his case. The jurors grew if possible even more stony-faced. The discouraged lawyer finally sat down and gulped a glass of water. He had earned his fee.

Judge Belden glanced at the clock. It was slightly after four. The judge looked at me. "Does the prosecuting attorney think that he can make his closing argument in time for me to charge the jury this afternoon?"

I arose: "The People will be very brief, Your Honor," I said.

"Very well," Judge Belden said. "We shall take a five-minute recess—and then proceed."

During intermission I ignited another Italian cigar, went to the can, combed back my drooping forelock, and planned a fishing trip for the next day, a Saturday.

Recess over I arose before the jury to make my closing argument. "Ladies and gentlemen," I began. The jury remained as grim and impassive as ever. For a few seconds, that is. I was pouring it on at a great rate when suddenly I noticed one of the lady jurors smile and glance at her female companion. Soon the faces of the entire jury were wreathed in smiles. Perplexed, I kept doggedly ramming home my points. Soon the jurors were practically laughing out loud and several nudged each other. Perhaps, I thought, they were just getting my button joke so, crass opportunist that I was, I got off another clumsy one on the buttons. This time I really convulsed them and, getting into the spirit of the thing, I wound up my argument in a shower of falling buttons.

Judge Belden charged the still mirthful jury. The smiling jury retired and popped back in ten minutes and smilingly delivered a verdict of guilty as charged. It was all very strange. As they filed out to go home they turned and smiled at me. Not to be outdone I grinned right back. Wonderful, good-humored, appreciative, sensible people. In view of the implications of the case the judge gave the defendant a pretty stiff prison sentence, little Doris went home with her parents, and true to his promise Big Mac, the chief of police, lumbered over to my table and presented me with the stuffed rabbit. "Here's your memento of the only rapist in history that got convicted for stealing a rabbit," he said.

"Thanks, Chief," I said, taking the rabbit.

Then the chief thrust the sewing basket of buttons at me. "Better take these buttons along, too, Johnny," he grinned.

"Buttons? What for?" I asked, puzzled.

"Just in case you continue to have trouble with your zipper when you argue cases like this to a jury."

I looked down and saw just why the absent-minded D.A. had convulsed the jury after the recess. "Thanks, Mac," I said, reaching red-faced for the buttons—and the yawning zipper.

Chapter 20

IN A MIST

SOME OF YOU may be mildly wondering what sort of an egotistic monster is writing this book. "Look!" you are doubtless grumbling, "why is it this fellow Traver always contrives to tell us about the big cases he *won!* Why doesn't he tell us more often about the times he stubbed his toe and lost?" It is a fair question, and to keep from appearing to brag on this score I must instead brag a little on another. The reason is simple: I *lost* but one felony case during my last ten years as D.A. Most of my felony losses prior to that were recorded in earlier D.A. stories I have written, so I can't very well rehash them, and, alas, by now I've conveniently forgotten the details of the others, they happened so long ago.

While writing these disorderly memoirs I have sometimes almost wished I had lost more of my recent cases so that I could tell about them here. It might tend to make this narrative more interesting, more balanced—and possibly even more instructive. At the same time it might also permit its author to appear less of a stuffed shirt, less drearily infallible, less of a precious little Napoleon among D.A.'s. (Behold! Here is a former D.A. bewailing that he hadn't lost more cases! Mark it well, for in this incarnation you are not apt to again witness such a phenomenon. Now you have seen everything!)

At least this circumstance of my losing so few felony cases serves one useful purpose: it illustrates beautifully, almost brutally well, my uneasy suspicion, growing into a conviction, that our present system of determining criminal guilt or innocence is in

209

many respects imperfect and unjust and should be changed. The Lord knows that in saying this I am not trying to be sensational or flippantly cute. This is no District Attorney Confidential. I've pondered the subject for years and I venture to speak from considerable experience. Let me explain myself.

First off, it is remarkable and also disheartening to realize how much depends upon the lawyers in the trial of a criminal case; upon the D.A. and his legal opponent, their relative competence or incompetence, whether they are on the ball or not. Too often, I feel, the result in the trial of a given case depends entirely too much upon this theoretically irrelevant factor. I have a companion grievance. Most big criminal trials in our day have become nothing more or less than a talent show, a forensic duel between two glittering legal personalities—however thrilling the duel or compelling the personalties—with the judge reduced to a master of ceremonies and the bewildered jury frequently awarding the prize to the side which puts on the better show. This would all be very well and even amusing if it did not happen to involve vital interests of the public as well as the fate of an anxious defendant. As it is we happen to be dealing with a clash between two of the most pressing concerns of our lives: the public welfare and the freedom and liberty of an individual human being.

This complaint does not apply to all criminal cases, of course. There are some prosecutions that the D.A. is occasionally forced to bring where the natural equities are so far with the defendant that the D.A. could never win, however brilliant; others so revolting to the public conscience that the D.A. could never lose, however stupid. Such cases are not in the majority, however, and the bulk of criminal trials usually present a fairly close issue of disputed fact and law. There's the rub. But whatever the case I have long been disturbed at the way the outcome can be influenced— yes, even manipulated—by the adroitness of counsel, including the adroitness of the D.A. himself.

Stated bluntly a good D.A. is a legal specialist in a complex field. He is an expert. He has learned the hard way—by trying criminal cases—the dope that isn't and can't be printed in books. When he gets experienced enough and good enough he is awfully hard to beat. The average lawyer who but occasionally undertakes the defense of a criminal case doesn't have a fair chance against him. He simply doesn't know his way around. It is a case of Ben Hogan stacked against the pedestrian pro at your local golf club. Ben could usually beat him using only a putter. This situation may be all right in the dreary world of golf, but in a courtroom it is unfair, an unfairness which in turn breeds another inequity: as between defendants it creates an unfair advantage for the lucky or well-placed or gang-sponsored defendant who, regardless of his guilt, can raise enough money to hire the services of an equally adroit defense magician. (Get back there, soapbox!) And when this happens the resulting trial is apt to be more of an indoor carnival than a sober judging of guilt or innocence; a bitter clash of a pair of panting and posturing and easily wounded legal prima donnas. During the subsequent absorbing drama Justice, a rather modest lady, is frequently crowded into the pit or forgotten altogether.

I am certain that as D.A. I have convicted in cases defended by inexperienced or inept counsel that I would have lost to a legal smoothie. There were times when I was tempted to take some of these poor groping inexperienced fellows aside and tell them in a fatherly way how to do it—the way, the opening, the argument, the revealing question—all seemed so apparent to me. How could they miss it? They missed it, of course, because they weren't trained to see it, or seeing it, to appreciate its significance. Moreover I am also morally certain that with my experience and training I could have successfully defended most of these identical cases against these same gropers, had they instead been D.A. This is not being immodest; I am not here talking on that level; it is a simple statement of fact and I wish it weren't true. I'd feel a lot better about the work to which I have devoted so much of my legal career.

Time and time again, as I naturally began to meet more fledgling lawyers spreading their trial wings, I became convinced that the deciding factor in their losing trials was simply my superior experience, nothing more. I swear the criminal element should have long ago banded together and raised a slush fund to hoist me to hell out of office. All these thoughts do not comfort me—and I can suggest no cure unless perhaps the whole *competitive* theory of prosecution and defense is scrapped and the guilt or innocence of criminal defendants is henceforth examined into, say, by some sort of an impartial board of inquiry. I would still preserve the jury, of course, as the ultimate judges of guilt or innocence. But the present *star* system of trial, these thrilling courtroom battles of gifted professional pleaders seeking to build or enhance a reputation, to extend a record of conviction or acquittals, to gain some political notoriety or advantage—all this may tend to make an exciting show for the bystanders and sensational newspapers and TV but has damn little to do with the business at hand: the quest for Truth and Justice.

I recall one criminal case that I won, believe it or not, simply because I had a timely drink of whisky. If I hadn't had that drink of whisky a luckless defendant who would otherwise almost surely have gone free instead went to prison. It was as simple as that and the thought has haunted me sometimes in the still of the night. The case illustrates, almost too well, one of the main points I have just tried to make. It was a murder case and I don't recall too much about the trial facts now except that there was a long list of witnesses on both sides; the defense was self-defense; and the opposing lawyer and I had tugged and hauled and objected for days to get in the mass of conflicting evidence. It was a hard case, rather close on its facts, and it was late afternoon of the fifth day when I again muttered, "The People rest," and the tired opposing lawyer muttered, "The Defense rests"—both of us nearly on the ropes with exhaustion—and Judge Belden sent us packing home to get a good night's rest before the big argument the next day.

I know of no fatigue quite like trial fatigue, and in my day I've chased game, fish—and mermaids—all over this Peninsula. After a long, arduous trial one is not only physically tired, but the over-churned mind itself seems to grow buttery and numb; the emotions become blunted; and the whole effect is one of a sort of stupid giddiness, like a tired old boxer reduced to a sparring bag.

At any rate, in my own stupid giddiness I stopped at a roadhouse on my way home to try to banish my trial flutters with a leisurely double Scotch. *One* certainly wouldn't hurt me, I told myself, and then I would slowly eat—and so home to bed.

As I sat there sipping my lonely drink, trying to put the whirling thoughts of my case out of my mind, a man emerged from the shadows and quietly sat at a battered upright piano against the far wall and began to finger the keyboard. There were little rippling blurts of notes. "Hm . . . listen to that left hand," I murmured. "Ah, a disciple of Earl Hines." Then he leaned negligently away and began to play in earnest. I held my glass poised. He hadn't played three measures before I recognized "In a Mist" by Bix Biederbecke, one of my favorite jazz piano pieces. But this fellow was *really* playing it, just like that audacious old man with a horn, Bix, did on his precious battered old piano record that I had home virtually preserved in a time capsule.

I rang for the lurking barmaid. "Give that lovely man what he wants," I told her. "And please tell him not to stop." The Scotch was divine; the music heavenly. After playing two or three more of my old favorites, during which I felt morally obliged to have just one more double Scotch, the piano man came over.

"Hi," he smiled. "Thanks for the drink."

"Hi," I said. "Won't you sit down and have another?"

"I will if you will," he said, sitting opposite me. He was a ravaged-looking character, possessing the telltale coppery glow and moist pursed lips of a dedicated lush.

"I don't mind if I do," I said, blissfully forgetting about both my cases—my case in court and my case of courtroom jitters. "Look, you either knew Bix or you know his phonograph record," I said. "That was awfully nice going."

"Both," he said wearily. "Over a million years ago." He didn't want to talk about it and sat silently turning his glass.

"Well, anyway, here's bumps to a beautiful piano man," I said. *"Dolores!"* I shouted. "Two more for the bears in the buckwheat!"

He looked at me uncuriously. "What do you do?" he asked, making talk.

"I'm a sort of a kind of a cop," I said. I didn't want to talk about it either. There was music in the air—tomorrow was time enough to play D.A. again.

I shall draw a charitable veil over the rest of that misty musical evening. The piano man and I moved over to the upright and tarried and reminisced over our doublers and the longer we tarried the lovelier he played. The man had it. And he could also drink ambidexterously, never missing a note. He'd had lots of practice at that, I guessed, because drinking seemed to be his trouble, all right. But that night it was good trouble; it made good music. As Robert W. Service would say, "My God! how that man could play!" And my God how Bix, Jr. and I consumed doublers, far into the night, two starved and happy men.

The next morning I tottered into court with pounding temples, dark glasses, a two-day beard and a fantastically soiled shirt, reeking of wintergreen, peppermint, spearmint and all the other mints mingled with heavy overtones of Scotch peat. (This was in the primitive days before chlorophyll gum.)

"Hear ye, hear ye, hear ye," the sheriff sang—and the quaking D.A. was tossed to the lions.

"May it please the Court, and ladies and gentlemen of the jury," I croaked. I didn't fare so badly in my opening argument because that, as always, was mostly a review of the evidence. And I had taken copious trial notes, which I followed slavishly, like a stagestruck child who'd forgotten his lines and had to read his Christmas poem. Done with that I groped to my seat and the able defense attorney got up and proceeded to give one of the most brilliant, devastating arguments of his career. He ripped and slashed into my case, mounting argument upon argument, while I took rebuttal notes furiously, biting my coated tongue. When he was done I felt like joining the jury and voting for an acquittal. He had been superb but it was a lead-pipe cinch he hadn't listened to or been "In a Mist" the night before. I sat there in a sick and defeated daze.

"The People will now make their closing argument," Judge Belden prompted me, looking at me with suspicious concern over the tops of his rimless glasses. "That is, unless for any reason they wish to waive."

To have waived the argument would have been to throw the case, and I had never thrown a case in my life. I lurched to my feet and again shambled before the jury. "L-ladies and gen'emen," I began, and paused. There was so very, very much to say, and so little time to say it. But I was stricken dumb; the words didn't seem to come. I *knew* what I wanted to say but it was as though I were standing spectrally outside of myself, listening to some fatuous stranger muttering to the jury. Groping for words, I at length automatically mumbled a few legal platitudes, instinctively, like a stricken boxer sore hurt but still keeping his guard up.

"My Gawd!" I said to myself, gaping. For there was the entire jury, box and all, turned upside down, *grinning* at me. Oops! The jury was revolving now, turning over and over, faster and faster, in grotesque Fourth of July cartwheels, all the while grinning and grinning and grinning . . . "Duck, Traver—they're spinning the other way now . . . Lord, the lights are going out!" I lurched to one side and crashed blindly against the stenographer's desk and managed to turn toward the judge. "Sick, sick," I said. "Wanna recess."

It was the opposing lawyer, bless him, who grabbed me and led me to my office and locked the door and sat me in a chair and loosened my collar and then my shoelaces. I sighed and sat back, thinking he was going to give me a shave and a shine. "Shick," I muttered. "Too mush work." I wanted to curl up on the floor. The attorney reached in his old leather briefcase—always the lawyer's Aladdin's Lamp—and produced a pint of pantherized cooking whisky. "Cut out the bull, Johnny, and take this hair of the dog that bit you. I'll get some water. Don't try to fool an old campaigner like me—I knew your trouble the moment I laid eyes on you this morning."

"I don't know whash you're talkin' about," I tittered giddily, "but anyway hersh bumps, skoal, thanksh million, Erin go bra, Gaw blesh you." I tilted the bottle and played a long trumpet solo to better days.

In fifteen minutes I was back before the jury pawing and snorting like a fixed horse in the fifth at Pimlico. "You may proceed," Judge Belden smiled, and away I broke from the barrier, up to the first turn before the rest got away from the post.

The whole plausible but false argument of the defendant's lawyer now lay before me like a jigsaw puzzle—a faulty jigsaw puzzle. One by one I removed the pieces and held them up to the jury and explained why they did not fit. I did not rant, I did not rave, I did not foam—I coldly destroyed, piece by piece, section by section, the entire specious fabric of the defense. Judge Belden, not given to pitching bouquets, told me later it was the most masterful argument he had ever heard me make. And the poor man had heard me spout plenty. "Whatever the medicine was you took during recess, I want some." His eyes twinkled. I drew in my breath. "Thanks, Judge," I murmured, hastily putting on my dark glasses.

After the jury had convicted the defendant and the courtroom was deserted, the other lawyer came over and shook my hand. "Congratulations, Johnny," he said, smiling ruefully. "Here I save your goddam miserable life—and then you bounce back and beat the pants off me. What a pal. That's gratitude for you!"

"Thanks, chum." I grinned weakly. "You've been a real pal. Let's go find a drink. You've certainly got a big one coming on me."

(NOTE TO WHOM IT MAY CONCERN: Deponent first being duly sworn on oath deposes and says that he is not now nor has he ever been in the employ of any distillers of spirits or malt beverages, foreign or domestic; nor does deponent now advocate or has he ever advocated the overthrow of law enforcement by recommending that D.A.'s swiggle before they argue their cases. R.T.)

Chapter 21

THE VIOLATOR

THE U. P. in general and Iron Cliffs County in particular constitutes one of the best hunting and fishing regions in Michigan and perhaps rivals any in the country. I say perhaps because, smugly enough, I've never had to *look* elsewhere. And the Lord knows I am not one of those doggedly joyful community-uplifters putting in a free chamber-of-commerce plug for the home team. The fact is I am reluctant to divulge this information and do so only because it is pertinent to what follows. Alas, I sacrifice everything for my art. For my part all wandering gunmen and fishermen can stay to hell out of here. At any rate, as a consequence of its outdoor attractions the game and fish laws frequently take a beating, not to mention the game wardens themselves (besides frequent maulings, three of them have been murdered in my county alone). It follows that the investigation and trial of conservation cases formed a considerable part of my work as D.A.

One of the circumstances that prevents this fabulous neck-of-the-woods from being a leaping paradise for game and fish is the activities of the violator. This pathologically greedy slob works day and night, in season and out, to make sure that he gets more than his share of all game or fish by fair means or foul: dynamiting, netting, head-lighting, spearing—the list is endless. On the few occasions he cannot find anything to slay illegally he will gravely bombard the moon. This charming fellow is a first cousin to the hoggish polph that hordes scarce goods in wartime. He is frequently a man of substance and often belongs to that and this organization and even to this and that club. He sometimes screens his activities by joining a sportsmen's club, the final irony. Operating from this front he is a great one to loudly support resolutions demanding more enforcement in one breath and more game and fish in the next—so that he can hurry out and ravish them.

To the violator a legal bag limit marks an absolute minimum which, if he does not exceed it every time out, casts grave doubts on his virile masculinity. Violating somehow massages his curious juvenile ego: he crows over his ability to outbag other sportsmen; he exults over his ability to outwit the game wardens. He is a giant with the mind of an amoeba and the moral stature of a gnat.

He seems not to have the faintest inkling of what is meant by sportsmanship; the concept genuinely puzzles and dismays him. He does not realize that, from the very nature of things, a sportsman *must* be on his honor; that to violate in the loneliness of the woods is the easiest thing in the world; that the very essence of the pursuit is the triumph over difficulties, frequently self-imposed He is craftily aware, however, that there can't possibly be enough game wardens to follow the violators, just as there can't possibly be enough police to guard every bank and grocery store. And he takes endless advantage of this state of affairs.

When the violator is caught he usually lacks the good grace to take his medicine like the man that he isn't. He is one of Nature's ignoble men. As you may be beginning to suspect, I have nothing but utter contempt for the violator and all his works. The only thing I like about him is that he affords me my favorite gripe. He is so bad he should—*he should be made to live in a large city!* That is the worst fate I can wish on any man. But I grow waspish. On with the case of one lovely violator.

One evening in mid-May two unarmed conservation officers, Saville and Laughton, were patrolling a woods road which runs along Rainbow River some distance south of Iron Bay. There had been rumors of illegal spearing of rainbow trout in the river during the spring spawning run. As Saville drove, Officer Laughton watched the sides of the road for evidence of fresh tire tracks turning off on side roads. At the top of the steep hill before the dip down and across the river itself, Laughton spotted such a fresh

track turning off to the left. Saville stopped the car and Laughton
ran in on the side road. Around the first bend out of sight of the
main road he found a locked and parked car. He took down the
license number and returned and told his fellow officer of his
discovery.

"Let's go look at the brook," Officer Saville poetically suggested.

The officers parked and locked their car and walked down the
hill and cut in to the river on the left. Gaining the river they
found and followed an old fisherman's trail downstream for
quite a distance. By this time it was growing dark and the two
officers sat on a fallen log along the shore and quietly awaited
developments. They made their plans in whispers. The only sound
was the rushing river. Ten minutes passed, twenty minutes, then
half an hour. A night chill had descended with darkness and the
officers sat wondering whether to tough it out.

"Look!" Officer Laughton whispered, clutching Saville's arm.
Downstream about a hundred yards away the firefly gleam of
two lights came winking and bobbing through the intervening
shrubbery. As the lights slowly neared the officers they saw two
men, each bearing a light, one walking slowly upstream in the
water and the other walking along the shore. The officers crouched
farther back in the shadows. As the two men drew closer the
officers saw that the man on the shore was carrying a bag flung
over his shoulder and that the man in the river was splashing
along carrying a spear. They could even hear the occasional clink
of the steel spear grating against the submerged rocks. The two
violators slowly drew nearer and nearer. . . .

"We're conservation officers!" Saville shouted, both officers
starting forward, Saville into the river after his man, Laughton
after the man with the sack. The latter dropped his sack and
turned and fled back along the trail, Laughton tight on his heels.
As Saville jumped into the icy river the man with the spear drew
it up, aimed it javelin fashion, and hurled it at the officer. Officer
Saville ducked just as the spear whistled past his neck and clanked
on the rocks behind him. The man turned and ran for the bank,
Saville close after him. Just as the man was clambering up the
bank Saville clutched a strap of the packsack he was carrying and

dragged him back into the river. The two men stood there knee deep in the icy water and grappled in the darkness.

Meanwhile Officer Laughton had overtaken his man and flung him to the ground. As he groped to light his flashlight to examine his quarry he heard a frantic scream from upstream: "Jesus Christ, Lottie, help me! He's trying to drown me!" Laughton fled his man and tore upstream to his partner while his violator scrambled off into the darkness. Arriving, all he could see was the solitary man crouching down over the rushing black water. Laughton made a running flying tackle at the man, from the shore, and hurled him to one side. Officer Saville then emerged from the rushing water, spitting and choking, nearly done in.

Laughton fought it out with the man, who kept furiously trying to drag him in to the bank. Laughton managed to grab Saville's arm and the powerful man dragged both of them in. The man turned, still full of fight, and Laughton recognized him. "Pelto, the traveling man!" he shouted. This discovery seemed to calm him down enough so that Laughton could help his tottering partner out of the water. Once out Saville could scarcely stand up, and began coughing and throwing up. Pelto thereupon took off again, pulling Laughton after him up the steep bank. Saville, game to the core, grabbed up the evidence—the fallen sack—and came staggering after them, coughing and retching.

Laughton managed to hold Pelto until Saville caught up and then the raging Pelto towed them both up the steep hill. Several times Saville fell down with weakness and nausea, but still clung gamely to his precious sack. Halfway up the hill the officers heard a car start and gun on its way. That would be Pelto's partner escaping. At last they gained the locked conservation car. By this time Saville was so spent that Laughton had to support him with one hand and restrain Pelto with the other. He had to let go of one or the other to unlock the car. He released Pelto who turned and broke for the woods. His wet hip boots weren't designed for sprinting and Laughton overtook him in 50 feet and brought him down and hauled him back to the car. He guarded Pelto in the back seat while Saville, shivering violently and wretchedly sick, somehow managed to drive the car in to the jail. Depositing Pelto there, Saville was taken immediately to the hospital and put to bed.

Officer Laughton and another officer then returned to the scene of the wild arrest and found a carbide light and the spear in the water near where he had pulled Pelto off the submerged Saville. The burlap sack was found to contain three large rainbow trout, the bloody spear marks still fresh in them. They were carted off to a deep freeze to await Pelto's trial.

This placid rural idyll confronted me when I came down to the office the next morning. A D.A. never knows just what will greet him on the morrow—except that it won't be good. . . . Officer Laughton told me the harrowing story and further told me that the defendant Pelto had a previous record for illegally spearing rainbow trout. He also told me that Pelto had acted like a wild man. Laughton, an active young man of nearly 200 pounds, had had all he could do to subdue him. Pelto, considerably older, was even a bigger bruiser. Saville, of slight build, weighed around 150 pounds. In sheer guts, however, I guess he weighed all of 1500.

We waited several days for Saville to recover, which he did, and then arrested Pelto for an aggravated assault. There were brutal implications in the case that might have warranted a murder charge, had Saville been killed. It was not nice to contemplate what might have happened had Laughton been out of earshot of his partner's frenzied SOS.

Pelto finally pleaded guilty and told who his partner was. It was the same man whose license number was on the parked car. (We were saving *that* intelligence for a little surprise in the event of a trial.) He was fined heavily for his part in the illegal spearing. Then, after a long and spirited presentence discussion, Pelto was sentenced to a long probation without jail, a $500 fine, and forbidden to hunt or fish for a period of two years. It was little enough punishment, the Lord knows, and if it were not for the pleading of his loyal wife and the forgiving natures of the two plucky conservation officers he would surely have gone to jail.

NOTICE

Are there any addled young men who'd like a job as game warden in Michigan? The hours are long but the pay is good—and we guarantee there won't ever be a dull moment. Applicant must be *able-bodied*, fearless—and preferably able to work under water!

Chapter 22

POP GOES THE JURY!

IT ALL STARTED quietly enough as a routine drunk driving trial in justice court in Chippewa. The defendant was Jacob Niskanen, a dignified old Finn from the iron-mining ghost town of Nestoria. He sat quiet and unblinking as I rolled in the People's testimony.

It seemed that while he was driving through Chippewa the Saturday night before he had rammed his car into the rear end of a parked car; that, amidst much clashing of gears, he had then backed away from this annoying obstacle and continued calmly on his way; that the outraged occupants of the rammed car had given chase; that they had overtaken the defendant's weaving car on the outskirts of Chippewa and forced it to the curb. It further seemed that the defendant had thereupon staggered from his car and taken off cross country in the general direction of one of the iron mines; that two of the men in the rammed car had continued the chase on foot; that they had finally overtaken the fleeing defendant, who had thereupon stood his ground and taken a highly successful swipe at each of his pursuers; that they nevertheless held him there until the cops had come and led him away; and, finally, that he was as drunk as a skunk.

The D.A. presented this sad and harrowing tale to a stolid six-man justice court jury by five witnesses: the three occupants of the rammed car, consisting of another old Finn called Kivisaari and his daughter and son-in-law, Mr. and Mrs. Willis Taskila, and the two arresting cops. (The defendant could also have been charged with leaving the scene of an accident—"hit and run"—and also assault and battery, but the People, who must stop somewhere, were quite willing to settle for drunk driving.)

"The People rest," I finally said in the quaint legal jargon that meant that I had completed my proofs. I thumped to my seat to demonstrate that the weary representative of the People was "resting." I sat looking wistfully out the courtroom window at the big dumpling clouds folding slowly across the sky before a soft west wind. What a day to fish! I was bored to tears and feeling sorry for myself. Judge Williams turned to the defendant and cleared his throat.

"Mr. Niskanen," he said, "you do not have a lawyer so it is my duty to explain to you that the time has now come for you to put in such defense as you may have. You may now call any witnesses you may have and you may, if you wish, also take the stand and testify in your own behalf. Do you understand?"

Old Jacob Niskanen thoughtfully blinked his pale blue eyes. He pursed his lips and finally spoke. He possessed a beautifully modulated bass-baritone voice. "Oh sure, Yudge—you mean it's my turn now for tell *my* story." I perked up my ears. Old Jacob had succinctly cut through all the traditional legal double talk to the core of the situation.

"Well, yes," Judge Williams admitted.

Old Jacob arose and stood straight as an arrow, holding up his right hand for the oath like a field marshal saluting his troops. "I do," he said. He turned and regarded the jury with his kindly eyes with their tiny crisscrossed life wrinkles. "Vell, yentlemen," he began in that lovely voice of his, "it's dis vay. My name is Yacob Niskanen—N-i-s-k-a-n-e-n," he spelled. "Yacob Niskanen come on here from ol' country young man on nineteen-o-seven. He 'Merican citizen long long time. He work many years undergroun' miner. Yacob Niskanen now retired miner on da sosall security." He paused and his voice shook a little. "An' dis be very firs' time his life he ever get pinc'ed by police gop.

"Vun day in mine Yacob Niskanen he's get hit on top his head by chunk of falling ore." Here Jacob paused and tenderly felt the top of his pate. Jacob then shook his finger at the jury to accent his words. "Ever since dat day, yentlemen, Yacob Niskanen he got dat bad pain for his head—buzz, buzz, buzz. Some days pain he so bad he stagger roun' like 'runken man. Funny t'ing—same day he get pinc'ed he's stagger like son-o-bits, dat pain *so-o-o* bad!"

The members of the jury grinned a little but recovered nicely. Jacob turned and pointed an accusing finger at me. "Dis young lawyer fellas—wat he say? He say Yacob Niskanen 'riving his car 'runk; dat he hit nudder car in da nass; dat nudder car he sase Yacob an' ketch Yacob an' Yacob try for run away; dat Yacob hit dem nudder Finn fellas his fist; dat Yacob very very 'runkard man."

Jacob paused and turned his attention back to the jury. "Wat Yacob say? Hm . . . Yacob say he never hit dat nudder car in da nass. Yacob say dat nudder car he's back up quvick into Yacob. Yacob say he never try for run away; he never hit dose nudder Finn peoples his fist; an' he never never be 'runk 'riving on dat day." Jacob paused and delivered his eloquent summary. "Yacob say dis whole monkey bizness case be nudding but da pullsit!"

I stole a look at Judge Williams to see how he was weathering it. The jury wasn't doing too well. Two spots of red glowed on Judge Williams' cheekbones. He rapped his gavel and urgently cleared his throat.

"Mr. Niskanen," he said sternly. "I realize that you have no lawyer, and that the English language is not your native tongue. But there are certain words we do not permit in a courtroom. I must warn you to be more careful of your language. Do you understand?"

Old Jacob was sweet reasonableness itself. He nodded his head in quick agreement and smiled benignly at the judge. "Das okay, Yudge—I only be dis country—le's see—fordy-some year, an' I never have da sances like you going on school. Anyvay I try for talk da best Englis' what I can talkit." Here he frowned and gestured at the People's witnesses. "But Yacob Niskanen don't like dat ven dose vitness peoples tell dat big pullsit story!"

Judge Williams turned to me, his voice grown a trifle shrill. "Does the prosecutor wish to cross-examine the witness?" He was struggling not to have to cite this earnest and dignified old man for contempt of court.

Ordinarily I would have been quite content to let the case rest right there on Jacob's bare denial, and let her go to the jury without further questioning. That would have been smart strategy. But by that time old Jacob had completely charmed me; he was my man. It wasn't that a perverse and somewhat gutty D.A. wanted to tease one of his favorite police-court judges; I simply wanted to hear Jacob's beautiful melodious voice just a little longer. Fishing or no fishing, I hated to see him pass out of my life.

"Why yes, Your Honor, please," I said with bland innocence. "I would like to ask the defendant a few clarifying questions."

Judge Williams shuddered in quiet dismay. "Ah . . ." He squinted a suspicious eye at me. "You may proceed, Mr. Prosecutor," he said with anxious skepticism.

"Mr. Niskanen," I proceeded gaily, "you live in the town of Nestoria, do you not?"

"Dat's right," Jacob answered, nodding agreeably.

"Are you married?"

"No—I'm a vidow man."

"And you live west of here?"

"Dat's right."

"Alone?"

"Dat's right."

"Now you were driving west when you were arrested, were you not?"

"Dat's right."

"So you were on your way home?"

"Dat's right."

Jacob was yessing me to death. I'd have to make him say something else. "Where had you been that day?"

"I be Hematite all dat day."

"Hematite is the next town east of us, is it not?"

"Dat's right."

"So you had already driven through Chippewa once that day, on your way down, and you were on your way through Chippewa for the second time that day when you were arrested—on your way home?"

"You bet. Dat's right." Jacob kept nodding amiably through all this exchange of punts.

"What time did you leave home that day?"

Jacob was quite positive about just when he had launched his busy day. "Nine-dirty o'clock in da morning, A.M.—s'arp on da dot!"

"And you were arrested about that time that night?"

"Dat's right."

"So you had been away from home about twelve hours when you were arrested?"

"By golly—dat's right."

"Why did you drive to Hematite that day?"

"Hm . . . Le's see, now. Oh! Vun Finn man dere he owe me money long time I borrow him. I go dere to find him an' get my money back what he owe me."

"Did you find him, Jacob?"

"No siree!" Jacob shook his head regretfully over his bad luck. Things were getting tough all over.

"What places did you look for him?"

"In tavern places." Confidentially: "He's pretty bad soak man, you know."

"How many taverns did you visit looking for him?"

"All of dem, of course."

I did some rapid mental calculation. The result was faintly astounding. "That would make nineteen taverns you visited in Hematite that day, isn't that right, Jacob?"

"More or less," Jacob admitted with easy indulgence. "Das close enough."

"Jacob, what time did you start hunting your friend in the first tavern?"

"Le's see, I get dere 'bout 'leven o'clock dat morning, A.M.—s'arp on da dot! I start looking right away."

"What time did you visit the nineteenth tavern?"

"Le's see, now. Hm . . . 'Bout nine o'clock dat night, P.M. Finally I give up—no more taverns. I guess my friend he have bad hang-over dat day an' never come for town."

"I see. So you spent ten hours that day visiting the nineteen taverns in Hematite?"

"Dat's right."

"That would average about half an hour to a tavern, wouldn't it?"

Smiling: "Hm . . . By golly, dat's right." Jacob was favorably impressed with my prowess as a rapid calculator.

"Did you eat anything during all that time, Jacob?"

"Oh, I have vun bag salty peanuts. I too busy lookit for dat soak man what owe me money."

"Hm . . . Did you have anything to *drink* in any of the taverns you visited, Jacob?"

"Oh, yes, I meet lotso ol' miner friend I know. Ve talk 'bout dem olden days. Some dey buy me drinks, some I buy dem."

"What did you drink?" I felt sorry to see my skillful legal net closing over this delightful old man. He shortly banished my concern.

"Bop."

"Pop?" I repeated incredulously, foiled.

"Yes siree, bop. I never take vun drop of visky. Not even beer even." Jacob reflected a moment. "Le's see—I never be 'runk now since vay las' Ford Yuly."

"I see. What kind of pop did you drink, Jacob?"

"Dat white bops—wat you call?—soda bop."

"Pop in every tavern?"

Jacob nodded gravely. "Oh, yes—sometimes two three bops vun place."

"So you drank at least nineteen bottles of white soda pop on your visit to the taverns in Hematite, Jacob?"

Airily: "Oh yes. At leas' dat. Maybe dirty-eight." Jacob could add, too.

"Jacob," the mean and unfeeling D.A. said, "you kind of like white soda pop, don't you?"

Jacob gagged at the very thought. He involuntarily pouted out his cheeks, strangled a burp, but recovered magnificently. "Oh yes," he answered gamely, "I love dat white bops."

By that time everybody was having a grand time: the D.A., the jurors, all the witnesses, the few curious spectators, even the janitor—everybody, that is, but an apprehensive Judge Williams. With sound judicial instinct he was waiting for the next blow to fall. And the D.A. was doing his damndest to justify that anxiety.

"Jacob, when you had this accident with Mr. Kivisaari's car— however it happened—why didn't you stop?" I thought that was a pretty shrewd question and I was pleased with myself. I waited complacently for his answer.

Old Jacob shot a quick look at the judge and lowered his voice. Confidentially: "Well, now, young fellas, I 'rink lotso bop dat day, like I yust tell you, an' natserly by den I got to go quvick to bat'room. I got no time to stop."

"I see," I said, foiled again. "Now, Jacob, is it true or not that after the Kivisaari car caught up with you, you got out of your car and started running away, they caught up with you, you struck each of them with your fist, and the officers finally came and took you away?"

Old Jacob shook his head gravely. "No siree, young fellas," he said. "You still got dat all balled up. Is it okay I *show* you how dat really happen?"

"That's okay, Jacob," I said, wondering evilly what was coming next.

Old Jacob stood up before the jury. "Yentlemen," he said, rolling his syllables in his deep booming voice, "like I say I got to go bat'room like son-o-bits. Ven dat—wat you call dat ol' Finnish man?—Mister Kivisaari ketch up my 1941 Sev car in his ol' Ford A model sedan box, I can't vait no any longer. Ve happen to be under street lamp so I valk—not *run*"—here old Jacob walked over and stood close to and facing the far courtroom wall under the clock, speaking to us over his shoulder— "over in da dark an' take a little biss." Here Jacob demonstrated in pantomime a man performing that ancient rite.

"Vile I standing dere taking a little biss dat—wat you call dat little ol' Finnish man?—Mister Kivisaari—I never see *him* before —he come running over on right side for me an' bodder me, so I change hands like dis"—illustrating—"an' give him little puss my free han'. He fall over *boop!* But I no hit him my fist. If I do he never vake up yet to come here on court today an' tell all dese big pullsit lies. No siree!"

The jury was cracking up badly. I didn't dare look at Judge Williams; after all, a gavel *could* be thrown. I yearned for a camera to capture some of the magic of that moment. Old Jacob continued hurling his testimony over his shoulder.

"Vell, I still standing dere taking a little biss an' dat Mister Kivisaari's son-in-law, Mr. Willis Taskila—I never see *him* before neider—he come running over on lef' side for me an' bodder me, too, so I change hands like dis"—illustrating—"an' give him a little puss my free han'. An' he fall over *boop!"* Jacob turned around and dusted his hands. "An' dat's all dere vere to it."

The pantomime over, Jacob with great dignity walked back before the jury. He spread his hands wide. His voice sounded as soft and persuasive as the muted strains of a pipe organ. "Yentl-men, I yust give you da 'traight dope." He smiled tolerantly. "Dis t'ing he can happen to anybody—I guess you fellas all be in dat bad kind fix before." He raised a warning finger aloft. "Country going to hell fast if citizen man can't biss in beace!" He leveled his finger at the jury. "Anyvay, now is your sances to give dat ol' Yacob Niskanen of Nestoria vun good break. Dank you, please."

They did. I heaved a sigh of relief and went fishing. That day even the trout seemed to dance for joy.

Chapter 23

MURDER WILL OUT

THE BRAVE RINGING PHRASE "Murder will out" is surely one of the finest fallacies with which man, the articulate ostrich, comforts his way to the grave. Every prosecutor knows this. Ah yes, savor its dark poetry on your tongue—*"Murder will out!"* Congreve stole it from either Shakespeare or Cervantes who in turn amiably stole it from each other or from Chaucer ("mordre wol out") who stole it from Aeschylus who doubtless stole it from the roof of a damp cave.

The grim fact is that most murders have to be dug out by main strength and awkwardness. Millions of dollars are spent annually, and often vainly, trying to pin murders on their uncooperative perpetrators. With their unblinking denials these murder suspects or murder defendants seem never to have heard of Aeschylus. And the annual toll of totally unsolved murders in this and every other so-called civilized country in the world would stagger the imagination. It would make a dainty project for a thesis in sociology. Our grisly tabulator would resolve his cases into at least three broad categories: where the fact of the murder is apparent but no murderer has been found; where both the fact of the murder and the identity of the murderer remain officially shrouded in doubt; and, finally, in that large class of cases where no legally actionable suspicions whatever are aroused, that is, in the completely successful murder.

It is upon a phase of this last class of murders that I now wish to dilate. I like to call them "psychological" murders because I have a suspicion that the most successful of them are truly that.

231

Let me tell you about the "murder" of Orion Fry. In a sense it is fictional in that it is frankly pieced together from the unreliable and colored back-stairs hints and rumors and chance gossip of the various maids, gardeners, cooks, scullions, chauffeurs, butlers and valets that worked for him.

Orion Fry descended upon this neck of the woods out of nowhere shortly following World War I. Some said he was a war-profiteer, some said he was a retired munitions manufacturer, some said he was a draft dodger. I don't know. Perhaps he was all three. Certainly he was a man of mystery. That he was also immensely wealthy no one doubted because, through his agents, he quietly purchased a large and valuable wooded estate along the rocky shore of Lake Superior. There he laid out elaborate grounds and built an immense, rambling ranch-type log house— called Orion's Watch—which commanded a splendid view of the restless lake and of Old Baldy, a granite knob lifted high over the lake a mile or so up the shore from the big house. A solitary towering Norway pine crowned its otherwise naked crest, like a single hair rising from the pate of a Kewpie doll. "Old Baldy" was good.

As nearly as we natives could tell the mysterious Orion Fry spent most of his waking hours sitting in his library staring out across vast restless Lake Superior and at Old Baldy. (He kept a rack of binoculars at his elbow.) That and listening to music. He possessed all manner of phonographs, radios and assorted music boxes. The walls of his library were lined with hundreds of albums of records, rafts of sheet music and scores of books devoted to musicians and musical subjects. He owned a grand piano as long as an oversized ping-pong table or a small bowling alley. Whatever else he may have been, Orion Fry was also an advanced musical soak. His tennis courts gathered leaves and his rockhewn swimming pool was largely a haunt of the sea gulls.

Further evidence of the man's wealth and fanatical devotion to music was the fact that practically all of the guests at Orion's Watch were professional musicians currently prominent in the world of music. They were a motley international group and their names would compose an impressive and fairly complete list of the musical great of the last quarter century. Many of them—it was learned later—were paid prevailing concert rates and even more simply to come to Orion's Watch and perform for this lonely and eccentric old man.

Then shortly before Pearl Harbor a brilliant young European pianist was invited to come to Orion's Watch. She accepted. To avoid international complications we shall simply pick a typical Anglo-Saxon name and call her Sonja. It seems that Sonja was very beautiful and very talented. The combination apparently proved irresistible; she came and played and conquered—and remained on at Orion's Watch as Mrs. Orion Fry.

Following this strange marriage Orion's Watch rapidly became a sort of musical mecca. It was said that one could not stroll along the rocky shore without stumbling over at least one recumbent concert pianist. Even darker kitchen rumor had it that one might even occasionally stumble over a mixed *pair* of concert pianists locked obliviously in the drollest of duets. This was doubtless a canard sponsored by the musically insensitive.

As time went on the gracious and beautiful mistress of Orion's Watch, Mrs. Orion Fry, surrounded herself with all manner of hopeful musical protégés. Some of the younger and more obscure and impoverished of them remained on as more or less permanent fixtures. By and by there got to be more metronomes ticking about the place than clocks. Despite a severe heart attack aging Orion Fry continued to sit in his vast library and listen to the music and stare out at Old Baldy through his powerful binoculars. He paid the bills, swallowed his heart pills, and said nothing.

"Keep him very quiet," the physician warned the beautiful Mrs. Fry. "Nothing must excite him—except possibly music, without which of course he could not live."

"Ah, yes, Doctor," Mrs. Fry gravely assented. "He shall remain very quiet."

Shortly before the master had suffered his heart attack a talented and handsome compatriot of Mrs. Orion Fry's had arrived at Orion's Watch as a guest. It seems that Mrs. Fry had known him as a student in Paris. To avoid international complications we shall pick another typical Anglo-Saxon name and call him Boris. At any rate Boris and Sonja instantly rediscovered what might be termed a complete musical affinity, an instinctive appreciation for each other's considerable musical talents. They frequently played the long gleaming grand piano for each other to their mutually delighted cries of "bravo, bravo!" They played piano duets by day while old Orion Fry sat in his chair listening and staring out the window at brooding Old Baldy. They played candlelit duets far into the night, long after old Orion Fry had rung for his man and finally retired. They even took long hikes together along the rugged lake shore presumably discussing music and kindred interests while Orion Fry swallowed his heart pills and stared at them morosely through his binoculars.

Then one bright day they left old Orion Fry sitting in his library with his battery of binoculars, as usual staring out of the broad windows. Slowly they prowled the shore, hand in hand, and finally scaled Old Baldy and lay under the lone pine in the glittering sun. Hours later when they returned they went immediately to the library. There they found the contorted body of old Orion Fry lying sprawled in his chair before the open window, staring sightlessly out at Old Baldy. One likes to guess that Sonja and Boris glanced quickly at each other and perhaps even smiled. Smiled frostily, we believe is the accepted fictional formula. The old man's favorite binoculars dangled from a strap clenched in his whitened hands. Ironically enough, they were a recent gift from Sonja. As for Orion Fry, alas, he was quite dead.

"Heart attack" read the death certificate. Heart attack it doubtless was. But was it not also murder?—what I choose to call "psychological" murder? This dark thought would never have occurred to me if a drunken tavern keeper in the village near Orion's Watch had not told us later, much later, that in an unguarded alcoholic moment Orion Fry's valet, just before he left Orion's Watch, had told him that it was really *he* who first discovered the dead body in the library; that it was *he,* grown suddenly curious, who had knelt and raised the binoculars dangling from his master's cold hands; that it was *he* who had looked out at distant

Old Baldy and there witnessed a certain tableau involving a man and a maid—a spirited tableau that had little or nothing to do with the more formal aspects of music.

We inquired about the valet but could not find him. He was last traced into war-shrouded England. As for Sonja and Boris, they had promptly sold out and reportedly left together to pursue their musical quests in the quiet English fishing village of Minsk. That, we found, was approximately ninety-seven *versts* from the village of Pinsk. But even if we could have proved all these things, and could have laid our hands on the musical pair, would we still have had a legally provable case of murder? We would not have. Any second-year law student could have sprung them. That is what is so devilishly diabolical about it. Yet, if the story is true, old Orion Fry was murdered just as surely as though the two lovers, Boris and Sonja, had aimed a Tommy gun at his heart and fired point-blank.

Will murder really out? It is to laugh. Old Aeschylus should have been arrested for circulating false rumors.

Chapter 24

INSULT AND BATTERY

HE SAT ACROSS THE DESK, his aggrieved and unblinking pale blue eyes looking out at me from two of the loveliest shiners I have ever beheld. Black eyes are among the commonest symbolic badges of a D.A.'s job; they hover about him always like a gloomy sort of occupational halo—but this candent pair seemed to shine out from some loftier realm, not unlike the afterglow of a double sunset on a surrealist desert. They were superb.

"Yes?" I prompted, curious to learn the identity and source of inspiration of the artist.

"Ay am Olson da grocer from Yopling," he explained. Jopling was a little iron-mining village down the line. "Me an' my portner Yonson ve run da big department an' grocery store down dare," he added, getting in a plug for the home team.

"Yes, Mr. Olson," I said with infinite professional patience, "you are in the grocery business." I had ruefully learned that one could never hurry the autobiography of a black eye. "What can I do for you?"

He smiled grimly. "Vell, by da looks of t'ings Ay tank Ay vant a varrant."

By the looks of the things I was inclined to think the man had something there. "Go on, Mr. Olson," I said.

"Ay tank Ay vant a varrant for—what you call?—insult and batt'ry," he went on.

This was an engaging variant on the prosecutor's old friend, assault and battery. I brightened perceptibly. "How did it happen?" I asked. "What's his name?"

237

"She veren't no he," Mr. Olson snorted. "She vere da Vidow Petterson." He blinked his pale eyes rapidly over the memory.

"My, my—a *lady* . . ." I marveled, leaning forward. "But how did she do it?"

"Vit her big ledder purse—dis vay!" Mr. Olson leapt to his feet and whirled through the extravagant motions of a discus thrower —winding up one inch from the nose of the startled D.A.

I quickly sat back and studied the sunset at close range. "Hm . . ." I mused, expertly squinting, weighing, appraising— finally concluding that the Widow Peterson's big leather purse must have harbored an anvil. "Tell me about it," I said.

Mr. Olson continued to lean across my desk, still poised in his role of the disarmed discus thrower frozen at the point of release. "Vell, Mester D.A., it all happen dis vay."

"But first sit down—*please*," I said, groping warily for an Italian cigar.

The Widow Peterson ran the boarding house on the hill over-looking the Volunteer Mine. The general merchandising firm of Olson and Johnson had just bought out the old Levinson department store at the foot of the hill. They sold everything from asparagus to zippers. Upon taking inventory the new partners discovered a lot of slow or obsolete items dangling from the rafters and clogging their shelves: things like mildewed horse collars, shoals of hand-cranked ice-cream freezers together with bulging and dusty sacks of rock salt to go with the freezers, scores of assorted lanterns and coal scuttles, racks of faded linen dusters of the vintage of the "horseless carriage," boxes of men's yellow button shoes with bull-dog toes, rigid rows of what at first looked like armored vests but turned out to be corsets with whalebone stays, discreetly covered enamel chamber pots with wildflowers painted on the sides. . . .

So they decided to hold a big clearance sale.

A few days later the Widow Peterson studied a large ad in the *Daily Mining Journal* announcing, among many other things, that the new grocery firm of Olson and Johnson was prepared to give away one free hand-painted chamber pot with each purchase of a pound of coffee. The big sale was to start sharp at 9:00 A.M. the very next morning, a Saturday. What with ministering to the needs of twenty-six hungry male boarders, all miners, it was well past the noon hour before Mrs. Peterson charged down the hill and sailed breathlessly into the store clutching her big black leather purse. At the moment Mr. Olson was on duty taking care of the trade. Mrs. Peterson rummaged in her purse and produced the ad and triumphantly waved it under his nose.

"Mester Olson," she panted, "vere it trew like it stood hare in the *Daily Mining Urinal* dat iff Ay buy vun poon of coffee Ay get vun free slop yar?"

"Dat vere certainly trew, Messus Petterson," Mr. Olson said, rubbing his hands. "Only ve call dem shamber pots."

"Hm . . . An' verc it also trew iff Ay buy tew poon of coffee Ay get tew free slop yars?" Mrs. Peterson, a practical woman, was not to be lured by the dainty euphemisms of commerce.

"Dat vere certainly trew," he gravely assured her. "Ve vant to stamulate bizznass."

Mrs. Peterson snapped shut her purse and complacently folded her arms. "Very vell, den," she announced, "Ay vill take twenty-sex poon of Maxswill House coffee."

Mr. Olson was worried. Sales of coffee had been rather brisk that morning and quite a procession of flowered chamber pots had moved across the counter. He was awfully afraid that he and his partner might not be able to meet this belated demand for such a large number of free chamber pots. Yet he certainly did not want to offend one of their best customers.

"Axcuse me, Messus Petterson," he said, "while Ay step out tew da back room an' hold a confulscation vit my portner—he vere busy out dare still taking inwentory, yew know. Please axcuse me, please."

Mrs. Peterson composed herself in rapt contemplation of a jar of pickled pigs' feet while the worried Mr. Olson hurried out to the back room to hold a consultation with his partner. There he remained for nearly a half hour. When he finally returned, red-faced and perspiring, Mrs. Peterson had wrenched herself away from the pigs' feet and stood before him with pursed lips, tapping her foot impatiently. There was fire in her eye.

"Mester Olson," she snapped indignantly, "Ay vill haf you understand Ay am a voman of decession an' my time were waluable! Ay din't come hare to be tinkered vit! Dew Ay or dun't Ay get da twenty-sex poon of Maxswill House coffee an' da twenty-sex free slop yars? Yass or noo? An' remember," she warned darkly, "Ay can always take my boording-house bizznass across da street to da Finnish co-op!"

"Now dun't be hesty," Mr. Olson tried to placate her. "Please dun't be hesty, Messus Petterson. Yew vill get the coffee all right, 'cause ve vant da bizznass. But four poon of da coffee vill haf to be Hills Brudders—ve vere running little short on Maxswill House."

"Very vell, den—but how about the twenty-sex free slop yars?" Mrs. Peterson persisted grimly.

"Yew vill get da coffee, all right," Mr. Olson repeated, " 'cause ve vant da bizznass. But Ay yust had a little confulscation vit my portner an' ve been hunting high an' low all over da joint looking for slop yars—an' den ve 'phoned up da Consolidated Fool an' Lumber Company—an' tew-t'ree Svede carpenter besides—an' ve got astimates an' bids—"

"Yass?" Mrs. Peterson interrupted ominously. "Vat den?"

"—an me an' my portner ve decided dat radder dan try an' round oop twenty-sex free slop yars it vould be quvicker an' sheaper for us to build yew a new outhouse instead!"

Chapter 25

THE HAUNTED ELECTION

I HAD BEEN D.A. for nearly fourteen years. That made seven two-year terms, a long time to survive the buffetings and uncertainties of popular election for one of the "hottest" jobs on any local ballot. Another election time was rolling around and I had to decide whether to run for an eighth term. The decision was not easy. I was weary of campaigning, that is, going out every two years and scouring the county for votes, all the while grinning and backslapping and kissing all the babies within reach—over twenty-one. There was no doubt, too, that I was weary of the job itself, weary of the endless round of Trouble, weary of the thrice-told tales of poverty and sorrow and swinishness that confront every prosecutor in the land. And I was sure the job was quite as weary of me.

What I really wanted to do was to hang up my gloves like Gene Tunney and be the retired champ. I guess I was doing all right enough at the job. I had lost but one felony case in the last ten years—probably some sort of record in D.A. circles—but the novelty was beginning to wear off. I was getting bored with my work. That was not quite fair either to me or the job. Why not quit while I was ahead? I had long since begun to repeat myself, over and over, until at times it seemed that I was retrying the same old criminal case, term after term, the only change being in the cast of unhappy characters.

Contemplation of the abrupt change from the highly specialized job of D.A. to that of the general practice of law scared me a little. I was shocked when I realized that I had devoted nearly a third of my life learning to be a competent prosecutor. The sobering fact was that I had done little else since I had gotten out of law school. Faced with the actual decision of voluntarily giving up my D.A. job—with its assured income—I found I couldn't take it. I reluctantly decided to run again—"just once more." Accuracy compels me to add that my decision was considerably eased when I learned that an unsolicited salary boost was planned for the coming term.

Yes, I would run again. After that, come what may, the younger crop of lawyers could fight it out among themselves to be my successor. I would hang up my gloves for good and turn my attention exclusively to the private practice of law—not to mention some attendant vices I had acquired along the way, such as fly fishing for brook trout and prospecting for uranium. Perhaps I would even write another book. . . . "Veteran prosecutor runs for eighth term," the leading newspaper unfeelingly announced. Old Man Traver winced and combed the burrs and wood ticks and miscellaneous tobacco shreds out of his beard. There was "politicking" to be done.

My opponent was a pleasant and personable young lawyer from Chippewa. He was also a veteran of World War II and, in addition, had starred in basketball in high school and had made the regular varsity team at Ann Arbor. While these distinctions might possibly prove of dubious assistance to a prosecutor during the awful loneliness of a knockdown drag-out criminal trial, I was realistic enough to realize that they could help out quite a bit in those biennial carnivals of sentiment, the American election.

Of course, I had my points, too. During the First World War I had fought with the Strawberry Hill Bicycle Corps in the Battle of Chippewa Grammar School and during World War II, being slightly overripe, I had fought valiantly and with distinguished success in the battle for the B-gas coupon. My opponent and I were both civilians in World War 2.5. We were at least even there. And I, too, was a noted athlete: noted, that is, for one historic play. In high-school basketball a hard-pressed coach had once put lanky Traver in the game. Traver was dismayed to suddenly find himself with the ball, so he wheeled and immediately sank a difficult long shot in the opponent's basket—*swish*—neatly racking up a score for the opponents, of course. The coach, not to be outdone, deftly shot Traver into the showers—*swish*.

I was in a real horse race this time and I knew it. But I hadn't seen anything yet. Since elections are decided by votes, when people who formerly voted for one get mad and vote for his opponent, the luckless candidate is in a sense losing two votes instead of one. At any rate, apparently a hell of a lot of people suddenly decided to get mad at Traver. Someone always has it in for the D.A. but right then I found the timing particularly unfortunate. Let me tell you a few of the highlights.

Just before the election a lady from the village of Spring River (the scene of the romance between old Frank Paquette and Rosie LaBeau—remember?) was rather unceremoniously propositioned one night, flung to the ground, and thereupon had by a male visitor from Illinois. The next morning she came to my office with the state police seeking a warrant for rape.

Rape is the forcible ravishing of a woman against her will. It is one of the most serious crimes on the books, in Michigan carrying a penalty up to life. Rape unfortunately does take place, and perhaps all too frequently. But it had been my observation that true rape, at least in my neck of the woods, was comparatively rare. So I questioned the woman carefully.

She was separated from her husband and was in the process of obtaining a divorce. She lived with her children in a modest home on the outskirts of Spring River. That night, Sunday, she had been to church. It was dusk when church got out and she walked home alone. When she got home she found that a distant relative of her husband's, younger than she, had arrived from Illinois in his truck. He had brought some bundles of clothing for the children and he asked her to help carry them into the house. She agreed.

It was a warm autumn evening and while they were lifting the bundles out of the truck the young relative, who had been drinking, suddenly got amorous and began making advances to her. (Perhaps he had his mind set on bundling.) She resisted his advances and continued to try to help him. According to her story the young man was not to be put off. He suddenly threw his arms about her and threw her to the ground beside his truck. There in the darkness he had intercourse with her.

Further questioning developed that they lay there some fifteen or twenty minutes; that during that time a neighbor boy walked past on the other side of the parked truck. She did not cry out for help or seek to attract his attention. Asked by me why she didn't she stated that the defendant had already choked her, she had cried out then, and he had warned her to shut up. She was afraid he would choke her again—and anyway the boy was too small to be of much help. That seemed reasonable enough. So far so good. Further questioning developed that soon after that her oldest daughter was driven home by a neighboring farmer and his wife, accompanied by their own daughter. The farmer was a big husky Finn who could probably have broken the defendant in two.

"How long did these new arrivals stay outside your house?" I asked.

"Maybe five or ten minutes," the lady answered. "I could hear my daughter and their daughter talking. The two are good friends."

"How far away from you was the farmer's truck?"

"Just on the other side of the parked truck where we lay."

"What were you doing during this time."

"I was lying on the ground. X had removed my pants and was trying to have intercourse with me."

"What do you mean 'trying'?"

"He seemed to be having trouble—ah—getting underway."

"Hm . . . Did you know then it was your neighbor who was in the second truck?"

"Yes, I knew he planned to drive my daughter home—and I recognized his truck. I even told X who it was."

"You mean that while you lay there with X having—or trying to have—intercourse with you—raping you—you recognized and told him who had driven up beside the first truck?" This was a most interesting development, and I went baying along the scent.

"That is correct."

"What tone of voice did you use to convey this message to X?"

"I whispered to him."

"Why didn't you cry out for help?"

"I was afraid—he was choking me. He had already warned me to keep quiet."

"He couldn't have been choking you very hard when you were able to whisper to him who the new arrivals were, could he?"

"Well, no—not just then."

"Why didn't you cry out at that time, then?"

No reply.

"Why didn't you cry out?" This was vital and I had to know her answer.

"I don't know. I was afraid."

"Will you please show me the bruises on your neck where he choked you?"

"They haven't appeared yet."

"Do you have any marks or scratches or bruises on your body anywhere as a result of this assault?"

"Well, no. But I'm stiff and sore all over."

"Was X armed? Did he have a stick or a club or any weapon?"

"Not to my knowledge. I think not."

"What happened then?"

"My daughter finally went in the house and the truck drove away."

"Yes?"

"Then still another car drove past and then a little later a man walked by on the far side of the parked truck."

"Did you seek to attract the attention of either the occupants of the second car or the man?"

"No."

"Why not?"

"I was afraid."

"I see. . . . What happened then?"

"X finally finished his job and drove away. I went into the house."

"How did you break the news of what happened?"

"My daughter saw that I was mussed up and my clothes were

soiled. She wondered what had happened and I told her. She got excited, I guess, and ran for the minister. The minister came—and here I am."

"Getting back to the assault, did you at any time during the period you lay there speak above a whisper?"

"No."

"And is it not true that all during that time and on four separate occasions a total of at least seven people passed within a few feet of you, you recognized five of them, and still you made no attempt to attract their attention or seek their help?" This was the sixty-four dollar question and she realized it.

Sullenly now: "I was afraid."

I glanced at the state police and they shrugged and rolled their eyes up at me. Our "rape" case had flown right out the window. However shabby and wrongheaded the conduct of the defendant may have been (and I do not seek to defend it), and whatever the degree of assault of which he might have been guilty, it was certainly not rape. *That* was the offense we were considering. Perhaps the lady was a disciple of Confucius, who did not say: when rape appears inevitable relax and enjoy it.

Under the law a woman being ravished need not struggle and raise a hue and cry if she is in reasonable and imminent peril of her life or great bodily harm. She must, however, do all that she can safely do to resist and frustrate her attacker. The law and Confucious do not see eye to eye. At any rate, here was a woman that was being made in a leisurely fashion by a half drunk and unarmed man. On four occasions she could have flung an old hot water bottle at her rescuers, they were so close, but instead she lay there whispering to the fumbling defendant. She watched her help go away while her faltering assaulter finished his task. That was not rape in my book.

I carefully explained all this to the poor woman. She had been through a harrowing experience and had told us the truth; she at least deserved candor in turn from me. I told her that no jury in the land would convict for rape on the basis of her own story alone and that few judges would ever let the case go to a jury on that charge. Aside from any question of the rights of the defendant, it would have been wrong to have let her go ahead and uselessly blast her own character and reputation and the peace of mind of her growing children, and I gently told her so. The woman took all this reasonably well. I told her that we would book the man on an aggravated assault charge while we completed our investigation, but that in no event would there be any rape charge. I asked the state police to drive her home. "Thank you," she said, and they went away.

A wily politician playing all the angles could have arrested that man for rape, continued the trial of the case until after the election, and then either have lowered the charge or booted the case out of court on the grounds that "further investigation" showed no rape. It's been done before and it will be done again. I knew that I would probably be severely criticized for not burning this "city slicker." I also wistfully remembered that in the past the voters of Spring River township had been very kind to me at election time.

But this was not rape; as an experienced prosecutor I knew it was not rape; and, goddamitt, election or no election, I wasn't going to blow it up into a rape. While a few noisy men in high places, notably in Washington, seemed to disagree with me, I felt that no man—prosecutor, senator or peasant—had any right to play politics with the destinies of his fellow men. It also seemed to me that a defendant was just as much entitled to receive the benefit of the doubt before an investigating prosecutor as he was later before a jury; and that when such a reasonable doubt plainly existed, it was the D.A.'s duty to "acquit" the man across his battered desk rather than force him through the useless expense and turmoil of a public trial. That was not only honorable; it also happened to be sound law. That way also permitted a prosecutor to bear down with vigor and a clear conscience when he *did* go to trial; jurors would come to sense that he meant business. Perhaps this attitude accounted partly for my unsought record of convictions. But I grow garrulous and, heaven forbid, begin to sound like a senator.

I don't know what story my lady went home and told her minister and friends and neighbors. I don't even know that she told them anything. At any rate, she was scarcely in a position to tell them the whole story. Whatever happened, it soon became evident that my name was mud in Spring River township. When I went up there campaigning old supporters snubbed me on the street. I slunk into the nearest tavern and sensibly buried my nose in a beer.

Ah, yes—Traver was the friend of the rapists; the flower of womanhood of Iron Cliffs County was no longer safe in his keeping; heave the blackguard out. And I was trapped. There wasn't a thing I could do. I obviously couldn't "try" my pending case on the street corners and simple decency, if not legal ethics, forbade me from exposing the true story of the "rape."

The autumnal skies began to look a little bleak for Traver. . . .

About then a poor lady from a neighboring town suffered that age-old family misfortune: her daughter was pregnant—and unmarried. The mother came to me and said she wanted to swear out a bastardy warrant for her daughter's boy friend. She was undertandably disturbed, and very angry to boot. She most definitely wanted the young man to writhe in prison. I inwardly sighed and patiently explained that in bastardy cases jail or prison was a last resort; that the statute specifically provided that the defendant, if found guilty, should first be given an opportunity to pay for the expenses of the confinement and the future support of the child. He might be jailed for his ultimate failure to pay, I explained, but never for begetting the child.

I also explained to the mother that it was the usual practice, and a rather desirable one, to first give the defendant a chance to settle out of court; that frequently the young man, seeing that his number was up, married the girl if she were willing, thus giving the child a name. (I did not tell her that some of the most successful marriages I knew had been launched under these auspices.) I told her that I had been obliged to handle scores of bastardy cases and that I had been driven to the conclusion that no amount of settlement money, however great, could quite take the place of legitimatizing the innocent child; that it struck me that most people had quite a rough enough time in life as it was without beginning the adventure under that added handicap. I urged her to do nothing precipitous that would spoil that chance.

The woman calmed down considerably before my Eddie Guest brand of philosophizing. She finally agreed that I should first write the young man and explore the possibility of marriage, and, if he wouldn't marry the girl, that I should try to reach a money settlement usual in such cases. She went away. I wrote the young man. He came in with his father. As is usual in these cases there was much palaver. I listened to the case history of a blighted romance between two childhood sweethearts. Minutes ran into hours. Great bitterness seemed to exist between the two families. The young man wouldn't marry the girl. I then told him that he would have to make the usual settlement or face a bastardy prosecution. He— or rather his father—agreed to pay the figure I named.

I wrote the mother that the boy wouldn't marry the girl (no American law can *make* anybody marry anybody), but that he had agreed to pay the usual settlement, naming it. I prepared and enclosed the settlement papers. She wrote back that they had thought things over and concluded that the amount was inadequate; that they wanted approximately twice as much. This wasn't quite cricket, I knew, but I wryly concluded that perhaps there was inflation even among the poor little bastards. . . . I called in the boy's father and again laid it on the line. The boy's harried father agreed to meet the increased amount. So I changed the figures in the settlement papers and again wrote the mother of the girl.

The next thing I knew the mother sailed into my office in a high dudgeon and said they had again changed their minds; that they didn't want to settle out of court for any figure; that they were sick and tired of all the delay; and that they now wanted the boy promptly arrested and prosecuted for bastardy. Feeling was evidently running higher on both sides. In the meantime as prosecutor I had been placed in a rather ticklish position. I had in good faith devoted many difficult hours to reaching a settlement. Now the woman wanted me to kick all that overboard and arrest the boy. During our discussion, which generated considerable heat, she suddenly accused me of selling out to the other side. I stared at her. Accusations continued to pour from her. She said that she had since heard of my shady dealings; of all the money I had made as my cut on crooked gambling in the county and in fixing cases. But I couldn't pull the wool over their eyes. The reckless torrent of words went on and on. . . .

I continued to stare at her. I leaned back in my chair and shut my eyes. My main feeling was one of utter weariness. So this was my reward for fourteen years of professional rectitude that had grown almost into a phobia? My friends even joked about it: "Honest John," they called me. I counted ten and stoutly quelled the impulse to grab this chattering magpie by the neck. After all, she was a distraught and sorely troubled woman. So instead I told her that it struck me that all good citizens who were in possession of knowledge that their prosecutor was crooked owed a distinct duty to themselves and to their community to pass the word on to their attorney general and circuit judge. I invited her to do this. I also did something I had never done before: I invited her, in the meantime, to get the hell out of my office. I could no longer bear the sight of her. She got—and my ears burned for days.

Things looked bleaker for Traver. . . .

There were a couple more cases nearly on a par with these two. I can't remember the details but it does not matter. I do remember that in each situation it would have been much easier and more timesaving for me to have O. K.'d a criminal warrant. And it most certainly would have helped me as a candidate. But I had always conceived that a prosecutor was something more than a spineless warrant granter. One important aspect of his job was to protect people, sometimes even from themselves. The simple fact is that it frequently takes more guts on the part of a prosecutor to turn down a criminal warrant than to grant it.

About then I was doing some serious soul-searching about my work. Could I have been dead wrong about my job for all these years? It was not impossible. Still I felt and still feel that the prosecutor's treatment of his cases should never be divorced from the social realities of the situation. He cannot operate in a legal vacuum; he happens to be dealing with *people*. Nor was the "just" way to handle his cases always to be found lurking in thick books. A good part of it—perhaps the most important part—had to spring from his own heart and head. . . . At any rate I was sure of one thing: in trying to breathe some life and meaning and humanity into the blind abstraction of Justice, I had instead only managed to maneuver myself firmly behind the eight ball. I went out and buried my nose in a flock of tall beers—purchased, of course, with some of the swag from my many fixes.

2.

All this was as nothing to what shortly befell my candidacy. Most prosecutors run on a party ticket and I was no exception. Since my opponent and I were not opposed in our respective party primaries, we wasted no time or money on that. We saved our ammunition for the big show in November. But the first bad omen for me was that two of my usual party running mates for county office were unopposed. In other words there was no contest for their jobs, either in the primary or in the general election in November. They couldn't lose. Since both were popular candidates and efficient officers, their lack of opposition at the election meant that many voters who would normally have walked on their hands to get out and vote for them—and who presumably would at the same time have voted for me, since I was on the same ticket as their favorite candidates—would instead stay at home on election day. Why bother to go and vote? Our people will make it O.K. . . . It was one of the breaks of the game. There was nothing I could do about it but campaign all the harder. I campaigned all the harder.

To spice things up a little more, the usually moribund and pompous county organization of the opposition party chose that very moment to draft new and younger men. The new blood promptly threw the pomp away and got out and slugged. I must say that these friendly "enemies" conducted their county campaign cleanly and with vigor and intelligence. They wisely made me their main county target. If they could isolate and knock off tough old Traver that would be a good entering wedge in their efforts to breach our entire party wall. "Traver is a good guy and a good prosecutor, but . . ." was their refrain. I grinned, not too hilari-ously, and campaigned all the harder.

All this was still as nothing. We did have a primary contest for one important county job on my ticket—and, believe it or not, the winner was then an inmate of an insane asylum. He had gone insane after he had filed for the office. Everybody had assumed that he would naturally be beaten at the primary. An insane can-didate couldn't possibly be nominated. Of course he couldn't. But we were the ones who were daffy. He won big. An insane man was to be my running mate in November. The dazed election commission appealed to the dazed D.A. for advice. What to do? I turned the election laws upside down and came to the reluctant and astounding conclusion that under our laws nothing could be done. Nobody had ever thought of such a weird contingency.

I wrote the attorney general and he agreed. He added that the decision to run or not to run was up to the insane candidate him-self, and that if he wasn't too nuts he could decide to withdraw; but that if he was too nuts he'd be too nutty to form an intent or possess the capacity to withdraw. I was naturally enchanted by all this legal double talk. It somehow charmed me that the nuttier he was the less we could do. Perhaps we were all a little nuts. . . .

A delegation went to see the candidate in the asylum. The poor addled fellow struck a Napoleonic attitude and said: "I choose to run." The delegation came away. Added immortality was ours: our party's good fortune made the front page of the *Chicago Tribune*. I guess maybe it was news, all right, and anyway, the Colonel's sharpshooters wouldn't overlook that chance to heighten our party's prestige. I began doggedly to campaign by night as well as by day. My dreams grew troubled and bizarre. I saw my-self trying cases in a strait jacket. "I choose to run, I choose to run . . ." was all I could say. A looming, frowning figure had be-come my judge; a figure which nightly looked more and more like Colonel McCormick.

One more nightmare awaited me. Our party's candidate for Congress was from another county. I had never met the gentle-man. As far as I knew he was a reasonably good, garden-run candidate for Congress. Then suddenly, just before the election, there appeared in the newspapers a facsimile reproduction of an election petition he had signed some years before seeking to place the Communist Party on the Michigan ballot. *Res ipsa loquitur* we say in the law: the thing speaks for itself. There it was neatly signed with his name and address.

I went out and waded up to my hips in beer.

I tottered around in the dismal November electoral rains doing my stuff to the bitter end. Though I felt beaten already I wanted the decision to be clearcut and without regrets. Came election day; the waiting files of silent and preoccupied voters (many of them unmindful of the age-long struggle that preceded this miracle of free choice); the endless sorting and counting; the spasmodic and garbled midnight radio reports: "Bulletin: Seventh precinct: For prosecutor: Traver, 361; his opponent, 337. Sorry. Correction! Traver 261; his opponent, 337." He's up; he's down; he's in a neutral corner. . . .

Our opponents swept the county. The Little Match Boy finally succumbed to the chill autumnal electoral winds. I lost by 36 votes. In retrospect the miracle was that it wasn't much worse. I did not dispute the result. I sighed with relief. The people had finally made up my mind for me. The battered D.A. was now the ex-D.A. Like old Joe Louis I had lingered too long; had fought a hard fight; and had finally got knocked out by a younger man. Oddly enough, once it was done I somehow preferred it that way.